HOLLOW BROOK MUTANTS

HOLLOW BROOK MUTANTS

First edition published by Blended Mix Publishing.
Contact us: www.blendedmixpublishing.com

Cover magic by InspireMind
Internal layout and typography by Meg Delagrange-Belfon

ISBN: 979-8-9913884-0-5

PRINTED IN THE UNITED STATES OF AMERICA

HOLLOW BROOK MUTANTS

JESSICA MERCIER

*To Alex, Jenny, and Stephen,
who I couldn't have written this book without.*

*(Just kidding, this book is actually dedicated to my
husband Justin, who is my venture capitalist, and
to my daughter Hensley, who is my best girl.)*

01.

I DIDN'T WANT to meet these guys.

"Alex Bailey and Stephen Wright are coming over tonight." Grandma sat next to me on the porch swing and wrapped her arm around my shoulders. "I think instead of hiding in your room, you should introduce yourself. They'll be in all your classes this year."

I'd spent the summer ignoring the impending fact that I'd have to start school in a new town. Hollow Brook sat in the middle of a green farming valley, known mostly as the only gas station between Medford and Willow City. The community revolved around planting in the spring, growing crops in the summer and harvesting fields in the fall.

"It won't be easy." Grandma had a habit of smoothing out her apron whenever she talked about my parents.

"Your mom and dad would want you to start living again. Go to school, make friends, and be happy. It's time for the rest of your life to happen."

My eyes trailed to the red barn across the gravel drive. It was the end of the summer. The air was finally cooling down and getting ready for the fall season. I didn't want a long talk about my parents right now. I let out a sigh. "I'll try, okay?"

"That's all I'm asking for." She patted my hand and then smoothed her apron again after she stood, disappearing into the house.

My dirty sneakers skidded softly along the gray wood plank floor as the porch swing moved. Grandma was always worried about me. I'd spent the summer in bed. Grandpa didn't push me, he had his own silent way of grieving. Aunt Sarah called me a few times each week from Coral Beach. She'd often asked me if I'd wanted to go to therapy or talk to someone professional, but I always told her no.

I knew they were all trying to do their best to help me with my grief, but all the emotions were cooped up deep within me in a way that nobody understood. I couldn't explain to them that even I didn't understand the way my mind processed the world around me.

Nothing interested me. Nothing tasted good. Nothing excited me.

My summer had been full of nothing and I didn't want to talk about it.

Later that evening, sprawled across my bed, I stared up at the ceiling. The sound of a diesel engine told me a truck was coming up the private lane to Grandpa's farm. I peeked out the window to find a pretty woman in a light-blue summer dress get out of the passenger seat. She was holding a casserole dish. It was Mrs. Bailey. Mr. Bailey slid out of the driver's seat, looking every bit the farmer in his classic blue jeans and flannel.

My grandparents smiled and greeted them warmly.

Two boys shut a door on either side of the truck.

Earlier this summer, I'd figured out that the light brown-haired guy was Alex Bailey. He was tall and on the leaner side. He had Mrs. Bailey's hair color and walked in the same way Mr. Bailey walked. Stephen Wright was about the same height and build as Alex, but his skin was dark. He wore his curly, floppy locks longer. I didn't know anything about Stephen's parents, they hadn't ever visited my grandparents since I'd lived in Hollow Brook.

Grandma told me they were the only teens who lived in the farming valley, near enough for us to walk to each other's houses. On Saturday nights, the two guys got a ride to our farm so they could grab their fishing poles and walk to the creek at the edge of Grandpa's property. She'd told me they were nice boys, always very polite to her. I couldn't take Grandma's word for it. Obviously, they'd be nice to a sweet, old lady like her.

Alex seemed quieter, usually laughing and shaking his head at his friend. Stephen was the one always talking in a quick, excited way. They joked and punched each other in the arm and seemed to have a solid friendship between them.

At least, these were things I'd learned from my bedroom window.

Once, I'd had my white lace curtain pulled back as they got out of the truck and I swore Alex's eyes flickered to my window. I'd dropped the curtain and stepped back, my heart pounding in my chest.

Grandma was wrong. I was sure of it, they'd never want me to bother them. I didn't want to go down there. I'd told her I'd try, but I didn't tell her I'd try hard.

I waited until the adults were settled in the kitchen before I slipped downstairs and snuck out the front door. The boys weren't in the yard. I was relieved, I figured maybe I wouldn't have to meet them tonight. Maybe they were already off to the fishing spot.

After a lengthy debate in my head, I decided to go into the barn and groom the horses. Grandpa said that caring for horses was pure therapy for some people. I wasn't sure that they'd been therapy for me but brushing them was something to do when I couldn't stand my room anymore.

"My mom said we have to talk to her."

I stilled. One of the guys was outside the barn door.

There was a groan from the other guy. "It's not our fault she's not coming down here. I mean, she's been here all summer. It's weird. She's weird. I want to go, man."

"You can go fish. I'm going to wait a little bit longer. I told my mom we'd meet her so she knows someone at school on her first day." The barn door swung open. "I left my line in here last time—"

Alex Bailey's mouth dropped open, his bright blue eyes wide. Stephen Wright stopped short behind him a second later, "Dude—Oh."

I'd spent all summer trying not to feel things. In a space of just a few seconds, I felt so much. I felt lonely because I had no friends in this town. I was frustrated and angry that my parents were gone. In that moment, I felt my stomach flip because Alex's gaze was locked on me in a way that made my heart race in my chest.

I couldn't show them any of those feelings, so I pulled out the biggest weapon I could think of and let sarcasm drip from my words.

"Hey there, I'm Weird Girl. Nice to meet you."

"Ah." Stephen scratched the back of his neck. "I didn't mean that. I just said it."

"It's whatever." I turned away to brush one of the horses, waiting for them to leave so that I could go on contently living my life alone again. I'd be able to tell Grandma I talked to them.

"Uh, well, do…" Stephen seemed to be scrambling, blurting out his words to try to cover what he'd said when he hadn't known I was listening. "I mean, uh, do you want to go fishing with us?"

"No thanks," I said. "I'm good."

Alex cleared his throat. "Why not?"

I looked at them again. His blue eyes cut through me and my honest thoughts tumbled out of my mouth. "You're only talking to me because your mom made you. I get it, it's all good."

The two friends looked at each other for a long moment. Alex raised his brows at Stephen, giving him the slightest nod in my direction. There was an exchange between them, something Alex was telling Stephen that I couldn't decipher.

"I'm Stephen Wright," he said with a sigh. I wasn't going to tell them I already knew their names. I wanted them to believe I had absolutely no interest in them. "This is Alex Bailey."

I didn't say anything. I was still waiting for them to leave.

"Come fishing with us," Alex said, sticking his hands in his pockets.

It took me several seconds to say, "I don't have a fishing pole."

"You can use mine." Alex shrugged.

Stephen nodded. "Yeah, we can pass our fishing poles around. Easy."

"I don't know how." I set the brush on the ledge of the stall and stepped off the stool.

"We can teach you. There's nothing to it." Stephen waved me off. "I didn't mean what I said. I just want to go fishing. Come on, let's go."

I looked between them, I supposed Stephen sounded like he genuinely wanted me to go. I quickly glanced at Alex. He gave me a half-smile and a nod. I really didn't have anything else to do. "I guess I can come watch."

"Cool." Stephen punched Alex in the shoulder. "She's coming. Let's go, bro."

Alex rolled his eyes at Stephen. They grabbed their fishing poles from behind the barn door. Stephen didn't waste time and took off with a red cooler swinging in his hand.

Alex glanced at me as I fell into step next to him. "I'm Jenny."

"Nice to meet you, Jenny." He gave me another one of those easy smiles.

I didn't know what else to say. I hadn't actually talked to another person besides my grandparents and Aunt Sarah in three months. I didn't think cashiers at the grocery store asking me nosey, small-town questions counted.

Alex walked with me, holding his fishing pole in one hand, but he didn't talk again. Stephen led us. He started babbling about fishing spots he knew and something about types of bait that were best for this area. I think he was talking about bait for other areas nearby too, but I wasn't following at all.

We walked a path between Grandpa's tall corn stalks, away from the farmhouse. I was sure this invitation to hang out with them was temporary. I decided to make peace with that and enjoy the evening air. I liked the smell of the farm, the sound of crickets chirping all around us, and I dug my hands into my little jean shorts as I walked.

We turned at the edge of the field and took another path. After ten minutes or so, we stopped where the trees got thicker. We slid past tall bushes and it opened up to a little bank of pebbled sand. The water pooled deeper into a larger pond. Stephen walked out onto a big flat rock and shifted his fishing pole to get ready. He waved me over to come stand next to him.

Stephen went right into explaining. "All right, so you get a little slack. See here? Then you push this button, whip it back and let it go."

That was fast. I'd need him to explain it again.

Alex joined us. He readied his pole slower, not saying anything.

"So, how did your parents die?" Stephen asked as he reeled in the line until it was taut.

The question rattled me, but I tried not to show it. "I don't really talk about it."

"Okay." Stephen shrugged. It was nice that he didn't push it.

Alex cast his line with a graceful flick of his wrist like he'd done this for years. He took a deep breath next to me before he turned and held out his fishing pole. "Want to hold it?"

My hands went up. "Oh, I don't want to take it from you."

"We fish all the time." Alex shrugged. "It's not taking anything from me."

After another few seconds of eyeing the fishing pole, I nodded and took it. Alex stayed close. I was ready to hand it over to him the second something crazy happened.

"Okay. Like this?"

"Perfect." Alex's tone was patient. "Good job."

"Thanks. I'm just standing here. But, thanks."

Both guys let out a laugh. We waited for a long

while and eventually ended up sitting down. Stephen cast his pole a few more times, rambling aimlessly to fill the silence. Alex scooted closer to me to explain more in-depth about what to do. I practiced casting more and more as my confidence grew. The light was fading when Alex said, "We should head back soon."

Stephen frowned. "Yeah, a few more minutes. Fishing sucks right now."

Alex shrugged and leaned back on the palms of his hands next to me. He was giving off a subtle tension, like he had something to say but the words weren't coming out.

I let the quiet settle as I held the fishing pole. The sky was a yellow-orange that reflected against the calm pond. Frogs and crickets started humming, with the occasional splash at the edges of the water. I figured I wasn't going to be invited to hang out with them again, but knew I wanted to come back by myself to think sometime soon.

Lost in my thoughts, I felt a big tug on my line. "Oh!"

"Ah, she's got a bite!" Stephen said cheerfully.

I stood, feeling something at the end of the line. Alex shot to his feet with me, his hands over mine and standing close behind me. "Okay, give it a good pull. Good, and then here." He pressed my hand against the handle. "Reel it in. Slow and steady."

I did as he said, feeling a jolt of warmth inside with his other hand on my back, trying to let his experience with fishing settle my nerves. Then there was a fish dangling and flapping over the water. Stephen took it off the line for me and held it up, "Nice, your first fish, right?"

"I've never done that before." I was smiling and breathless. I'd faked-smiled to appease the adults in my life a few times this last summer, but I hadn't smiled a smile I'd felt since I'd last seen my parents.

"I'll clean it." Stephen turned to open the cooler he'd brought with him.

I turned too, wanting to give the fishing pole to Alex, but he was standing so close we bumped into each other. "Oh sorry." I said, still smiling.

Alex wore his own big grin that sent a storm of butterflies through me. "Yeah, I got it." He took the pole from me. "You did great. I'm impressed."

As we walked back together, Stephen talked about my fish. He went on and on about my good luck. I walked with my arms crossed, feeling empty after feeling so much back by the pond. Alex stayed quiet, not looking at me or saying anything. It was nice that Stephen was talking so much.

"These are the four corners of our farms." Stephen stopped us at a path that branched north, south, east, and west. "That farm there is your Grandpa's." I nodded, studying the faded yellow farmhouse with the gray-brown roof that peeked over the tall corn stalks.

"Alex's farm is that way." Stephen pointed to the large, fresh white farmhouse with its modern black tin roof. It was the largest farm in the area. I could see it in the distance from my bedroom window.

"That's Stephen's farm," Alex said, gesturing more north of us. From what I could see over the tall cornstalks, his house was a small dark blue one-story home. The house was older, but charming in its own way.

Stephen jerked his chin toward the only other house in the valley. "We call that the Mystery Farm."

"What do you mean?" I asked, squinting, it was north of where we stood, set right up against the edge of Grandpa's farm. The farmhouse seemed normal enough, a simple, older, white two-story home. There were several sections of tall white fences and three white vans surrounding it, but there was something sterile about it too.

"No one really talks about that farm." Stephen's eyes went big. "We have our theories."

"They have all that land surrounding it, but they don't grow anything." Alex glanced at me, his eyes darting over my face as if he were curious about something, but I couldn't puzzle out what he was thinking. "Why have all that land and not do anything with it?"

"Cars go in Monday through Friday, but no one is ever there on the weekends." Stephen crossed his arms, scratching his jaw with his hand. "I keep a close eye on it."

"That's so weird." I wanted to know what the farm was and decided I'd come back to this spot during the week to see what Stephen meant about cars coming and going. The mystery of it drew me in, making some part of me come alive, giving me something to look forward to in a way I hadn't since before my parent's death.

Alex looked at Stephen with a raised brow. "Come on, we're supposed to be back at Grandpa's farmhouse by dark."

"Yeah, yeah." Stephen sighed.

They started to walk away, but I kept my gaze fixed on the mystery farm.

"Jenny?" Alex said, turning to look back at me.

"Coming." I caught up with them, but the mystery farm seemed to call to me as I walked away.

02.

I MISSED MY MOM.

Over the last three months, there were several times I thought I might die from crying. I spent most of my time thinking about my mom and her big smile. I missed my dad's laughter when my mom did silly things. She always had music on, especially when she cleaned the kitchen because she hated cleaning and needed dance breaks. Dad would sail into the room and spin and sway her around in pretty circles. He'd reach out to twirl me on the white tile floor until he planted his feet in front of the sink to finish the dishes while Mom and me moved on to a new song to dance to.

Today, I had a fresh memory to dwell on.

I laid in bed all Sunday morning, looking at the ceiling and thinking about catching that fish. I liked Stephen's laughter, full of life and ease. I'd never seen kindness in a teenage boy the way I could see it in Alex's blue eyes. My thoughts about the boys and the fish always circled back to the mystery farm.

I didn't have the energy to go look at it myself yet. Grandma made me come down for lunch when she got back from church with Grandpa. But then, I'd fled upstairs again.

A familiar aloneness settled over me, dark and cold and empty. It was one of those days where the grief threatened to swallow me up. I imagined the ache within me might split open my chest. I didn't know if letting the grief float into the air would free me or kill me.

I was staring up at the clear sky through my window outside when something small hit the glass. Several seconds later, it happened again. I sat up and slowly leaned forward to find Alex and Stephen standing below on the gravel drive.

I opened the window. "What are you guys doing?"

"We want to show you something." Stephen grinned. With just one phrase from Stephen, all the grief and all the loss faded like sunshine clearing dense fog. "Come down and let's go."

"Show me what?"

Alex did a one-shoulder shrug. "It's a surprise."

"Why didn't you knock?" I tilted my head at them,

still confused and a little stunned that they were here right now.

Alex rolled his eyes. "Stephen thought it'd be cool to throw rocks at your window."

I didn't get it, but I said, "All right, one minute."

"Yeah!" Stephen clapped his hands.

I slipped my dirty white sneakers on and looked in the mirror. I tried to imagine what Stephen and Alex might think of me based on my looks.

I studied my big brown eyes under gently arched dark brows and the freckles across my straight nose. My legs were long like my dad's, but a bit scrawny since I'd grown a few inches in the last year. My lips reminded me of my mom the most. They were pouty, but a little too big for my younger, thinner face. I didn't know what to do with my unexciting long brown hair. I usually pulled it back in a hairband.

I tugged at my shirt because it was wrinkled from lying in bed. I didn't want to be obvious and put on a summer dress, but it also seemed pointless to take another shirt off the hanger and change into it.

Fifteen years old was a weird in-between place. I didn't know if I was a pretty girl or a pretty woman, but I knew instinctively I wanted to be pretty, even if I couldn't explain why I wanted to be pretty, or who I wanted to be pretty for.

With a sigh, I decided my white T-shirt and jean shorts were fine.

———— ×❖× ————

I didn't understand why these guys wanted to hang out with me.

Stephen led the way again. Alex and I followed behind him. Stephen talked about a spot they wanted to show me. "It's past where our farms meet. It's at the edge of the foothills hidden where the tree line starts."

"That's where our clubhouse is," Alex said. "We've put a lot of work into building it over the years."

"It's cool," Stephen glanced back. "Then, we're going to check out the mystery farm."

"We're just going to show Jenny from the clubhouse, right?" Alex said.

We turned, walking along the drainage ditch through Grandpa's field.

"I want to see what's behind the white fence." Stephen spun around, looking at us with wild eyes. "Mystery and intrigue!"

Alex stopped. "That's trespassing. My dad said he doesn't want us on other people's land anymore. Not like the last time when Mr. Thomas got his shotgun out to scare us."

Stephen shook his head. "That's not like this. They won't be there."

"I thought we were going to show her the clubhouse." Alex wasn't moving. "We aren't going to trespass."

"Do what you want, Alex Bailey." Stephen rolled his eyes and then raised his brows at me. "We'll leave Alex as a lookout back at the clubhouse."

"No, you're going to get Jenny in trouble." Alex crossed his arms, his jaw tense.

I didn't want to get in trouble, but I thought about my dark summer and remembered what doing and feeling nothing was like. My parents were there with me one day and then they weren't. I didn't want to be afraid anymore. I didn't want to hide anymore. Alex and Stephen claimed they wanted to hang out with me. I was going to make the most of it, in case they decided to ditch me when school started.

I walked past Alex, declaring with a little flare in my voice, "*I'll* go see what's on the other side of the white fence."

"Yes!" Stephen cheered and picked up his pace as he started to walk again.

I looked back at Alex, giving him a big smile. "Come with us."

"It's stupid. Stephen is stupid." He frowned.

"It's fun," I insisted, hoping to convince him.

He gave me a long, flat stare. He looked away, swallowing, dropping his arms to his sides. "All right. I'll come."

I ran to catch up with Stephen. Alex ran behind me. We came to a rocky point where the stream passed between property lines. Through trees and rocks, we followed a rough path until a big haphazard clubhouse came into view.

"Wow, you guys worked a lot on this?" The wooden fort climbed up and around the tree. I spotted a ladder to climb all the way up onto a small platform built into the branches.

Stephen nodded, ducking into the clubhouse. "Since we were, like, seven."

"It's so cool." I felt like I wasn't invited to go into it. Something about it felt sacred.

Alex laughed, digging his hands into his pockets. "Thanks for saying it's cool. It's kind of a kid thing to do. We still like to build on it, like a hobby when we're bored."

I took a few steps back to get a better view of the balcony they'd created higher up on the tree. "Really, I love it."

"Come on. We'll show you." Alex waved and then he ducked in.

I smiled to myself at the invitation and followed

behind him. The inside was bigger than I thought it would be. I could fully stand under the wooden hut-like structure because they'd dug up the ground. A bunch of random treasure junk lined a crude shelf along the wall. I started touching things. A yo-yo, a Rubix Cube, a hammer, and a rusted screwdriver. Dusty hot wheels lined one of the makeshift bookshelves, sports memorabilia was everywhere.

Stephen rummaged through a box. "I had binoculars in here. We might need them."

"Want to go up?" Alex pushed at a piece of the roof of the clubhouse.

I nodded and followed him up the wooden ladder rungs nailed into the side of the tree. He held out a hand to help me onto the platform. We were too close when I stepped up. We seemed to both go still because of it. We stood there for a long second, his eyes moved over my face.

I jerked my gaze toward the view. "Wow."

"Yeah, here." It was a small platform, but he stepped back to let me move forward a little. "You can see all the fields. They'll harvest everything soon and it'll be just dirt."

I rested my hand on the railing.

"Don't lean into that piece of wood," Alex said from behind me.

My hand came up. "Thanks," I said with a breathy laugh.

He scratched the back of his neck. "We built it ourselves. It's probably not safe."

I glanced back at him. "You're the responsible one, huh?"

"What do you mean?"

"Stephen does all the crazy stuff, comes up with the adventures and the things to do when you guys are bored." I looked him over from head to toe. "You make sure to follow the rules and keep you guys from killing yourselves."

His face flushed pink, his voice changed a little, went deeper, "I mean, I've gone along with Stephen's crazy ideas before. I'm not perfect. I usually give in—"

"I had a friend back home, her name was Rachel," I said quietly with a bit of a smile because it was the first time I'd thought of her without hot pain searing across my chest. "She was the one with crazy ideas. Once we broke into her neighbor's pool while they were on vacation. It was past midnight. We jumped in with all our clothes on. It was fun, but some college guys who lived in the neighborhood too showed up. I convinced her to leave because I was scared of them. Her mom caught us sneaking back into the house, but she wasn't even mad because she couldn't stop laughing at us in our wet clothes. She had a point, like, we didn't think through that part."

"That's funny," He laughed, a warm smile spread across his face.

"I'm the responsible one too."

"Every crazy kid needs a responsible kid, huh?"

I nodded, it was easy talking to Alex. "I think every responsible kid needs a crazy kid too."

"Yeah," His smile got bigger. He looked away and nodded. "I like that."

"Found it! Let's go!" Stephen said from below us.

———————— ✕ ◆◆◆ ✕ ————————

A thrill zipped through me as we followed Stephen into the cornfield that would lead us to the mystery farm. Alex walked behind me, his hands in his pockets and his head down. My hand hit the green cornstalk leaves as we went. Stephen was talking again about his theories of what was behind the white fences. "I think they have oversized giant fruit. Or maybe it's a new kind of food they're developing."

"Maybe it's something really crazy," I said, having fun. "Maybe they're growing limbs."

"Gross." Alex was laughing behind me.

Stephen spun to look back at us, "That's epic."

Soon, we were at the edge of the field. I studied the simple white house. Stephen was right. There was no one in there and it seemed like it had been converted into some kind of lab or business by the looks of it. Three white vans lined the side of the red barn. Between the barn and the house was a huge square area of tall, bright white, closed-off fence.

Stephen whispered, "Let's go."

"Wait—" Alex pulled Stephen's arm, looking around. "Make sure there's no security or something."

"It's totally quiet." Stephen said. "You and I already staked out if there were cameras weeks ago, and there aren't. Besides, we're stupid teenagers to them. The worst is they'll chase us off if someone is here."

"That's not the worst. The worst is jail." Alex glanced at me. "Or them bringing us to your grandpa."

My heart was pounding, doubt threatening my nerve, but I pushed myself to say, "Let's get to the fence, but stay low. Right?"

"Right. Good plan. See, Alex?" Stephen's smile was big and excited.

"Fine, you go first, Stephen. Give us the signal and then we'll come." Alex said, as if it was non-negotiable.

"Right." Stephen crept low, running across the gravel area until he pressed his back against the solid white fence. Nothing stirred. No one was here. He waved us over and uttered a hushed whisper again. "Come on."

Alex made a low growling sound in his throat. He was still frustrated by the whole scenario. I gave him a smile, wiggled my brows, and ran for it.

Nothing happened again. We found a door, but it was locked.

Alex shrugged. "Welp. Good try. Let's go home. My mom made pie and said she'd save some for us."

But Stephen and I were looking at each other. "Hoist me up. I've done gymnastics and cheer club since I was, like, three."

"Yeah, perfect." Stephen nodded.

Alex stepped toward us. "No—"

Stephen had already crouched, clasping his hands together in front of himself. In one smooth motion, I put my sneaker in his hand and jumped, pulling myself up to peer over the fence. "What do you see, Jenny?"

"Uh, plants," I said in a loud whisper. "It looks like a normal garden. Why is it behind the fence?"

"None of us know. Get back down, Jenny." Alex said from below.

I thought about asking Stephen to help me down, but instead of satisfying my curiosity, glimpsing the mystery garden only fed it. I lifted myself up by my arms, my foot coming out of Stephen's hand.

Stephen's voice was suddenly unsure. "Uh, what are you doing?"

"One minute." I swung my leg over and dropped to hold the other side of the fence with my feet dangling. Dropping with a small thud to the ground, I turned in a quick circle, observing about a dozen square patches of different fruits and vegetables. There was room for a small path between each squared-off area. Since it was the end of summer, everything was green and leafy and big, but there didn't seem to be anything special about it.

"This is all your fault." I could hear Alex say to Stephen.

"It's not my fault. I didn't want her to go over."

"Guys. It's all good." I walked through the garden down one of the paths and stood at the gate. "Come here. I think it opens from the inside." I pushed through the door and found a frowning Alex shaking his head, standing next to a jittery, grinning Stephen.

"Yeah, it does look like a regular garden." Stephen nudged past me to bend down and read the labels of the different plants.

Alex leaned in the doorway with his arms crossed.

I knelt next to a patch of strawberries. "Looks good though."

Without thinking about it, I picked one and plopped it into my mouth.

"You're going to go ahead and eat the mystery fruit, huh?" Stephen laughed, kneeling next to me.

"It's really good. Such a perfect strawberry." I picked another and handed it to Stephen. "Try one."

He took it from me and ate it. "Okay, that's a good strawberry."

Reluctantly, Alex squatted next to us. "I'll try one too."

Stephen and I watched him eat one. Alex shrugged, admitting it was good.

"Okay, so, boring garden." I stood and looked around again. "Maybe the fence is to keep the deer away."

"I don't think so. I mean, my mom has a shorter fence and it keeps them away." Alex circled the square of strawberries. "It's kind of overkill."

"Abilities," Stephen said, holding a tag attached to the plant. "Each of the labels says *Abilities* on the back of them. I assume that's a company name."

"Could be the nursery the plants are from," Alex said.

I pulled at a tag too, finding a barcode and numbers on the opposite side. "I can look it up online. Maybe see if it's like a business or a lab. Or, like you said, a nursery."

"We can look it up together." Alex's eyes flickered to mine.

I liked the thought of doing something together in the future. I gave him a little smile with a nod back. I stood up and turned to Stephen. "Well that was fun. Not groundbreaking, but I guess it was worth the adventure." I turned to Alex. "Your mom has pie?"

Relief washed over Alex's face. I understood it because I was a responsible kid too. He grinned at me. "She really wants to meet you. She wants you and Stephen to come over."

"Cool." I glanced at Stephen. "Let's go eat pie."

Stephen shrugged, but he whipped around to face the open gate door. The distant sound of a rumbling truck engine sent my heart into a gallop. Before I could blink Alex slid past me to shut the gate door. The engine sound was getting louder. They were coming up the private drive of the farm.

"What do we do?" Stephen said, his eyes wide.

Alex pressed his back against the gate door, drawing in deep breaths. "We can't stay here. They can't see us now, but they might come in."

I turned in a circle on my heel, stopping to face the wall I'd climbed over. "We can jump the fence, run back into the fields—"

Stephen shook his head. "What if they see us?"

"I don't know!" I threw up my hands. "We just keep running, right?"

"Right." Alex strode across the garden. Standing next to the wall, he crouched down and clasped his hands together. "Stephen first, Jenny next, and I'll get myself over the fence."

I was down for that plan. We didn't have many options. I looked back at Stephen, who still seemed stunned as if he were trying to process the best thing to do. The engine was closer, gravel crunching under the truck's wheels. I whispered harshly to Stephen, "Let's go, bro."

Stephen blinked. Leaping over a square of plants, he set his foot in Alex's hand and swung himself over the fence. Alex's eyes were wide when he turned to me, gesturing for me to move faster. I didn't hesitate. Two steps later, my foot was in Alex's hand, and then my hands were on the fence. I propelled myself over the fence so hard my teeth hurt when my feet hit the ground. I heard Alex jumping over behind me, but I was already running.

I was halfway across the open area to the tall corn-field stalks when a man with a deep voice shouted behind us. "What the hell—Hey!"

I whirled around, afraid of being in trouble, ready to accept the consequences that came with trespassing. The man had seen me. We were caught. Grandpa would know soon. I wondered if I'd be in jail tonight.

Alex gripped my hand and pulled me along. We

ran through the rough dips and ridges of the cornfield between the tall green stalks.

My shins began to ache as we ran and a pain in my side screamed at me to stop, but I wasn't going to slow down until I knew we were safe.

Stephen stopped first and looked back at Alex and me. His chest heaved. "Don't say it—"

"I absolutely told you so, Stephen Wright." Alex said, out of breath and glaring at his best friend. He turned to me, giving my hand a squeeze. "You okay?"

"Yeah." I slid my hand out of his, rubbing away the warmth he'd left on my skin. "I'm okay."

Alex shook his head. "I've never had a good feeling about the mystery farm." He glanced behind us, as if making sure we weren't being followed. "We're never doing that again."

Stephen winced. "I mean, it was fun though, right?"

I barked out a laugh, "Next time you suggest doing something dangerous, I'm taking Alex's side."

Alex's laugh was a huff. A grin spread across his face and a flush of pink crept up the back of his neck. He held my gaze for a few seconds longer than necessary. We both looked away as Stephen declared he wanted Mrs. Bailey's pie.

I'd lied. I was totally down to adventure with Stephen again, he was cool. I didn't know what to do with the way Alex made me feel when he looked at me, but I was desperate to find out everything I could about him.

03.

Mrs. Bailey's Kitchen was white with black hardware. It was the cleanest kitchen I'd ever seen. My mom's kitchen had been warm and comfortable, with butcher block counters and an orange, oversized bowl that always overflowed with fruit. Mrs. Bailey's kitchen was like a picture from a magazine, seemingly staged and unused.

Mrs. Bailey also talked a *lot*.

She asked me endless questions at her kitchen table while Stephen, Alex, and I ate her pie. Mrs. Bailey had short brown hair similar in color to Alex's. She was a classic beauty and moved like she knew it, with painted nails and bouncy curls that rested heavy over her shoulders. "Was your school big in the city you're from?" she asked, running a white washcloth over her pristine island counter.

I didn't mind her questions. But, it was a little awkward with these two boys I'd only met yesterday at the table too. "Yeah, like ten times as big as the one in this town. I'm nervous, but I know it'll be okay."

"Oh, you'll have a great time. I told Alex to keep an eye on you and help you with your way around the school. You'll most likely have the same classes, it's that small. I remember sophomore year. I loved it. You really grow up when you go from fifteen to sixteen." Mrs. Bailey winked at me. "At least girls do. Boys take a little longer at everything."

I glanced at Alex across the table because I felt him watching me. He shot me a nervous little smile. We were both obviously uncomfortable with his mom's rambling.

"Can I have more, Mrs. Bailey?" Stephen asked, distracted by the pie that he'd consumed very quickly.

"Oh sure, Stephen." Mrs. Bailey seemed happy to cut another slice and bring it to Stephen. "And you had friends where you lived before?"

"There's a group of girls I hung out with sometimes. I had a best friend named Rachel—"

"Had?" Mrs. Bailey's high-pitched tone almost startled me. "What changed?"

Stephen stilled with his fork in his hand between his plate and open mouth, a bite of pie hovering in midair. Alex raised his brows, looking a bit incredulous by her question because *What changed?* should have been obvious.

I'd been okay talking about Rachel to Alex an hour ago, but a familiar heavy pressure filled my chest now. I didn't know how to tell Mrs. Bailey that I'd fallen off the face of the earth when my parents died last spring. It was difficult to explain to adults that the sound of Rachel's voice reminded me of slumber parties when my mom would make us popcorn and we'd watch a chick-flick late into the night. I knew I'd hurt Rachel when I cut her off, but I'd needed her to move on and find new friends. I needed everything from the city I lived in before to disappear.

"I haven't talked to her since…" I swallowed, the rims of my eyes stinging. "I mean, I didn't finish out the school year when my parents—"

"Oh!" Mrs. Bailey's hand flew to her chest. "Of course, honey. That makes sense," she continued, bubbly and moving on from my small moment of panic. "It'll be nice to have Alex and Stephen on Monday. First days of school are hard enough, let alone walking in as a new kid. My family was military so I got used to moving schools a lot." She laughed to herself as if she was remembering something fondly, but I didn't know why the memory of moving around a lot would be a good one. "That's why I married a farmer. Bound to the land. We've lived in this house since Mr. Bailey bought it when we were twenty. I've remodeled it a few times through the years, but I love it."

"Yeah." I nodded. I figured it would be nice to know Alex and Stephen on the first day of school, but I still wasn't sure yet if Alex was being nice to me because he wanted to, or because his mom was forcing him to. "I guess no one likes to start a new school."

"Mr. Garrison is a good teacher. He's your homeroom teacher. I think he teaches your history and science classes too." Mrs. Bailey glanced at the clock. "It's almost dinner. Stephen, are you staying?"

Stephen glanced at me with uncertainty in his eyes. He seemed to decide that he didn't mind if I heard what he was going to say. "I stopped by the house after church. Dad was working on fixing the UTV. He told me to find myself dinner tonight."

"Sounds good," Mrs. Bailey stood and opened the fridge to pull out some sort of casserole. "Jenny, you're welcome to stay too. I'll call your grandma and ask her."

"Oh. Sure. Thanks."

Alex was scratching the back of his neck. "You want to see my room, Jenny?"

Mrs. Bailey waved us away. "You guys go off. This will be done in a little over half an hour."

"Uh, sure." I stood and pushed the chair in.

"Come on, Stephen."

We headed up the stairs and entered a cream-colored room with blue accents. There were glimpses of boyhood with a light blue baby-ish baseball lamp. The same blue was woven into the quilt on his twin bed, which I noticed also matched the curtains. But the posters were from official sports teams. Football and baseball gear were piled in the corner by his closet. A coffee mug used as a pencil holder and an antique lamp that had probably been his dad's at one point sat on a dark-brown desk.

The room told a story of a young boy transforming into a young man.

Stephen settled into the window seat with baby blue pillows. Alex fell into the bed and sat cross-legged. I felt like the safest place for me was to sit on the swivel desk chair.

"This room is cool," I looked around and then added, "Clean."

"Way too clean." Stephen threw a ball into the air and caught it. "He's a neat freak."

"I'm not a neat freak," Alex made a face at Stephen. "I like to walk through my room. Unlike your room."

Stephen rolled his eyes. "My room is perfect. I know exactly where everything is."

Alex's voice was all sarcasm. "That's true. It's laid out

on the floor, ready to use when you need anything."

"Exactly." Stephen jerked his chin at me. "Is your room messy or clean?"

I thought about my room before I came to Hollow Brook. There was always clean laundry in my chair next to the closet. My mom used to bring my clothes into my room, drop them in the chair, and tell me it was up to me if I wanted wrinkled clothes or not. She'd always said it with humor dancing in her eyes because she hated putting laundry away herself. The thought made me ache for my mom and that chair I had to leave behind.

"My room is usually clean, but it's cheating because I don't do anything to mess it up and my grandma puts my laundry away for me."

"You lucky duck." Stephen shook his head at me with a grin.

I shrugged. "What can I say? I live a life of luxury."

"What do you do then?" Stephen asked as he threw the baseball up and caught it again. "Why isn't your room messed up?"

I couldn't tell him that I did nothing but lay in bed all day. Instead, I pulled one leg up, wrapped my arms around it, and set my chin on my knee. "Sorry. That's classified information. I'd have to kill you if I told you."

I watched Stephen and Alex exchange a look I didn't

understand. It was like they knew something I didn't. Stephen gave Alex a shrug. "A little mystery in a girl is fun."

I couldn't tell if Stephen was mocking or flirting. I wasn't going to tolerate either. I gave him a level look, my voice dull but impatient. "Don't be weird."

Stephen barked out a laugh.

Alex was obviously annoyed with his friend. "Dude. She's right. Don't be weird." He turned to me with a smile. "Feel free to tell him to shut up whenever you want."

Stephen snorted, but there was amusement in his expression.

I gave them both a warm smile. These guys were cool. They weren't playing some cruel joke on me. They were boys who were trying to grow up and figure stuff out. Just like me. My mom's face flitted through my mind, but the thought was only passing. Her memory was quick and not as painful as usual.

I played with my shoelaces, still thinking, and then I looked up to ask, "What's Hollow Brook High like?"

"Small. Old," Stephen said absently.

"I know that," I said in that dull tone again. "I mean, like… what's it like?"

"Stephen and I mostly keep to ourselves." Alex scooted over to sit with his back to the wall. His long legs stretched out until his feet hung off the edge of the twin bed. "I don't really know what it's like for girls. You'll have to meet Emma, Meg, and Suzy. They're cool."

Stephen caught the ball in his hand before going still. I watched him distinctively dart his eyes over me. He looked thoughtful as he said, "She's going to be too pretty for Emma."

"Dude. Stephen. We just talked about not being weird." Alex glared at him. He turned to me. "Emma has a big personality—"

I was confused. "Wait. Who's Emma?"

"A girl we've known all our lives." Stephen threw the ball up in the air again. That absent tone was back. "You can hang with them, but I know, for a fact, Alex wants you to hang out with us."

Alex threw a pillow hard at Stephen. Stephen caught it with a grunt and a laugh. "What he means is you're welcome to hang out with us—You know, if you don't have anyone else to hang out with."

"Thanks, it'll be nice to—" Nausea washed over me. I held my stomach, feeling like I was going to barf all over Alex's floor. I tried to push the feeling down.

"You okay?" Alex sat up straighter. "Your face just went pale."

Stephen was looking at me funny too, his head tilted.

"Oh my gosh, I'm so sorry." I stood, feeling my stomach lurch again. "I think I'm going to throw up."

Alex stood up and pointed. "The bathroom is right across from my door."

I was deeply embarrassed as I ran and then threw up into the toilet violently. The second time I wretched, I didn't care about what anyone thought because it was painful and I just wanted to stop. I didn't care that the sounds coming from me as I emptied my stomach were unattractive. I wouldn't have blamed them if they never talked to me again. When my stomach gave me a moment to pause, I could hear Alex talking in the other room. "Dude, grab my trash can."

From where I sat across the hall, I watched Stephen fall to his knees and vomit into Alex's trash can. Seconds later, Alex dropped on the ground next to me to reach for the bathroom trash can and began throwing up too. I didn't really care because I was busy losing my stomach contents again.

Mrs. Bailey came up the stairs, clearly flustered. She looked between the three of us. "Was it my pie?"

Like the good mother she was, she quickly sprang into action and gave us wet washcloths. She called my grandma and told Stephen she'd leave a message for his dad that he was staying at Alex's house for the night.

As I waited for Grandma to come, I sat back against the side of the bathtub, holding my stomach and waiting to be sick again. Alex was next to me and Stephen sat in the hall outside the door with Alex's blue baby-ish trash can. We smelled horrible, each of us covered in sweat, taking turns to dry heave every few minutes.

When I got a moment to breathe, I said, "At least I'm not alone."

"The bright side." Stephen's face was twisted. "Oh, this sucks." He threw up again into the trash can, it sounded like a dying animal. I noted he'd eaten most of the pie and had more to empty from his stomach than Alex and I did.

Alex looked over at me, pale and exhausted. "We've never brought anyone else to the clubhouse before."

"What?" I had no idea why he said that. I was so sick and that made no sense.

"He's trying to say you're in." Stephen grinned at me. "Good luck getting rid of us now."

Then he threw up again.

Alex tried to smile despite the sounds Stephen was making, but his face turned into a grimace as he vomited again. The smell of it hit me and sent me into another dry-heaving session. We were miserable, but I wouldn't have changed anything about the last two days.

04.

*I*WAS IN BED for three days after I left Alex's house. Grandma called Alex's parents and Stephen's dad to get updates. They were in the same position as me.

"No one but you three ate Mrs. Bailey's pie. She feels horrible about it." Grandma held a washcloth and wiped my brow.

"I'm feeling better though." I sat up, propping myself up on my elbow. "Are they feeling better?"

"Mrs. Bailey and I are going to keep you guys in bed till morning." Grandma stood up, smoothing her apron down, and I knew she was thinking of my parents. This was the first time my mom wasn't here to take care of me while I was sick, but neither of us were going to say that out loud. "I'll come back with soup."

The next morning, I felt great.

I was gathering up my bed sheets to put in the wash when I heard the tap of a rock hitting my window. I dropped the sheets on the floor and rushed to open my window. "Hi!"

"My mom said you were better." Alex was grinning up at me with Stephen at his side. They were in T-shirts and board shorts. "Come swimming with us. We're going to the waterhole."

"There's a rope we can swing from and jump in." Stephen had a towel draped over each of his shoulders.

"Okay. I have to put laundry in and make sure it's good with Grandma." I shut the window and rushed to put the laundry in the washer. Swinging around the doorway from the hall into the kitchen, I found Grandpa. "Can I go to the waterhole—that's what they called it—with Alex and Stephen?"

Grandpa was reading the paper. He took his glasses off to see me better. He didn't look immediately happy about my request. "Alex Bailey and Stephen Wright?"

"Yeah."

"Those are boys, you know." His tone was stern, but his eyes were teasing.

"I know they're boys, Grandpa." I smiled sweetly at him.

He raised a brow at me. "Can't you find any girls to be friends with?"

"I haven't found any girls yet." I shrugged.

He let out a sigh, laying his newspaper flat. "Here's the thing. Sit with me real quick."

"Okay." I slid the chair out and sat down. I was a little nervous, Grandpa hadn't acted like this with me before.

"You don't go off with one of those boys alone. Especially the Wright one. Make sure that Alex boy is there." He wrapped his hand around his coffee mug. "You don't have to go around telling everyone I told you that. Just do it."

"Okay." I didn't understand his advice, but I was going to agree to anything if I could go swimming with Alex and Stephen. "Sounds good. I get it."

"Good." He took a sip of coffee, flipping the newspaper in his hands again. "All right, go have fun. Take water."

"Thanks, Grandpa." I kissed his cheek and went off to grab my bag and change.

I pulled up my purple one-piece swimsuit, the straps tight over my shoulders. It occurred to me that I hadn't worn this swimsuit since last summer. It fit a little different around the new curves and hollows of my body. I slid on athletic shorts, but I didn't bother with a shirt. Following Grandpa's orders, I packed a drawstring bag with water, sunblock, and a towel inside.

We walked to the waterhole together, Stephen was ahead of us, wanting to lead and take charge. Alex fell into step next to me.

We strolled past the Bailey farm to get to the waterhole and I realized they had backtracked to invite me to come along. They'd gone out of their way, and that made me ridiculously happy. But I had to remember to play it cool because I didn't want to say something stupid. They didn't need to know they were changing my life with every step we took.

The waterhole sat between a set of jagged rocks, a pretty waterfall that spilled into a natural pool. Older teenagers were down the way, splashing and playing. There were girls in two-piece swimsuits laying out on towels and guys wrestling in the water.

Stephen's face fell, his voice deflated, "Did you know they'd be here?"

"No, or we wouldn't have come," Alex said, rolling his eyes. He pointed at them. "My older brother Mark is the one in the green swim shorts. He's a junior. That's his group he hangs out with."

"I didn't know you had a brother," I said, trying to recall any family photos in his house, but all I could remember was fancy decor and expensive-looking pictures of fields.

"We used to like each other." He gave me a little sad

smile. "Then he turned seventeen and got a girlfriend. Now he only talks to me when I'm taking too long in the shower and he needs pomade for his hair."

"Oh yeah," I said, pretending to hold a serious expression. "That makes sense, girls love pomade on a guy."

Alex laughed, rubbing the back of his neck as he eyed the group of older teenagers. I could see debate behind his eyes. I was curious to know why it was a big deal that his older brother and his friends were here, but I wasn't sure how to ask about it.

Stephen shrugged. "Let's go this way so they don't bother us."

"Cool," Alex said, following Stephen.

I glanced back at the group of teenagers once more. They'd paused and were looking at me. I blinked, realizing they were also talking about me. Nervous, I turned to follow Alex and Stephen. Sticking with them seemed like the best idea.

"Hey! Wait!" I turned to find one of the older boys jogging toward us.

Alex's brother Mark was behind him. "Brandon, come back."

"We all want to know your name," Brandon said, skidding to stop in front of me. His smile was obviously mocking. His brown eyes were narrowed on me.

"Uh, Jenny." My heart pounded in my chest. I didn't want trouble, but I could sense it coming. "Jenny Phillips."

"Go away, Brandon." Alex took half a step forward, placing his shoulder in front of mine.

Stephen was on the other side of me. "Seriously, leave us alone."

"Hey, *chill*, just wanted to know Jenny's name here." He was studying me, his gaze fixed on my face. There was a definite difference between Alex and Stephen and Mark and Brandon. Stephen and Alex were just past puberty, an inch shorter than the other guys. They were lean but hadn't built any kind of muscle yet. While Mark and Brandon were both toned, muscular. "Are you new to Hollow Brook?"

A pretty, older girl with curly hair spoke up, "Leave her alone, Brandon."

"You guys." Brandon's hands went up. "Only curiosity."

I could tell by everyone's reaction that Brandon had a history of causing problems and maybe bullying. I scrambled to think of a way to ease out of the situation. Alex's shoulder brushed mine as he pinned Mark with a look that said, *Help me or you'll be in trouble if you don't.*

Mark cleared his throat. "Come on, Brandon. You got her name. You can tell everyone—"

"How old are you?" Brandon asked, his gaze pointedly roaming over me.

Heat washed over my face, I'd never had an older guy look at me like that. I wrapped my arms around myself, hoping I looked more defensive than insecure. "I'm fifteen. I'm going to go swimming." I wanted this to stop, and so I started to turn. "Nice to meet you, though."

"Are you Alex's girlfriend?" I looked back to see him smirking.

Mark groaned. "Brandon, that's enough. Let's go."

"Has he kissed you yet?"

Out of the corner of my eye, I could see a blush creeping up Alex's neck and behind his ears. I didn't know the history between Alex, Stephen, and Brandon. I didn't know how Brandon would react if I said any number of the sassy things I wanted to say so I could put Brandon in his place.

Stephen crossed his arms. "You want to go, Brandon? Cause we can go."

Brandon ignored Stephen. "So he hasn't kissed you yet?"

As the rest of Mark's friends started to gather around us, it dawned on me that not only did Brandon want to humiliate Alex, he was playing with everyone's thoughts about me too. Either Alex wasn't man enough to have kissed the new girl, or I was the new girl who'd shamelessly let Alex Bailey kiss her over the summer. He was trying to write my story at school before I'd even stepped foot through the front door.

As Stephen had said, I realized I wasn't afraid of Brandon either. Alex and Stephen wanted to be my friends. If Brandon wanted to spread rumors about me, then he was just going to do it, no matter what I said right now. Alex had been nothing but kind to me.

I'd take the bullet for him.

Slowly, I smiled at Brandon, letting my lashes flutter and my lips part. My voice was soft and low. "Yeah, he has. It was really good. Tell that to all your friends. I'm going swimming."

Alex and Stephen whipped their heads around to stare at me, obviously surprised by my declaration. Mark and the curly-haired girl laughed with the others, clearly impressed by the way I hadn't let Brandon bully me and Alex.

Stephen whistled under his breath as we began to walk in the opposite direction of the group of older teens. "Okay, wow."

"Why'd you say that?" Alex asked, but he was grinning at me, pleased at what I'd done.

I shrugged. "They'll talk anyway. They'll say what they want. Let them talk." I spun, facing them and walking backwards. "What's going to happen? It's not like I'm not going to have friends on Monday. You two will be there. Right?"

"Stick with us at school." Stephen grinned, giving my shoulder a light punch. "Yep. We'll be there."

My stomach dropped and my eyes widened. Fear thundered through me as Brandon stormed toward us. I'd never seen the kind of fury I saw in Brandon's eyes as he pushed past Alex and grabbed my arm with a jerk that hurt. Spit sprayed from his mouth as he shouted, "We weren't done talking—"

In a whoosh of movement, Alex threw a punch at Brandon.

05.

THE PUNCH WAS in slow motion. Epic and glorious, but somehow fake at the same time. As if they'd staged it and were all playing some kind of big prank on me. Alex's fist collided with Brandon's face with an audible crack. Air whispered past my temple in a moment of insanity.

Brandon should have never, under any circumstance, jolted back so far like that.

Alex shouldn't have been able to throw a punch that dramatically, like he was in a scene from some kind of superhero movie. It'd been fast and slow all at once, Brandon landing with a hard grunt, sliding along the pebbled ground. I couldn't make sense of it, I could only gape at Brandon's limp body on the bank of the waterhole, now several feet from where I stood.

Stunned, I took three breaths before I screamed, sliding onto my knees at Brandon's side. Logically, I knew this punch wasn't my fault, but Brandon was hurt because Alex had punched him over me.

Brandon wasn't moving. His cheek was bleeding and his neck bent at an awkward angle. "Oh my gosh. Oh my gosh. Wake up, wake up—" My heart raced in my chest and my hands were shaking.

Mark was kneeling on the other side of Brandon. "Dude— Brandon."

"You hit him so hard…" The curly-haired girl gaped at Alex.

Alex and Stephen stood at Brandon's feet, both wide-eyed.

"I didn't mean…" Alex shook his head, breathing hard. "It happened so fast."

"Mandy." Mark looked up at the girl. Authority rang in his voice. "Get my keys. They're on the blanket next to the cooler. Pull up the truck and we'll get him to the clinic. There's no cell service here."

"Right." The girl turned on her flip-flop heel and ran toward a red truck in the distance.

Alex kept shaking his head.

"Go home, Alex." Mark glared at his younger brother. "Tell Mom what happened."

"Yeah. Okay." Alex nodded and looked at Stephen.

Stephen touched my shoulder. "Come with us, Jenny."

My hands were shaking as I pushed Brandon's hair back. "He's breathing, Mark, right?"

Mark looked up at me, his eyes soft. "Yeah, Jenny, he's breathing. He'll be okay. I need you to go with Alex and Stephen. All right?"

I nodded as Stephen grabbed my arm and dragged me to my feet.

We ran and didn't stop until we were panting on Mrs. Bailey's porch. Alex and Stephen's words were rushed as they told Mrs. Bailey the story, but they were honest and clear about what had happened. Mrs. Bailey rolled her eyes. "Brandon Thomas getting himself into trouble again. I'll call Mrs. Thomas and see what we can do." She looked at me. "Jenny, go wash your hands. You've got blood on them."

I did have Brandon's blood on them. I hadn't realized.

Alex gestured for me to come with him as Mrs. Bailey went into the living room to grab her phone. Stephen was on my heels. At the kitchen sink, Alex lifted the soap so he could squirt some in my hand. "Here."

"Thanks." I let the water wash away Brandon's blood and then used the hand towel hanging on the cupboard below the sink before twisting to lean back against the sink. We all looked at each other, but Stephen and I were mostly looking at Alex.

I spoke first. "That was a weird fluke."

"A *fluke*?" Stephen said it like he didn't know the word.

"It means, like…like, random. It was random," I said, trying to rationalize it.

"What did it feel like?" Stephen asked.

Alex shook his head. "I didn't even think about it. It just… happened."

"You hit him just right— Or he tripped when he went down." I didn't believe my own words. "It was a fluke."

We went quiet again. I crossed my arms, trying to steady myself. The image of Alex's fist flying past my face kept flashing again and again in my mind. Brandon passed out and bleeding was like a broken record player in my head.

After another minute, Alex said, "It felt good."

Stephen looked up at Alex, a small grin on his face. "Yeah?"

"I mean, like, it felt good to punch him. He's been bothering us forever." Alex frowned when he looked at me. "I was pissed off because he thought he could mess with you."

My cheeks burned. When Brandon had looked at me it'd felt gross, but when Alex gave me a certain look, everything inside me turned flustered. I stared at the white cabinet across from me. No one had ever punched someone for me before. And definitely not the way Alex had. I didn't know how I felt about all of it.

Alex continued when I didn't say anything. "I mean, uh, when I punched him... I can't explain it. It's like my body turned on or something." He shook his head. "This is too weird. I can't explain it."

"Try." I looked up at him. "We aren't judging you."

Stephen nodded.

"It felt like... I felt alive. Extra alive. So much strength...and power, I guess?" His eyes lit up as he thought about it. "I felt really in control of the swing of my arm."

"Huh." I blinked at him.

"It's like it's all buzzing through my body still." Alex's eyes drifted to the window above the sink. "Come on. Let's try something. Maybe I can show you."

Stephen and I followed Alex into the barn. Alex took a moment to think before stepping in front of an older tractor. As he studied the machinery, the sensation that this was all some kind of prank hit me again. I watched him shrug and bend over to lift under the metal frame of the tractor. He wasn't struggling or straining, looking as stunned as I felt. I kept blinking, trying to make what I was seeing rational and real, but I couldn't piece any of it together.

"Dude," Stephen said, his eyes wide, his voice barely above a whisper. "This is a trick or something."

It was effortless the way Alex continued to stand there with two tractor tires on the ground and two suspended in the air. "The feeling is buzzing like crazy through my back, arms, and legs. I don't know how else to explain it."

"Let me do it," Stephen said as if to make sure this wasn't a prank on him too.

Alex set it down. The tractor groaned, metal creaking as it rocked from one side to the other before it settled.

Stephen placed his hands in the same spot Alex had. The tractor tilted a fraction, but there was no way he was going to get the tires off the ground. "Dude. That's impossible. This is… This is *impossible*."

"I'm telling you," Alex hadn't looked my way since he'd lifted the tractor. "Something crazy is going on with me."

"Uh, do something else." Stephen started to look around.

My mouth was dry because it'd been hanging open. I cleared my throat and glanced over to see six rusty pitchforks up against the wall. "Does your dad need all these?"

"Probably no." Alex still wouldn't quite look at me as he moved to grab the metal pitchfork from my hand. "You try first, Stephen. Like, really try to bend it."

"All right." Stephen took it and tried to bend it over his knee. When that didn't work, he put it on the ground to try and bend it with his foot. "Okay, so that's impossible to bend. Stephen-approved."

I took a few steps forward. "Let me try. So I know you two aren't pranking me."

"Us? Prank you?" Stephen handed it to me. He was teasing me despite the fact Alex was in some sort of crisis that none of us understood. "Never, Jenny."

I did the same tests that Stephen had. It was solid metal that wasn't bendable at all. Not even Mr. Bailey or Grandpa could probably do it. I bit my lip as I held it out for Alex to take. We had the briefest eye contact as he took the pitchfork from me. After drawing in a deep breath, Alex bent the pitchfork in his hands like a child bending a plastic straw.

Stephen and I stepped away from him.

Alex dropped the pitchfork, stunned at his own strength. "Something crazy is happening to me, Stephen. I need to tell my mom." He picked up the bent tool again. "I need to go to a doctor or something."

"No. Nope. No way." Stephen stepped in front of him. "They'll test you and make you go to a secret government lab. Wait a minute and think about it."

I agreed with Alex. "No, maybe something is really wrong with him. Like he's aging really fast and needs—" I cut myself off. I had no idea what I was saying. "I think adults need to know about this."

"I think so too." Despite his own words, Alex kept standing there, staring at the bent pitchfork.

Stephen shook his head again after touching Alex's forehead with the back of his hand. "You don't feel sick. Nothing feels wrong. Wait it out."

I didn't say anything. This was up to Alex. I held my breath as I watched him wrestle with his thoughts. Finally, Alex met my eyes directly. I gave him a nod. I trusted him, I wanted him to trust me, and I'd do whatever he wanted me to do.

"Fine." Alex let out a long sigh. "Let's see what happens with Brandon. Then… when it's all calmer, then I'll tell my mom and dad. My dad is at an auction buying cows. He should be here when I tell them."

"Good plan." Stephen looked over at me. "Can you keep the secret?"

"I won't say anything to anyone." I said confidently. This wasn't my secret to tell.

"Cool." Stephen nodded, and then very casually, as

if everything that had just happened didn't happen, he said, "Let's go find lunch in Mrs. Bailey's fridge."

I stared at Stephen. Alex did too. I didn't feel hungry after what I'd seen Alex just do, but I had a feeling Stephen was always hungry. None of this phased him. He wanted to eat and that was next on his mind.

Alex and I exchanged a look, erupting in laughter, and we headed to the kitchen.

06.

STEPHEN AND ALEX stood on the front porch, waving at me as Grandma drove down the private drive. When we walked through the front door, Grandpa called me to come see him in the kitchen. He made me repeat what happened at the waterhole three times.

"Alex punched Brandon Thomas because Brandon wasn't being nice to you?" Grandpa sat back in his chair.

I nodded. "He didn't mean to. Like, he wasn't thinking—"

"He's a good boy. I like him."

Grandma smiled, giving a little shake of her head. "Well, I'm glad you're okay. I found out through the prayer chain that Brandon woke up on the way to the hospital. I guess he has a broken bone in his cheek and a concussion, but he should be fine."

"That scrawny little Bailey kid broke his cheekbone, huh?" Grandpa said, looking thoughtful.

I didn't dare say what I knew about Alex. They both moved on from the conversation eventually. I was relieved they'd stopped asking me questions.

The next morning after breakfast, I went upstairs and laid out on my bed to read my book. An hour later, I sat up after hearing the familiar tap of rocks hitting glass. I went to the window and found Stephen standing there.

"Hey," I said after I opened it. "Where's Alex?"

"He's grounded until the first day of school for breaking Brandon's face," Stephen said from below. "I'm bored, let's go do something."

"One minute." I shut the window and went to the mirror. I was in my usual summer uniform, little jean shorts, and a white tank top with my dirty white sneakers. It was too hot to do anything with my hair except pull it back into a plain ponytail.

I paused at the bottom of the stairs, remembering what Grandpa had said about Alex and Stephen being together if I was going to hang out with them. I counted myself lucky when I found Grandma in the kitchen. The sunlight poured through the window onto

Grandma's worn wooden dining table, making the chipping yellow cabinets feel bright today. I figured she'd suggest a way for me to follow Grandpa's rule without humiliating myself. "Stephen is here."

Grandma was distracted because she was baking something. "Oh, nice, dear."

"Grandpa said I can't hang out with the guys unless they're both there. But Alex isn't here because he's grounded."

She paused her whisking. "Okay. Um. Well, Grandpa is in town this morning. What if you stayed near the house? I think he'd be all right with that."

"Okay, thanks."

She went back to whisking, her eyebrows drawing together as she peered down at her cookbook.

I stepped out onto the porch. Stephen was at the bottom of the steps. He wore a pair of jean shorts and a red shirt that was a little big on him. He pushed his heavy dark curls away from his forehead. "Let's go to the clubhouse."

I sat down on the top step. "I can't. I have to stay here."

"Why?" He sat next to me.

"Because Grandpa doesn't want me to be alone with a boy." I wasn't embarrassed about it. It was a manageable rule, and I wasn't the rebellious type.

Stephen frowned, picked up a stick from the flower bed, and hit it against the wood step. "It's just me, huh?"

My gaze snapped to him. "No, I can't be alone with Alex either, or any boy. Grandpa is traditional and old. He's trying to make sure I'm safe. It's not you."

"Everyone in this town thinks I'm a bad kid," Stephen said. "It's okay. I get it."

"Why would you think everybody thinks that about you?"

He huffed and looked away.

"Do you do bad stuff?"

"Nope."

"That makes no sense."

"You're right," He shrugged. "It doesn't make sense. That's the point."

I almost pushed him to tell me more, but I realized Stephen had no problem with expressing himself verbally. He'd hardly stopped talking since the moment I'd met him. If he didn't want to spell out his meaning then I wasn't going to press him, especially since he'd decided to stop asking me about my parents the day we went fishing.

"We can't change the story of what's behind," he said, as if he were cosplaying some mysterious philosopher, a smile played at the edge of his lips. "But we can write the story of what's ahead."

"What?"

"That's something Mr. Bailey says." Stephen laughed. "He's always saying stuff like that."

I stood and stepped onto the thick wooden garden barrier, balancing on it as if it were a gym beam. Stephen stood too. He bent down and picked up a smooth rock from the gravel path.

"I've had Mr. Bailey in my life for as long as I can remember." He paused, glancing up at me. "The Bailey's are very involved in Hollow Brook's social circles. Which, before you ask, by social circles I mean basically church potlucks. My dad and Mr. Bailey are best friends, so Alex and I have always played on the same team in sports. The Bailey's take me on vacation with them every year. Alex and I always want to hang out, so they pick me up and take me with them to do stuff. Basically, every day I end up hanging out at Alex's house." He tossed the rock up into the air, leaning forward to catch it in his hand behind his back. "But my dad isn't really into social gatherings. He works hard seven days a week on our farm, he reads the newspaper while he eats all his meals, and he goes to sleep at seven o'clock every night. He and Mr. Bailey go fishing maybe once a month, and that's it for interaction with friends for him."

I swung my leg around, turning at the end of the beam to balance on it the opposite way. I tried to keep my voice light as I asked, "Why are you telling me this?"

"Lots of reasons," he said, scrunching his face to indicate that he thought my question was dumb. "First, Alex is forcing me to be your friend. Second, if we are going to be friends, you're going to have to know the dynamic. I'm not changing who I am just because you're a girl. Third… Third, is that I'd rather you hear about me from me first, rather than anyone else in this town. Because keeping to yourself like my dad does isn't bad. Not having a mom around isn't bad either, it's just different." He eyed the stone in his palm, bouncing it in his hand. "And fourth, I can't help it, I just talk a lot."

"Okay."

"Okay, what?"

"I won't listen to anyone about your life but you. If anyone else starts talking about you, I'll turn my ears off." I said, bending my knee to balance on one foot, my arms spread wide to keep myself steady. A few seconds went by, and I realized he was still chewing on my promise in his mind, but since he'd shared so much about himself, I said, "I don't know how to talk to people."

"Why?"

I turned toward him so that my toes were pointed in his direction. "I think I'm going to be too much for people." I hadn't realized I was going to say that. "And sometimes there aren't words for what I want to say. Like, I'm afraid people wouldn't understand, and they wouldn't know what to do with me if I tried to tell them what I felt."

Stephen dropped the stone on top of his shoe and kicked it up like a hacky sack, letting the rock jump from one foot to the other. "Yeah, well, you don't have to talk to people if you don't want to."

"But they want me to talk."

The rock dropped to the ground. Stephen frowned at the rock as if he'd failed at some great feat, but then he looked up at me. "Who says we gotta do what they say?"

"I don't know," I shrugged. "I guess, I don't want people making a big deal out of things."

"I don't think we owe the world our thoughts. I think the world should earn our trust by displaying good behavior." He pointed at me, eyes narrowing. But I caught the teasing behind his expression too. "By the way, I'm into conspiracy theories and they say to be careful of the government, the goons and the girls." He clicked his tongue with a shake of his head. "Especially, the girls."

Deadpan, I said, "You're going to have to switch to UFO's if you ever want a girlfriend someday."

Stephen threw his head back and laughed at that.

His laughter was so big and dramatic that I was caught up in the moment too and started laughing with him. I turned on my heel again, but the plank of wood I stood on wobbled, and I slipped.

Instinctively, Stephen lunged forward so I wouldn't hit the ground. I yelped at his touch and jerked away as a searing pain shot up my arm. His hands went up. His eyes were wide, confused by my reaction. "What— What?"

I held my arm, and we watched it turn red and blister. "What's wrong with your hand?"

"Nothing," His eyebrows scrunched together as he studied his palms. They looked completely normal. "Nothing is wrong with them."

"Your skin is super hot." I couldn't tear my eyes from my arm as the print of his hand continued to turn into a bright pink. The sting of it was faint, no more pain than as if I'd barely touched the edge of a hot burner. "Holy crap, Stephen. Are you okay?"

"I'm fine…" He placed a hand over his chest. "I mean, I feel like there's like pins and needles all over my skin, but in a good way."

"Alex," I said, swallowing. "You have something going on like Alex?"

Stephen shook his head, stepping away from me. "I don't know— How should I know?"

I rolled my eyes. Boys were so useless sometimes. "Come on."

Stephen followed me until we stood behind the house. I grabbed the hose and turned the spigot on. "Put your hand out."

"Uh, okay." He did as I asked.

As the water hit his hand and arm, it sizzled and steamed. We both looked up at each other with the same shocked expression. I pointed to a nearby bird bath. "Put your hand in that."

Stephen's eyes were wary as he put his hand in the birdbath. It bubbled and boiled, the steam rising again between us.

Stephen pulled his hand back, pressing his palm to his chest. "What's going on, Jenny? What's happening to me?"

"Probably something similar to what's happening to Alex. But apparently different." I rubbed my face, totally overwhelmed.

Stephen was silent, but then his eyes lit up. "The strawberry, Jenny. We all ate one. I don't think it was Mrs. Bailey's pie that made us throw up. I think we ate those strawberries behind the fence and it did something to us."

I stared at him, letting the connection settle within

me. The theory was crazy, but so was super strength and skin that boiled water.

"Okay, but nothing has happened to me," I said with my arms spread out.

"I can't think." Stephen dug his fingers into his curls. "We have to go talk to Alex."

"We can't." I wrapped my arms around my stomach, feeling out of control. "We have to tell someone."

"We promised Alex we wouldn't talk unless he agreed to it." He patted his cheeks. "I feel fine. I feel better than fine. I'm totally serious."

I was silent for a long moment, weighing out options in my head. But Stephen was right, Alex needed to be in on what was happening. "Okay, let's go talk to Alex. Wait—How do we talk to Alex?"

Stephen grinned at me. "I know exactly how we talk to Alex."

"His room is on the trellis side," Stephen said five minutes later. We were crouching in Mrs. Bailey's rose bushes. "I've snuck up there when he was grounded before. Remember how you climbed the white fence? I bet you can climb it too."

"Yeah, I can do it." I eyed Mrs. Bailey's white SUV

in front of the three-car garage. The Bailey's lawn was a spectacular shade of green, perfectly landscaped. There wasn't anyone around to see us sneaking in, but that didn't stop my heart from racing. "Let's go before my grandma realizes I'm gone."

We sprinted across the front yard of the Bailey's farmhouse until we tucked ourselves against a porch column to stay hidden. A white trellis covered in green vines clung to the side of the house. Stephen didn't say anything as he climbed it. He scanned the area around us before he signaled for me to follow.

As I climbed, I noticed the vines had shriveled at his touch. When I neared the top, he held out a hand to help me up. He obviously wasn't thinking things through. I wasn't about to grab his inferno hand.

I huffed. "Uh, no."

"Right." He winced, withdrawing his hand. "Sorry."

I pulled myself onto the roof, trying to find my balance on unsteady legs. I followed Stephen's lead as he scooted along the side of the house. He peered into Alex's room. "He's in there."

"Okay," I said impatiently. I wanted to get this over with without getting into any kind of trouble. "Knock on the window, James Bond."

Stephen tapped on the glass. Alex opened the window and leaned out wearing only black gym shorts.

"Dude." He looked past Stephen. "Jenny? What are you guys doing here? I'm grounded."

"Yeah, we know. We need to talk. Emergency." Stephen said. "Now."

"You're going to kill Jenny." Alex backed up and Stephen climbed in.

I slid against the wall until I was next to the window. Alex held out a hand for me. I took it and ducked into his room.

I drew in a sharp breath, taking in Alex's bare chest. Rationally, I knew it was completely normal for a guy to walk around with no shirt on. The problem now was that the backs of my bare legs were against the edge of his bed. My cheeks burned as I glanced downward. He glanced down at himself a second after I did, flushing pink as he turned away. He took a few steps, grabbed a light gray shirt from the top of the hamper, and slid it over his head.

"My mom is going to call me down to lunch soon." Alex said quietly, not looking at me, obviously trying to recover from also realizing I'd been standing in his room while he was shirtless. "Talk fast, Stephen Wright."

Stephen nodded. "Okay, so my skin is really hot."

"What?" Alex looked at me.

I turned, showing him the blistered handprint on my arm. "Stephen did that."

"We put my hand in water and it was, like boiling." Stephen said, bouncing from one foot to another. "So you got super strength. And…I got super hot skin, apparently. I think it's from the strawberries behind the white fence."

Alex's expression twisted in confusion. He wasn't understanding, he looked at me for help. I gestured to Stephen. "Have him touch your skin." I said impatiently.

Stephen held his arm out to Alex. "Right."

Alex placed four fingers on Stephen's arm. "Oh shit," He jerked his hand away. "Okay, that's extremely weird."

Stephen snorted. "Says the muscle maniac."

Alex ignored him and looked at me. "We all ate the strawberries."

"Nothing for me." I shrugged.

"Nothing for you… yet." Alex groaned and put his face in his hands. Stephen and I watched him for several seconds before he looked up again. "I haven't said anything yet, but I think we should tell my parents. Let them help us."

"No." Stephen shook his head.

Alex's eyebrows shot up, his eyes wide. "I have this weird strength thing. You have hot skin. What if Jenny's is like… What if she dies? We can't let her die without telling anyone."

"How do you feel? Right now?" Stephen asked.

Alex looked down at his hands. "Good. Better than good. It feels amazing."

"Yeah." Stephen smiled at his friend, setting his hand over his chest. "I do too. It feels like I can do anything. If she's got something coming for her, I bet she'll feel really good too."

The thought of me getting a strange power hit me in the stomach. I was overwhelmed. I didn't know what to say. This was all too much for my mind to wrap around. I wanted to cry.

"It's up to her if she—" Alex looked over at me, his face changing after seeing mine. "Dude, she's crying because of you."

"No." I brushed tears away. "I'm not crying."

"Stephen, you made her cry." Alex growled.

"So what?" Stephen scowled. "Girls cry. We have to deal with it if you want her in our group. I told you that."

Alex glared at Stephen. "We should tell someone."

"Fine." Stephen stood up. I swore the temperature changed in the room. A gentle wave of warmth washed over me, like I was sitting next to a portable space heater. "You have to be ready to be the weird kids. All right? We'll get shipped away and tested on and they'll put us on the news. We won't ever have a normal life ever again."

A normal life.

Stephen was right. Alex and Stephen would never be the same. If we told adults, they would take us to doctors and the doctors would take us to more doctors. These two guys I'd only met days ago would be taken from me. I hadn't known them long, but I wasn't sure I could survive losing them, just as I'd lost my parents. Desperation swelled in my chest, I couldn't think of anything I wouldn't do to keep them in my life.

"We'll end up in a secret military base or something. It's in every movie about aliens and superheroes." Stephen threw his arms up. "We won't ever see our families again—or each other."

Alex's eyes darted to me before his chin dipped down to study his fingers.

"At least we have control right now. Before we tell anyone. Maybe we can hide this a little longer and…" Stephen's shoulders dropped. "And maybe we can try and be normal."

"I can see your point," I said quietly, trying not to reveal how scared I was. "Let's wait a few days and see what happens to me. If something happens to me, then we can talk again and decide if we are going to tell adults or not."

Alex buried his face in his hands again. Silence stretched in the room before he ran a hand through his light brown hair. "Okay, we'll wait."

I turned to Stephen. "You're not sweating or any-thing. You look totally normal."

"I don't feel any different." He said, holding out his arm for us to observe it with him. "I feel a tingling all over my body. And a lot of energy. That's it, though."

Alex frowned. "By the way, I know Mark, Mandy and the others saw me punch Brandon, but I think we're good. Mark tried to explain to my dad how weird the punch was, but my dad brushed him off. I don't think he understood what Mark was really saying."

Stephen shrugged. "That's good."

I was relieved. I'd wondered what the others would say about Alex's superhero-like punch. I was still wor-ried about what it meant that they'd seen, but I pushed the thought to the back of my mind.

"Alex, come wash your hands." Mrs. Bailey's muffled voice startled me. She sounded like she was at the bot-tom of the stairs.

Alex jumped up, cracking the door open, and called down to his mom. "Coming."

I stood, desperately not wanting to get in trouble. "I have to get back before Grandma realizes I'm gone."

"What do you mean?" Alex asked, looking between Stephen and me.

"Her grandpa told her she can't be alone with me." Stephen rolled his eyes. "We both know it's not the first time a girl in this town has been warned to stay away from me."

I scowled at Stephen. "No, he doesn't want me to be alone with one boy at a time." I gestured to Alex. "So when you're not grounded we can go on adventures and hang out again. Until then, Stephen has to stay at my boring house."

"Or apparently convince you to sneak away." Alex raised his eyebrow at Stephen. "But that's cool with me. I don't have to miss out on anything fun while I'm grounded."

Stephen grumbled something I couldn't hear as he turned to climb through the window. Alex helped me as I stepped out onto the roof, steadying me. I looked back at him through the open window. "Sucks that you're grounded."

"It would have been longer but my dad was proud I punched him," Alex said, smiling at me. "Stephen and I will come get you on the first day of school. We'll walk to the bus together."

"Okay, sounds great." I felt a little breathless. I didn't want to leave. Stephen was fun, but Alex being with us made the friendship dynamic feel more complete. Alex and I stared at each other like a couple of idiots.

"Jenny, let's go," Stephen hissed at me. "Before someone sees."

I whispered, "Bye."

"Bye." He grinned.

I could feel Alex watching us as we climbed down. I hardly knew him, but something in me already missed him. We raced across the yard into Mrs. Bailey's rose bushes and then disappeared into the field of cornstalks.

07.

MONDAY MORNING, I grinned at the familiar sounds of small rocks tapping at my window. Stephen and Alex were early. I pulled back the white lace curtains and waved at them, a smile spreading across my face. Apparently, Stephen liked his tradition of throwing pebbles at my window instead of knocking on the door.

I liked it, too.

"They're here early." Grandma was looking out the living room window. "I made you breakfast."

"Thanks. Can I take it with me?"

"Let me bag up the food." She turned toward the kitchen. "You can take orange juice in one of Grandpa's travel mugs."

I swung my new light pink backpack over my shoulder as I walked through the front door, looking down at them from the top of the porch steps. "How does freedom feel, Alex?"

"Feels great, the last four days of summer in my room and now I get to walk into another prison." He shrugged, but smiled. "School."

Stephen turned to Alex, throwing his arms out passionately. "School is a prison, isn't it? Or more like a brainwashing institute. They make us go, teach us anything they want—even if it's lies—and mold our minds into what the American government wants us to be. That's how they control us." Stephen sighed, his shoulders dropping dramatically. "I hate society sometimes."

I nodded slowly, looking at Alex. "He's a lot of work, isn't he?"

"You have no idea." Alex shook his head, amusement in his eyes. "You should see him when he's hungry."

I laughed. Stephen's mouth fell open, "I know Jenny's in the group now, but you guys can't gang up on me."

"Sometimes, you need to be ganged up on, Jenny will be good for you." Alex laid a heavy hand on Stephen's shoulder, but quickly lifted his hand again. I assumed because he was startled by Stephen's body temperature. "Okay, I'm not used to that yet."

After Grandma handed me my breakfast all wrapped up, we took off down Grandpa's private lane. We didn't say anything until we were standing where the fencing ended and the main road began.

Stephen whirled around to face me. "We're here early to ask you if anything is going on with you."

"I don't think so," I said, glancing down at myself. I felt nervous about my first day at Hollow Brook High, but beyond that nothing was off with me. "I feel totally normal. Maybe it's not going to affect me or something."

"Maybe it doesn't affect girls." Alex shifted his backpack onto his shoulders, looping his thumbs in the straps resting on his collar bones. "That'd be a good thing, right?"

Stephen chewed on the inside of his cheek. "Maybe. I don't know."

"Do you guys both… you know, feel it still?" I whispered, even though there wasn't anyone near us within a quarter of a mile.

"I've been sticking my hand in room temperature water at random times," Stephen said. "It always boils. I've been trying to be careful about what I touch, stuff that isn't flammable, at least. I think I cool off a little if I relax, like when I sleep the bed isn't all melted or anything. I'm trying— " He paused, shaking his head with a rough laugh as he glanced at Alex.

Alex's eyes were wide. He looked as lost as I felt.

Stephen sucked in a deep breath and released it before he went on. "I don't know what I'm doing. I've been using hand towels to pick stuff up because a plastic bowl got all melty in my hand. I mean, let me tell you, trying to play video games with socks over your hands to hold the controller is a different kind of challenge."

I didn't know what all this meant. "Your dad? Has he seen, you know, the weirdness?"

"No." Stephen waved me off. "He just lets me do my own thing."

I shifted on my feet, looking to Alex who had a frown on his face. When he met my eyes, he winced. "I tore the door handle off our hall bathroom."

"Oh. Wow."

"My mom lectured me about being careful, but in the same voice she always uses when Mark and I do something stupid. I'm trying to be careful." Alex paused, holding out his hand to study it. "I've been bending things and crushing rocks to sand with my hands. I haven't felt tired at all. If I do nod off, I wake up feeling great."

"I feel really good too," Stephen agreed. "Like—alive."

"I guess I'll let you know if something happens to me," I said with an evenness in my voice that I didn't have within me.

Dozens of possibilities for what might happen to me exploded in my mind. I wondered if I'd get hot skin like Stephen, and what that would mean. Maybe I'd get really strong like Alex, but I hoped not. I wasn't sure I could handle constantly paying attention to my strength. I tended to be absentminded. My dad used to tease me, saying, *Tell me all the stuff in that pretty head of yours.* He'd let me babble on about all the things I was worried about, letting me sort out everything swirling in my mind verbally.

The more I thought about it, the more my chest tightened. My breath hitched. I opened my mouth to try and force words out, but they wouldn't come. I wanted to turn back to Grandpa's farmhouse and curl up under the covers in my bed.

Alex must have read something in my expression because his hand shot out and he squeezed my shoulder. "If you're hurt or something—"

His grip was just a little too tight. "Ouch—"

"Oh god," Alex snatched his hand back, his face flushing. "I'm so sorry."

"It's fine." I rubbed my shoulder. "It doesn't really hurt."

"I know, but…I mean, I gotta be careful." He stepped away from me, giving Stephen a glare. "We talked about it for a long time. If you're in pain or something bad happens to you, we're going straight to my parents."

"Yeah, of course." Stephen rolled his eyes, groaning. "Duh."

I bit my lip, but my thoughts calmed because I wasn't facing this alone. This past summer, my grandparents and Aunt Sarah had tried to help me with my grief, but they'd had their own mourning to do. I hadn't wanted to be a burden, I didn't know how to handle my emotions and theirs in the conversations around my parents.

Stephen's carefree bravery mixed with Alex's rational, steady blue eyes settled me, erasing the loneliness of this past summer. They would know what was happening if something bad happened to me. I felt like I could move forward knowing that.

"Okay," I said, taking a deep breath and smiling. "Sounds like a good deal to me."

✦

The school was small and a lot of it seemed out of date and old-fashioned. The interior looked like a fusion between the 1950s and the 1970s. It was as if they tried to do a remodel sometime in 1975, but gave up. There was one long main hallway and the other three halls stemmed from it. I took in rusting teal lockers, empty bulletin boards, and an old yellow drinking fountain that sat between the girls' and boys' restrooms across from the main office.

"Grandma told me I need to check-in at the office as a new student," I said as we entered the main doors. I wanted to let them off the hook if they wanted to ditch me. "So, I guess—"

"Right," Alex said, his eyes intense, insistent. "My locker is going to be right around the corner. It's in the B's so it's close to the front here. Last year, Stephen used my locker because the alphabetical lockers end at the back of the school away from all the classrooms. Go left down there and meet us at my locker when you're done."

"Okay." A rush of relief ran through me. I was still invited to hang with them. "I'll try and hurry."

"Cool," Alex said, grinning broadly at me.

Stephen pushed his dark mop of hair away from his forehead, giving me a friendly wink.

Five minutes later, I had all the paperwork I needed. It was some sort of orientation packet. The office lady asked for information I didn't have. She said Grandma could help me with it at home tonight. I just had to bring it back in the morning.

Pushing through the office door, I realized I needed to use the restroom, especially since I didn't know what the rules about using the restroom during class were.

I entered a vintage-looking bathroom, with old-fashioned sinks, and teal-painted stall doors. While I did my business, girl laughter cut through the silence. I told myself I had Alex and Stephen waiting for me, whatever came from my first interaction with these Hollow Brook High girls, I wouldn't be alone after it.

The three girls lined up at the only three sinks. They were doing makeup and chatting. The girl in the middle was pale with freckles across her nose and vibrant red hair that hung straight down her back. The other girls on either side of her were blonde, one with her hair up in a messy bun and the other had soft curls. It was obvious they were twins.

I cleared my throat, keeping my tone polite. "I just want to wash my hands."

They stopped chatting and turned to me. Surprise washed over their faces, each of them looking me over from head to toe and back up again. I knew the school was small. I figured Hollow Brook High didn't get new kids often. The girls looked at each other, I could see the unspoken assessment of me and I had a feeling it wasn't in my favor.

The girl in the middle flipped her long, glossy red hair over her shoulder. "Who are you?"

I could hear the mean girl tone loud and clear. I had dealt with girls like this the year before. Rachel and I had learned that the best way to deal with a bully was to give a strong first impression, a hefty balance of confidence and emotional distance. I forced myself to believe that I didn't need these girls to approve of me. My best bet for friends at Hollow Brook High were Alex and Stephen.

"My name is Jenny and I'm going to wash my hands. Please excuse me."

"Just so you know," the twin on the left said with her chin held high, "This bathroom is our bathroom."

The other twin smirked. "Feel free to use the one by the science classrooms."

"Oh." I had no idea where the science classrooms were, I figured it wasn't a convenient location, but I wasn't going to let these girls push me around. I crossed my arms, keeping my voice calm. "There wasn't a sign. It said Girls and I figured I was a girl and so I came in."

"Well, you've learned. Now you won't make the same mistake again," the redhead said with an annoying whine in her tone. "Bye."

I took a step toward the redhead girl. "I need to wash my hands." She gasped as I stepped around her, almost as if she was going to play off that I pushed her. I turned the water on, pumped the soap on the wall, and then didn't look at the girls as I washed my hands.

The redhead stared at my reflection in the mirror.

"You're the girl who kissed Alex."

I didn't like the way she said Alex's name. There was a familiarity in her tone that made my skin crawl. I turned the water off, grabbed a paper towel from the dispenser next to us, and smirked at her in the mirror. "Do you only listen to rumors or do you spread them too? I feel like it can't be one or the other with girls like you. It has to be both."

She made a squeaky gasping sound. "You are so rude."

"I'm rude?" Her comment sent a warm pulse of something through me. "You just told me a public bathroom was off-limits. I don't think I'm the rude one here."

I could see the flash of panic behind the mask she wore. This girl wasn't used to others standing up to her. She didn't know that my parents were dead. I cared very little about the things she cared about. I didn't need popularity. I didn't need a group of girls who talked about nothing all day. I wasn't interested in the games the pretty redhead with the cute freckles and perfectly winged eyeliner wanted to play.

"And I'll use this bathroom whenever I want."

She blinked, her mouth falling open. Her eyes went a little wild as she said, "Alex wouldn't kiss you."

Somewhere deep inside me, a switch flipped on. "You have no idea what you're talking about." Power and warmth danced along my spine. My arms turned numb. Something wanted to be released into the air.

"Maybe you need to ask Alex who he would kiss or wouldn't kiss. I don't have time for this."

I needed to get out of here—maybe go to the parking lot so I could catch my breath. Or find Alex and Stephen and tell them I was pretty sure whatever was happening to them was happening to me.

"Alex doesn't like ugly girls," the redhead spat.

I didn't look at them as I shoved past one of the twins.

"Everyone knows he's only being nice to you because his mom is making him."

I knew she wanted me to turn—to fight with her. I reached for the door handle, ready to push it open and run, but it was old and caught on the latch. My shoulder slammed into the metal door.

"Brandon's right." Her voice was almost a shout. "You're going to be the easy girl this year. Trust me, Alex won't stick around for that mess."

I whirled and exploded, willing her to stop speaking. The rush of something hummed through my body. The four open stall doors slammed shut. The swinging pendant lights above us flickered. We all stepped back, startled, and gasped. A second later, the room was still and silent again. Shock rumbled through me. I was just as wide-eyed and surprised as the other three girls.

Except, I knew that whatever happened was my fault.

Alex was strong. Stephen had hot skin. I'd just caused a minor earthquake.

08.

MY HEART pounded in my chest.

Trembling, I held my shaking fist at my side and reached for the edge of the sink so my knees wouldn't give out from under me. I'd been in my body one second and somehow everywhere in the next. After another blink, I'd been in myself again.

"Was that an earthquake?" one of the twins asked, her face pale.

Her sister had braced herself against a stall door. "We get earthquakes every so often. I mean, not like that. Whatever that was."

An earthquake seemed like the only possible explanation. I would have agreed with her guess if I hadn't known for sure that whatever happened a few seconds ago was because of me.

The redhead took a moment to look around, studying the room. Her assessing gaze landed on me. She gave me a smile with a cruel promise in it. "I'll tell everyone we met, put a good word in for you, set you up for the rest of the year. Especially if you plan on using this restroom."

Her shoulder clipped mine as she jiggled the handle to the bathroom, successfully opening it, and strode into the hall with the twins in tow. Silence filled the room. I laid a hand on my chest as my heart slowed again.

I realized I felt *good*.

I couldn't form words to describe what hummed in me. A lingering sensation sparked along my spine. I looked in the mirror, wondering if I looked as different as I felt. Nothing seemed different.

I frowned at the mirror.

It was hard not to look at myself and see how plain I was. The redhead and the twins had carefully crafted their outfits—jeans, crop tops with cute midriffs, and hair that they'd probably woken up early to do. Their makeup painted queenly masks that helped them rule Hollow Brook High.

I was in a T-shirt, shorts, and dirty sneakers. My hair was up in a practical ponytail to keep it out of my eyes so it wouldn't bother me while I took notes in class. I'd absentmindedly chosen my outfit, choosing the same kind of clothes last year when there were a thousand more kids in my school and it was easier to blend in.

A warning bell rang. I felt bad for not meeting with Alex and Stephen, but I found them outside the girl's bathroom. The redhead and the twins were talking to them with the sound of years of familiarity between them.

Some sort of Small-Town-Five situation.

Alex caught my eye over the redhead's shoulder. He looked more worried than I thought he should have been. "Hey, we couldn't find you."

"Did you feel that?" Stephen asked. "We don't ever get earthquakes like that here."

The hair on my arms stood up, sending a chilly sensation down my spine. I couldn't see any actual damage. It'd been a quick rattle for the building, nothing more. I glanced around, absorbing the general buzz of excited whispers of "We never have earthquakes," and "Whoa, that was crazy," and "You think they'll send us home?" Four teachers stood in the middle of the hallway, probably discussing what I'd done, too.

I swallowed the nausea threatening to crawl up my throat. My vision blurred at the edges. I'd done it. I knew my mind had somehow caused the school to shake—

"Jenny?" Alex's voice drew me back to the present.

"Yes," I said, nodding, agreeing to whatever they'd been saying.

Stephen narrowed his eyes.

"This is Emma Henderson." Alex gestured to the redhead.

I nodded again like a robot. Emma smirked.

"Suzy and Megan Johnson, they're twins." He laughed a little. "I guess you can see that because they look identical. Stephen and I grew up with them."

"Great to meet you." I couldn't hide the slight sarcasm in my tone. I needed to figure out the earthquake situation, not chat with mean girls. "I don't know where my first class is."

"Yeah, we'll show you." Alex glanced down at the watch on his wrist. "We have, like, one minute to be on time."

"Alex?" Emma's voice made us all pause and turn to her.

Alex looked as if he was forcing himself to be patient. He didn't want to be late for class. "What's up?"

"Megan, Suzy, and I are doing a homework thing after school every day at my house this year. I'll have snacks and sodas," she said sweetly, her eyes darting to me. "You and Stephen are welcome to join us."

Stephen shifted from foot to foot, confusion written across his face. He opened his mouth slowly, as if he were going to ask her to clarify what she meant. I knew what she was doing. I started to turn away so I could get to class and deal with my humiliation over not being invited alone.

"Dang." There was something in Alex's voice that made me turn back. "I'm doing the same thing at my house. But there's only room for Stephen and Jenny." His gaze shot right through me as he jerked his chin, gesturing for me to follow him. "We don't want to be late."

I didn't look back at Emma, I left her shocked expression to my imagination.

I followed the guys to our first class. Distracted by my mini natural disaster, I hardly noticed Brandon Thomas as he tried to step in my path, his cheek still a faint green-yellow bruise around a slice of scabbed-over skin. Brandon had opened his mouth as if to say something, but Alex shouldered him back and Stephen nudged me in the direction of the sophomore hall.

Emma Henderson and Brandon Thomas were the least of my problems.

I knew from my paper schedule that my first period

teacher's name was Mr. Garrison. He stood in front of the class, waving his hands. "Calm down, everyone sit and settle down."

"Is school canceled?" someone asked.

"Nope, school is not canceled."

A chorus of disappointed groans flitted through the classroom.

Mr. Garrison gestured for me to come to his desk. Alex slid my bag off my shoulder without saying anything. He and Stephen found seats in the back corner. Alex dropped my bag in the spot between them.

"Jenny Phillips?" Mr. Garrison picked up a piece of paper that appeared to have a list of student names on it.

"That's me." I shifted from foot to foot, glancing over my shoulder as Emma and the twins found seats in the other corner of the classroom.

Mr. Garrison was a tall and slender man with big glasses. His eyes softened. "I went to school with your parents. I'm sorry for your loss."

"Oh." I didn't know why I was surprised that he would mention them. "It's okay."

He gave me a quick smile. "If you need anything, let any of the staff know and we'd love to help you."

"Okay," I said, a little breathless. "Thank you."

"Go ahead and have a seat." He set the paper down on the desk.

A numb sensation washed over me, but my feet took me in the direction where Alex had set my bag down. I needed a minute to calm down or I was going to break a window or make the roof explode or something else terrifying. I closed my eyes and hid my face in my arms on the top of the desk.

"I'm going to pass out personality tests. Take the quiz and then we'll each get to share our results." Mr. Garrison started passing out papers.

I glanced at Alex, who was already reading the assignment, and then found Stephen watching me. He mouthed, *You okay?*

He was observant. I wasn't okay, but I flashed him a tight smile and nodded.

I could understand what Alex and Stephen had meant about feeling… good. A light, feathery sensation prickled along my skin and my muscles felt relaxed and tight at the same time. A gentle, warm current ran up and down my spine. The sensations calmed down a bit as I filled out the personality test.

Forty minutes later the bell rang for a fifteen-minute break. Stephen hunched next to my desk between Alex and I. "Something is happening with you, huh?"

Alex leaned forward from his seat, facing me and Stephen. "Are you okay?"

"Yeah. I'm good." I laid my head down again, the side of my face pressed into my folded arms. "Except that I'm the one who made the freaking earthquake happen."

"What does that mean?" Stephen whispered, his eyes wide.

"I don't know. I got—" I shook my head. Then my words came out in a rush. "Emma was trying to be mean and I wasn't having it. She said stuff and I got mad and stuff moved and then the doors slammed and the lights flickered and it felt different in the room for like three seconds."

Stephen and Alex exchanged a look. There seemed to be some sort of quick decision-making between them that ended with a nod of agreement, as if a silent plan had been laid in place.

"What?" I asked, wanting to be in on whatever thing they'd just decided. "I'm freaking out here."

Stephen raised his eyebrows at Alex, nodding toward the three girls whispering nearby. "I told you about Emma."

"Yeah, I know, I get it." Alex frowned. "We'll deal with that later."

"I can deal with Emma," I whispered harshly. "The important thing is my earthquake problem."

"What did it feel like?" Alex said in a way-too-calm voice.

"Warm and fuzzy," I said sarcastically.

"What?" Stephen scowled.

I sighed, "Uh, it felt like the hair on my arms was standing up, like static electricity. But warm, like you guys said. I felt really strong and warm and…powerful, I guess."

"Sounds about right." Stephen nodded.

Alex frowned. "How do you feel now?"

"I don't know, less warm and fuzzy than before." I was trying to stay as calm as they were, but I could hear the edge of panic in my own voice. "It was only a few seconds."

Alex shook his head. "Okay, I still think—"

"Wait, do you smell that?" I vaguely recognized the smell—like burning wiring or plastic. I leaned back in my seat to look around the room for the source, but Stephen's hand was resting on the back of my chair. The heat ate through the fabric of my shirt, I jerked forward. "Ouch."

"Sorry." His hand sprang off the back of the chair.

"The plastic is melted," I whispered, looking at the imprint of his hand on the back of my seat. "You melted the chair, Stephen."

Stephen's mouth fell open, his eyes darting between his normal-looking hand and the teal plastic back of the chair. His dramatic movements were almost comical. I had to bite my lip because none of this was funny.

Alex snorted, trying to stifle a laugh too. "Great work, Stephen."

Stephen's face flushed a subtle pink over his dark features. "The wood can handle it when I'm sitting. My clothes kind of act as a barrier, but the seat felt softer the longer I sat there. Like, it was melting slowly."

"Yeah, be careful," I said. "We all have to be careful. I don't know if whatever happened in the bathroom with me is going to happen again."

"Stay calm." Alex thought for a moment and then he looked up. "When it happened to me at first, I was really angry—I was emotional."

"Emotional." Stephen huffed.

Alex sighed. "You know what I mean." He turned to me. "And you, you were fighting with Emma when it happened to you. Same with Brandon, I was angry…" He looked at Stephen. "Were you mad when it happened to you?"

"Uh, no."

"What was happening?" Alex pressed.

"Nothing was happening." Stephen's tone turned defensive. "I was just hanging out in Jenny's yard with her."

"Were you guys fighting?"

"No, we weren't fighting." Stephen glanced at me, looking for help. "It just happened. No rhyme or reason. Right?"

"We weren't fighting." I shrugged. "As far as I know anyway."

Alex hummed, studying the floor before he looked up, his tone thoughtful. "You were really emotional though?"

"I wasn't emotional," Stephen insisted. "I don't know how it happened."

I thought back to the moment we'd discovered his hot skin. "I fell, remember? You caught me by the arm. That's how you burned me at first."

"You fell?" I almost laughed at the way Alex whipped around to look at me.

His concern was unnecessary, but absolutely adorable.

"I didn't actually fall." I gestured to Stephen. "You were talking about yourself. You know, how you grew up going on vacations with the Baileys and stuff."

Alex cracked a smile at his friend. "Awe, opening up to Jenny, huh? Sounds super emotional, bro."

Stephen's mouth fell open and he sputtered, "No— That's not—"

"Stop that," I swatted Alex in the arm, but I couldn't help laughing at Stephen's reaction.

"Emotions are manly too, Stephen." Alex said with a big, teasing grin. "It's only natural—"

"Guys, move past this." Stephen's voice rose a little. "I wasn't emotional."

"Come on, it's not a big deal to talk about stuff," Alex sighed, his tone more apologetic. "Can you at least explain what you were feeling when you were talking to Jenny?"

Stephen glared at him. "I wasn't feeling anything."

"Then what would be the reason—"

Stephen stood up, stomped to his desk, and slid into it. I felt bad that Alex and I had laughed at him, but before I could say anything, Stephen's hand landed hard on his notebook.

A burst of flames flashed under his palm.

He flung himself back, away from the fire. The lights in the classroom flickered as I stood up and gasped. Alex moved faster than I thought possible and threw his backpack on top of the smoking notebook with a loud whap.

There were two kids across the room watching us now, but they'd turned away from us before the flames had appeared. Emma, Suzy, and Megan had obviously seen it because they were gathered around Megan's desk, whispering to each other and glancing at us.

"Did you just light your notebook on fire?" Emma asked Stephen. "Why would you bring a lighter on the first day of school? Put it away, you idiot."

Stephen's face was green like he might get sick.

Emma rolled her eyes. "Suzy, open the windows. Mr. Garrison will be back soon." She pulled out a bottle of perfume and started to spray it around the room. "Hide your notebook, genius. You're going to get expelled on your first day."

I realized that Emma was helping Stephen. Alex stuffed Stephen's notebook into his backpack. I stood there, dumbfounded, watching it play out.

Mr. Garrison walked in seconds later. "Emma don't spray that in here. It's overpowering. Some people have allergies to perfumes like that."

"Oh, sorry Mr. Garrison," she said sweetly. She put the perfume back in her bag. Emma gave Stephen a wink.

I slowly slid into my seat, feeling useless and overwhelmed.

Alex leaned over to whisper to me, "The three of us need to talk."

I glanced at Stephen, he was staring ahead, looking a lot like I felt.

"Stephen and I have a spot at lunch—" Alex paused. "Do you want to eat lunch with us?"

I knew everything was a mess, but I couldn't help but smile. "Yes, please."

"Cool," Alex turned as Mr. Garrison wrote on the board, but he leaned forward to press his fist against his mouth, as if trying to hide his own smile.

I was incredibly happy to have a *spot* with friends for lunch.

09.

THEIR SPOT WAS under a tree near the back corner of the school. The tree was framed by a square cement partition. I followed Alex's lead and sat on the edge of the partition next to him. We faced away from the school toward a field of patchy grass that met a line of forested trees. A few other students were eating outside in the distance, but no one was close enough to hear us talking.

Stephen paced on the sidewalk in front of Alex and me. "I lit that notebook on fire."

"Yes, and I caused an earthquake." I said, deadpan. "I don't think we're even, Stephen."

"Hilarious, Jenny Phillips." Stephen gestured to Alex. "I was pissed at you. I didn't mean to— Holy crap, the notebook just went up in flames."

"How about you calm down so you don't light up on fire again." Alex's tone was impossibly even. "I think that would be a good start."

"How am I supposed to control this? What if it gets worse?"

"I don't know," Alex shrugged, then muttered, "That's why we should talk to adults…"

"No way." Stephen pointed at Alex. "No way. Never. I can't tell anyone about this."

"What are you talking about?" Alex threw up his hands. "You know my parents can help us."

Stephen let out a frustrated groan. "We're freaks now. Alex Bailey, we are freaks. You get that? Circus sideshow freaks."

Freaks.

The word ricocheted through my mind. Images of Alex picking up a tractor with one hand, Stephen's notebook lighting on fire, and the way the room had changed in the bathroom sent a shiver along my skin despite the warm afternoon.

Stephen was right. If people found out about us, it'd change our lives forever. We'd never be the same as everybody else. Doctors and scientists would study us. I could imagine the scientists in white lab coats with their clipboards in hand, taking notes on our every movement.

I wasn't sure where they'd have three freaks with weird powers live. I wondered if we'd have to move into a government facility with guards. If people found out about us, I wasn't sure I'd ever get to go to the mall again, or a school dance, or any number of the things on my secret bucket list.

Stephen began pacing again with his hands dug into his curls. Alex was looking down at his worn navy sneakers, processing what to say next. I was terrified of what was happening to us, but I wanted to hold onto what little control we had.

"I think…" I said, biting my lip, drawing their attention.

Stephen stopped, his feet planted in front of me, his hands still in his hair.

When I didn't continue right away, Alex leaned in and said, "You think what?"

"I'd like to think of myself as a mutant. Not a freak. Mutants are way cooler."

Stephen stared at me for a long several seconds before his face broke into a smile and he burst into emotional laughter. Alex was right behind him. I cracked too and we laughed together like insane people. There wasn't a clear reason why we were laughing, but it felt like the thing we needed, as if whatever thing happening within us needed it.

Stephen dropped to the ground, sitting with his legs sprawled out in front of him on the sidewalk. "Alex, mutants keep their identities and abilities a secret. Sideshow circus freaks are for everyone to come and see their deformities. I'm with Jenny, I want to be a mutant too."

"We do have each other through this," I said the words to them, but I was saying them to myself too, trying to reassure my unsteady nerves. "It's my first day here. I'm a mutant now and I'm already Emma's target to bully for the year. But you guys are here with me through it and it helps a lot. I think we should work together and come up with a plan before we tell adults. I mean, like figure out how we could control what's going to happen, even a little."

"Okay, I get what you guys are saying. Let me think," Alex wrinkled his nose and then touched on the other part of what I'd said. "I'm sorry about Emma. I didn't know she'd do that to you."

"It's fine." My gaze swept the school's lawn that seemed to be an old football field blended into an old baseball dugout. "She's probably territorial. I'm a threat to the Small-Town-Five thing you've got going on. Like I said earlier, I can handle her."

Stephen huffed. "You're not the only girl she does this too. Emma is a flirt to the guys, but she's a bully to the girls."

"Why did I not know this?" Alex frowned.

Stephen grabbed Alex's backpack and chucked it at him. "Because you're dumb."

Alex grunted as he caught the bag. "Well, that's not going to be a problem because Jenny is sticking with us this year." He paused, waiting for me to look at him. "Right?"

"Right." I smiled. The tension in my stomach eased. "Thanks."

Alex frowned. "About Brandon Thomas, Stephen and I have your back, okay?"

"Yeah," Stephen said, raising his chin slightly. "If Brandon bothers you, I'll let Alex punch him again."

That made me laugh. "I doubt he'll want to mess with Alex again."

"Well yeah," Stephen looked at me with wide, exaggerated eyes. "If he wants to keep his pretty face intact, he better not mess with us."

Stephen and I looked over at Alex, waiting for him to laugh or say something witty with us. But he looked ready to move onto the more important discussion.

"Ok," Alex said, setting a plan into place for us. "Every day we come home from school, do our homework, and then meet at the clubhouse before dinner. We can work on what's going on. Take notes of what's happening throughout the day. Every day we'll reevaluate when, and if, we're ready to tell adults. All right?"

"Sounds good to me." I shrugged. I was torn between telling my grandparents or not, but Alex and Stephen were going through the same thing as I was with this mutant thing. I didn't know them very well, but I did know in the few short weeks since I'd met them, parts of me had unfrozen and come alive again. I wasn't exactly sure what motivated them to keep the secret, but if I lost them, I would lose the only good thing in my life right now.

"What if one of us gets caught?" Stephen looked between Alex and I. "Or messes up really bad?"

"Then I think we should tell adults. Not one of us is alone in the freak show." Alex looked at me. "If one of us gets revealed and becomes a freak, we're all freaks. From there, even if that happens, we still try to help each other. We stick together."

I absorbed the way Alex Bailey was looking at me, but I didn't understand the intensity in his expression. I was slowly learning that Alex was a naturally very serious boy. My gaze swung to Stephen, a smile lifting the corner of my mouth. "Okay, if Stephen catches something else on fire with his body in public, then we go forward with telling adults."

"Oh great, thanks." Stephen groaned.

"Exactly." Alex laughed, his stiff shoulders loosening.

"Or if Stephen burns the school down, we should tell adults."

My eyes went wide as I shot to my feet, echoing the way Stephen had looked when he'd lit his notebook on fire in class. "Or if all of his clothes burn off—"

"Shut up!" Stephen fell flat on the ground, his arms and legs sprawled out. "I hate you guys."

10.

ᴘROGRESS REPORT. I'll go first." Stephen shrugged off his winter coat, always secretly warmer than the average human and now more comfortable in a forest green short-sleeved T-shirt. We settled on the ground near the clubhouse. Grandpa had told me the temperatures stayed below freezing during this time of year in Hollow Brook. We could see our breath in the air, but it hadn't snowed yet. "It's been officially eighteen days since I've burned or melted anything unintentionally."

We'd stuck to Alex's plan to meet up after school and on weekends. Those first few weeks we'd argued about telling adults or not, but we were realizing it wasn't that hard to hide our mutations.

I smiled wide and clapped. "Nice work, Stephen Wright."

"Thank you, thank you all." Stephen bowed at the waist from where he was sitting on the ground. "Alex?"

Alex wore a thick black winter coat with his gloves on, his legs sprawled out in front of him. He took a few seconds to think before he replied. "Nothing exciting from me. The big thing right now I'm working on is trying to match the pace and load of how my brother does his chores. I can lift a lot more, obviously. It's like my dad knows something is up with me but doesn't know how to ask me about it. And you guys already know I'm trying to be careful so I don't break another kitchen appliance."

In the last three months, Alex had managed to accidentally break off a sink knob, tear the microwave door off its hinges and shatter a coffee pot by setting it down absently on the marble counter.

Stephen's gaze landed on me. "Jenny?"

"Same." I shrugged under my pink winter coat. My "same" was that little things happened around me, like if I was upset, the lights might flicker. Once, Grandma startled me and the photo on the wall next to us fell down as if an invisible wind had whooshed past both of us. Sometimes when it was quiet and I was alone, I could feel it under my skin, find the top of my mutation, and sense its power and mystery within me. I always pushed it back down. "I'm still convinced my mutation isn't as strong as what you two have."

"You say that a lot." Alex shot me a glance, shifting to cross one ankle over the other. "My theory stands that our mutations are connected to our emotions. I think you're good at hedging your emotions. I think you're suppressing it or something."

"You say *that* a lot." I narrowed my eyes, a playful smile on my lips. He gave me a mischievous grin in return. But I jerked my chin at Stephen, "And what? You two are so in touch with your emotions, huh?"

"I need to stay focused. I make mistakes when I'm distracted." Alex took a second to think. "My mom nags at me, usually when I'm in the kitchen. She's going on and on about something, I get irritated, and I'm not paying attention to adjusting my strength. That's when stuff happens with me."

I gestured to Stephen. "What about him?"

"He's always emotional." Alex raised his brows, giving me a dramatically grim expression. "And it's unpredictable, thus Stephen Wright could combust at any second. He's the one we have to watch."

Stephen snorted and I laughed. Alex was joking, what he said about Stephen had been true that first month, but in the past few weeks he'd learned how to stay calm. He'd become aware of himself and his heat in a way that I hadn't.

"Stone cold, Jenny." Stephen mocked me playfully.

"What are we going to do with you?"

I fluttered my lashes at Stephen. We were used to this kind of banter after three months of friendship. "I'm not stone cold, I'm sweet."

"Yeah," Stephen countered sarcastically. "Like hard candy."

"Oh. Wow. Well, if I'm hard candy, you're a fireball," I said with a frown, a little disappointed in my lame comeback.

Alex saved me by saying, "Some people like fireballs, and some people can't stand them. That's a good description of Stephen."

"What can I say?" Stephen sat up straighter, laying a hand on his chest. "I'm too hot to handle."

I groaned. "Please, I'm going to throw up."

Stephen held up his hand. A wispy yellow-orange ball floated above his palm. "I'm getting good at controlling the flames."

I felt a twinge of amazement every time he did that. He closed his hand over the fireball. "We should get you really emotional and see what happens, Jenny. I'm so curious about your mutation." We'd decided to call it a "mutation" and we were "mutants" now. Not that it was technical, we just needed code words for it all. "Do you want me to make you angry or cry? I think I could handle either."

I threw a stick at Stephen. He dodged it easily. "Neither. Thanks."

"I'm curious too." Alex eyed me. "Try and do something."

I paused to consider what it would be like to casually lower the walls I'd built around my mutation, but nothing in me would budge. I had felt a burst of whatever it was that I could do in the girl's bathroom on the first day of school, but it had terrified me.

It was hard to tell Alex and Stephen about my fears. I wasn't sure they'd understand. They were courageous and bold about testing the limits of their mutations. I wasn't like that. Everything I felt was a tangled mess of thoughts and worries.

"Maybe later." I looked past Stephen, toward the open field behind him where I could see the mutant farm. We'd stopped calling it the mystery farm because of the little we knew about it.

Months ago, we'd looked up the company *Abilities* online and found one webpage that didn't tell us much, other than it was a medications lab. We'd staked out the farm for weeks, but we didn't dare go back and trespass again. On a cool, late October day, we found the mutant farm empty, all of the vans and signs of habitation gone. Alex had overheard his dad say that the company ran out of money for whatever they'd been researching and had closed down the operation.

When Alex pressed for more information, Mr. Bailey shrugged and said that was all he knew. The company had been very private.

Thoughtfully, I said, "Do you think they're ever going to come back?"

"I have no idea." Alex studied the abandoned farm. "My dad says it's not for sale or anything. *Abilities* still owns the land, though, whoever they are."

I stared at the ground, entertaining the idea of trying something with my mutation again, but I'd built a fortress of fear within myself. Stephen was right, I was stone cold in so many ways and I didn't want to melt. Besides that, right now, my behind was starting to get cold from sitting on the ground. I let out a long sigh and stood.

"Where are you going?" Stephen asked, making a face at me as if he were offended I'd even think about leaving early during our hangout time. "We just got here."

I shrugged. "It's cold out here."

"It's not cold." Stephen snorted.

I raised an eyebrow at him. "Says the human heater."

Stephen stuck his tongue out at me. "Hilarious."

I felt Alex watching me as I stuck my hands in my pockets. "I'm going to head home. It's getting darker earlier now. I'll see you guys at the bus stop in the morning."

"I'll walk you home," Alex said, standing too.

A weird stillness dropped heavy between the three of us. When we hung out at the clubhouse, I always walked home by myself. Alex and Stephen went to their own houses. The clubhouse was closer to my grandparents' house and in the opposite direction. I turned back to him, shaking my head, "It's out of your way."

Alex looked toward the empty open fields, thinking about it, and then said, "I want to walk you home."

I still felt something awkward dancing between us, but I didn't have a clear reason to argue. "Okay."

Alex and I both slowly looked at Stephen. Stephen was looking between Alex and me. I could see his mind working. He took a step back as his expression transformed into brotherly annoyance. "I'm not walking Jenny home. Waste of my time. I'll be online playing the game when you get home, Alex."

"Cool," Alex said with a nod.

I waved at Stephen as he started to turn away. "Bye. See you in the morning."

"See you, Jenny." He flashed me a smile, taking off down the path toward his house.

That left Alex and me alone to stare at each other.

11.

W E BOTH LOOKED AWAY at the same time. I let out a little laugh, "You know I can walk myself home."

"You're the one who said it's getting dark earlier." Alex glanced up at the sky. The clouds were starting to move and the wind picked up around us.

I pushed errant hair away from my face. "It's not exactly a bad neighborhood out here."

"You're right." He laughed, but then he jerked his shoulder toward the path to my grandparent's house, and started to walk. "We should do fun stuff for Christmas break."

I fell into step next to him. "Like what?"

"Sledding, snowmobiling..." He gave me a shy glance. "We could get hot chocolates at the gas station and get a ride from my dad into Willow City to see the Garden Show light display. I think you'd like that."

Christmas break was a week away. We'd take three weeks off and then start the next semester in January. I wanted to confirm with him that he meant we would be doing all that with Stephen, but I didn't have the courage. "I'm going to my Aunt Sarah's house for about a week during Christmas break."

"What dates?" Alex said with a touch of disappointment in his voice. "Will you miss Christmas? Your grandparents come to our house on Christmas Day for dinner every year."

I nodded. "Grandma told me about dinner at your house. I leave on that Sunday after school ends. I fly back on Christmas morning. I'll be here those two weeks after Christmas. We can do fun stuff then."

"Do you think Christmas will be hard?"

We stood in the middle of the cold, empty fields. The air and sky were blue and gray under the darkening clouds. "What do you mean?"

"Your first Christmas without your parents?" His gaze shot to the ground after he spoke and his hands went into his pockets. He looked up again, nervous. "I'm sorry. You never talk about your parents. I've been thinking about that lately."

Everything within me shifted and turned over. I pushed it all down to control what I was feeling. Alex and Stephen kept everything light and fun, never asking about my parents. Alex was crossing a line in our relationship, testing to see if I was ready to take our friendship deeper somehow.

I didn't know what to do with it.

The wind whipped a little harder around us. I tried to laugh and say the right thing to smooth his question over. Instead, what came out was a harsh and shaky breath. When I looked back at him, I opened my mouth to say something, but everything about me shuddered and I let out a broken sob as tears ran down my face.

Alex's face fell and he pulled me into a hug. "I shouldn't have brought it up."

"It's okay…" But I was sobbing into his coat.

"Oh, Jenny, I'm so sorry." Alex said softly as he pulled me closer into his chest, resting his cheek on the top of my head. "I'm so sorry it all happened. I can't even imagine what it's like for you."

No one in my life—not Grandma, Grandpa, or Aunt Sarah—had opened me up like this. I was good at burying the stuff inside me, just as I'd learned to bury the secrets of our mutations, but in a few words Alex had taken a shovel and dug up everything that hurt.

I couldn't sort exactly why, just that Alex was solid—

the way he looked at me and the way he lived his life, the way his voice was like velvet across my skin when he spoke. Alex Bailey was worthy of my trust, not only did I know that, but somehow the mutation within me knew that too.

Whatever power lurked beneath my skin, this force that hummed within me, every emotion that rolled in waves through me, knew he could handle me. I could sense Alex, the steady sureness of him was a brick wall that I wanted to hide behind.

"Your tears don't make me uncomfortable, you know," he said quietly.

I huffed, wiping my face with my gloves.

"You see"—he leaned back to look at me, his expression gentle—"my mom is a crier. She cries at everything."

Alex shifted, locking his hands around my lower back. It was a snug feeling to be tucked up against him in our coats like that. He kept me there, concerned blue eyes studying my face. It was cold, but everything about me was warm now. My blushing cheeks stung against the chill in the air. "What are you—"

"Hugging practice," he said with a wide smile.

"What?"

He gave me a little squeeze. "Comfortable?"

"Oh," I said, realizing he was asking for help with

his mutation—learning the proper feel of a hug. A few weeks ago we'd been sitting at the clubhouse when he'd grabbed my hand and made my heart jolt up into my throat. But he'd simply been asking about his mutation, learning how his brain needed to adjust to the appropriate pressure so he wouldn't hurt someone with his grasp. "Very comfortable. This hug is top-notch."

"Good." I expected him to let me go, but he didn't. "Who else do you have to cry with?"

"I don't know," My thoughts tumbled out of my mouth like a spilled bag of marbles. "I don't cry. I brush it off when my grandma asks me about this stuff. I mean, I guess she doesn't even really ask me anymore, but my Aunt Sarah does. I have a script, like lines in a play that I use when they ask me stuff. I guess I sort of push everything away. Like, you were saying earlier about hedging my emotions or whatever. You're right, my mutation is connected to what I'm feeling and so I don't—" I sniffled and tried to smile at him, to push down everything again. It wasn't an easy feeling for me to be open with someone like this. Alex's presence in my life since day one had seemed like a prank someone might be playing on me, as if they'd all jump out and reveal that Alex thought I was a joke. "I'm good though. I really am. I spent the summer crying alone in my room. When I met you and Stephen, everything wasn't perfect, but better. You know?"

"I get it. That's good." Alex said thoughtfully. I could see the wheels in his mind working as he took a few seconds to form a response. Something wet and cold hit my nose. We both looked up to find snow flurries around us. Alex grinned up at the clouds. "First snow of the year."

The seconds ticked by and I was still locked in Alex's embrace. I didn't know what to do. This wasn't normal Alex Bailey behavior. His hand moved, pressing me closer to his chest again, my cheek landed against his jacket. His chin rested on my head.

"I guess what I meant was if you need to cry on Christmas at my house, I'll find a quiet spot for you. You know, if you want me to go on a walk with you or something. If you need my help, I want to be there for you. That's all."

My whole body relaxed. He squeezed me a little tighter when he felt all my stiffness melt away. "Thank you."

The snow was falling thicker as I leaned into him and closed my eyes. I wasn't drowning under black water like I'd imagined if I opened up to someone. Alex was here with me, kicking his feet to hold us up so I wouldn't drown.

Alex sucked in a quick breath of air and whispered, "Jenny."

I looked up, realizing what he saw. The snow was

swirling. Flurries moved in a circle, a slow, pretty tornado around us. Despite the bit of natural wind, my mutation was moving around us, pushing air, creating magic.

"It's like a snow globe," Alex said, wonder in his voice. "That's incredible."

I smiled brightly at him, laughing happily. I was alive in Alex Bailey's arms and I had no idea how I'd ended up here. "I didn't mean to do that."

"Beautiful." He gave me a half smile, his gaze washing over my face. "Your mutation is so cool, I love it."

I couldn't handle that look on his face. I stepped back and shook off the mutation's effect running through me. I dug my hands into my coat pockets. We both watched the snow settle and turn back to normal. Snowflakes gathered in Alex's light brown hair. "You're a good friend, Alex."

He looked away with an uneven laugh. When he found my eyes again, he opened his mouth to say something.

"Jenny," Grandpa interrupted, walking up the path, "there's a snowstorm coming. You two need to get home."

I could hear Grandpa, but Alex's eyes had caught me. "You better get home too. This snow is crazy."

"I'll see you at the bus stop in the morning." Alex took a step back, but even as Grandpa approached, we kept looking at each other. He laughed, rubbing the back of his neck as his face flushed red.

"What?" My face broke into a smile.

He shook his head, grinning back at me. "Nothing."

"Jenny." Grandpa barked at me, just yards away with his arms crossed. "Get home."

"Bye," I said quietly, still smiling.

He held my gaze as he backed away. "Bye."

"Get home, Alex," Grandpa said gruffly. "The storm is supposed to be bad. Don't get caught out here."

"Yes, sir." Alex waved at Grandpa and then turned, sauntering toward his house. I couldn't look away yet. I watched the snow flurries gathering on his navy coat, imprinting the memory of our snow globe moment in my mind forever.

⋆ ◆◆◆ ⋆

I followed Grandpa home as the storm the grew into dark clouds and heavy snow, turning into a slant as the wind picked up.

In the entryway, I shrugged off my coat and slipped out of my boots. I was trying to downplay the goofy smile on my face. Grandpa stood in the doorway between the entryway and living room. "I'll be upstairs until dinner," I told him.

"Jenny." Grandpa's voice was low. It surprised me. I'd never been in trouble with him before. I couldn't think of what I would be in trouble for. I turned as he said, "I told you not to be alone with a boy."

"I wasn't alone," I said softly, confused, I leaned against the banister. "Stephen was there a few minutes before."

"I didn't see Stephen."

"He was there…" I shook my head. "I mean, Alex offered to walk me home. It was getting dark and the storm was coming. We were talking about our Christmas plans." I straightened. "I guess I don't understand the rule. Alex is my best friend, Stephen is too. Neither of them would do anything bad to me."

Grandpa let out a long sigh, making the wrinkles around his mouth more prominent as he frowned. "They both have birthdays in January."

"What?" I was so confused. "What does that matter?"

"It matters because they're about to become sixteen-year-old boys. You don't need to be hanging around them." As Grandpa spoke, Grandma came from the kitchen, listening to us. "You need to find girls to be friends with."

I looked between Grandma and Grandpa. "Why? I only want to hang out with them."

"She's fine, honey." Grandma said quietly to Grandpa. "It's a different scenario."

"What scenario?" I felt like this was some big secret no one wanted to talk to me about. "Are you talking about the way my parents went off and eloped at eighteen?"

Grandpa grumbled and stared at Grandma, raising a brow.

Grandma nodded, turning to me. "Sweetheart, Grandpa and I were boyfriend and girlfriend when we were very young. I had your mom when I was sixteen years old. It was a really hard time for us. We had to quit school, Grandpa had to work for very little money on a farm. We lived in a house that was small and wasn't good for a young wife and baby. It took us a long time to get where we are today."

"Where is this coming from?" My voice turned defensive. I knew my reaction was a little over the top, but I couldn't imagine life without Alex and Stephen. "What does it have to do with me? I'm not dating anyone. I'm not there with anyone. I'm not going to get pregnant—"

Grandpa cut me off. "Your mom and dad were asked to wait. They snuck around and pushed us away. Instead of being patient, they went off the day your mom turned eighteen and left us."

"We didn't see them again until you were born."

Grandma said, hugging me. She pulled back and held my upper arms as she smiled at me. "We're here for you, Jenny. We want you to stay friends with boys right now. That's all."

"No dating until you're eighteen," Grandpa said, his mouth set in a firm line. "I don't want you sneaking around with Alex Bailey."

"Sneaking around?" My stomach turned to lead as I realized they didn't trust me. They were acting like Alex wasn't the most caring, thoughtful, responsible, and respectful teen boy they'd ever met. "I would never sneak around with Alex or anyone else. Alex and Stephen are my friends…" A new wave of shock washed over me. "Wait. You're saying I can't go on a date with anyone? When I turned fifteen last spring, my dad said I could go on dates as long as I was open with them and we talked about it." I swallowed my anger, pushing it down, feeling something inside me build. "This isn't right. This isn't fair. I didn't do anything wrong—"

"Jenny. This isn't a discussion. This is the rule. We're done talking about it."

"But Alex would never—"

Grandpa's eyes flashed with a sharpness I'd never seen before. "If you want to live here in Hollow Brook, you'll abide by my rules. If not, you can live with your aunt in Coral Beach. I won't have this kind of defiance in my house."

I jerked backward, as if he'd slapped me.

Rare fury hit me. I was about to shout at Grandpa, but as I opened my mouth, the lights in the house went dark with the sound of a click-pop. My breath turned into a harsh rhythm. I knew the power was out because of me. It was as if the anger had ridden on the wave of my and Alex's conversation about my parents and Christmas. My body shook, I wrung my hands together to try and make it stop.

Grandpa's voice was tight as he said, "The storm, probably. I'll go down to the cellar and check the fuse box."

"I'll grab flashlights and candles," Grandma said, heading down the dark hall to the kitchen.

I ran up the stairs to my room, threw myself on my bed, and buried my face into my pillow. The old farmhouse groaned and creaked as the wind howled outside.

In my mind, it was early summer, just after my parents died and I was in this bedroom that wasn't mine. I wanted my dad to come as he'd always done after I'd argued with my parents. He'd hug me and rub my back. He'd tell me sometimes life was hard, but that's why my mom and him were here. They would always be there for me. It had felt like a promise.

It was a promise he couldn't keep. I was alone.

Grandpa got the power back on and Grandma tried to call me down for dinner. I ignored her and stayed in bed. I knew sometimes she didn't know what to do with me. I wondered if my mom had felt like this with Grandma, and if my dad struggled with my Grandpa before I was born.

My room was dark and cold, the industrial light on the barn outside highlighted the snow blowing in a slant outside my window. I was left alone to wonder what life would have been like if my parents were alive today.

12.

WINTER IN HOLLOW BROOK meant that it was still dark out when I left the house for school in the mornings.

My head ached at the memories of fighting with Grandpa the night before. He'd been gone when I woke up, out doing chores early. Grandma and I fell into normal tones. Neither of us brought up what happened.

As I got ready, I kept forgetting things upstairs, trying to make sure I had all of the snow gear I'd need. During the third trip up the stairs to grab my gloves, I heard the tap of rocks on my frosted window.

It was Stephen's signal that I was taking too long to come out.

I didn't go to the window because if I had, I was pretty sure I would have flipped him off. I didn't say goodbye to Grandma as I pushed through the front door. Grandpa had shoveled the path to the gravel drive, but I walked through the yard, trudging into fresh snow that went up to my ankles around my snow boots. Finally, I came to face to face with Alex and Stephen.

"You picked one heck of a day to make us wait outside," Stephen said with wide, dark eyes as he teased me.

I gave him the biggest eye roll of my life as I shoved past him.

"Whoah, what's up with Jenny Philips?" Stephen turned on his heel to walk next to me. "That's how you thank us for making sure you survive Hollow Brook's tundra season?"

Alex fell into step on my other side. "You okay?"

"Yes. No." I shook my head, but then remembered I'd promised myself last night that I was going to try and be more honest with them. "Something happened."

"What happened?" Alex asked, his tone gentle.

"I don't know." Stubbornness hit me in the throat, I apologized inwardly to myself, promising I'd try to open up to them another time, but right now wasn't the time. "Nothing really."

"Spit it out." Stephen demanded with a frown. "What happened?"

I was still going through it. I was angry at Grandpa for telling me I couldn't date. I was angry at myself for the way I reacted. And I was angry at my mutation for acting up when I didn't want it in the first place. "I don't want to talk about it."

"You can't say something happened and not tell us."

I smirked at him. "Uh, yeah I can."

Stephen shot Alex a pleading look. Alex held his gloved hands up. "Don't look at me."

We were still walking to the pick-up spot as the bus pulled up slowly in front of us. Careful of the snow and ice, I rushed up the steps toward our usual seats in the back. I always slid in first, Alex slid in next to me and Stephen sat in front of us. He twisted to look back at me as the bus moved. He spoke quietly so the other students couldn't hear. "Is it a mutant thing?"

I decided to offer Stephen a little nod of acknowledgment.

Alex shifted, bringing his leg up between us as he faced me. "What happened? Are you okay?"

"Grandpa and I got in a fight." My eyes darted between my two best friends. "We argued and I made the power go out."

"The power went out?" Alex asked at the same time

as Stephen said, "What was the fight about?"

"Grandpa thought it was the storm. I felt my mutation do it." I said and then I looked at Stephen. "The fight is classified."

Stephen tilted his head. "Girl stuff?"

I scowled at him. "Sure, if you want to tell yourself that. Girl stuff."

"Man, you're salty," Stephen laughed.

I crossed my arms and glared out at the snowy fields we passed as we headed into town toward the school. "I'm still…" My voice fell into a whisper. "I'm not ready to talk about it."

"That's all right." Alex slid his hand out of his glove to give my hand a quick squeeze. The warmth of his touch made me realize that I'd never put my own gloves on. "So, electricity. That's consistent with what happened with Emma and the lights."

"Electricity and air. And earthquakes, I guess." I mumbled but turned to Alex. "Did you tell him about yesterday with the snow?"

His eyes flickered to Stephen. "Most of it." I had a feeling Alex hadn't told Stephen the whole story of what I confessed but focused on what happened with my mutation. I was grateful for that.

"Super interesting." Stephen pushed his dark curls out of his eyes. "I knew there was more to your mutation."

I sighed, frowning at Alex. "I just don't want to talk about it right now."

Alex shrugged, settling back against his seat. "We're all allowed to have a bad day."

We were quiet the rest of the way to school. They let me watch the snowy fields in silence.

All morning, I tried to shake my bad mood.

I could hardly pay attention between thinking about Grandpa telling me I couldn't date anyone and the fact that I was painfully aware of Alex watching me in class. I could feel him studying me, his concern, and the questions he wanted to ask me, but he was determined to let me process alone.

At lunch, we stood at Alex's locker. "I'm starving." Stephen said. "Let's go eat."

"Sounds good to me," Alex said, as he shut his locker.

I didn't say anything and followed them like I did every day. I paused at the library door, remembering I'd reserved a book last week. I wasn't sure how long I wanted to give Grandpa the silent treatment, I figured having a book to entertain myself up in my room was a good idea. "I'm going to check if my book came in yet. I'll meet you there."

Alex nodded. "We'll wait."

Stephen's whole body sagged dramatically.

I snorted. "He won't make it. I'll be right there. I have a cold lunch again. You guys get through the line and I'll meet you at our spot."

Alex hesitated, but turned after I gave him one more assuring nod. Stephen was happy to be on his way to food.

After I grabbed my book from the hold shelf and checked it out, I made my way to the lunchroom. Once I stood in the open doorway of the lunchroom, I glanced at our favorite table in the corner where we sat when it was cold outside.

I was hit with another emotional bat when I saw Emma, Meg, and Suzy crowding Alex and Stephen. Alex rolled his eyes and shook his head while holding his tray of food, but he was smiling. Stephen held his tray with one hand and ate his sandwich with another while he listened to Alex and Emma talk.

The scene around me slowed as they all sort of laughed again with each other.

The Small-Town Five were right here before me. Alex was tall and handsome, rolling his eyes at Emma with a smile as if she were saying something ridiculous. Emma flipped her glossy red hair over her shoulder. She was definitely flirting. The girls had seen an opportunity with my absence and they'd pounced.

The mutation within me stirred.

I couldn't help it. The fear of losing Alex and Stephen jolted within me, confusing my mutation. I needed to calm down. I didn't want something to happen with all of these people around. I turned on my heel and headed down the hall. I didn't know where I could hide, but my grip tightened on the book in my hand and my feet took me back in the direction of the library.

I didn't pay attention to the other students scattered down the hallway as I walked. A locker slammed shut, laughter echoed in my mind, and darkness inched at the edges of my vision. I rounded a corner and slammed into a hard chest. My mutation slipped from my control—just a sliver of it—and papers flew everywhere.

"What the—" a familiar voice said as the papers fluttered like feathers to the ground.

Brandon Thomas's gaze darted around us, noting the way the papers in his notebook had landed in a wide swirling circle around us, a geometric shape, too perfect for coincidence. My mouth dropped open as we stared at each other.

"I'm so sorry," I blurted out, trying to pick up the papers and pushing them around so the formation looked more random. "I wasn't watching where I was going."

Brandon knelt by me, picking up his papers too. His gaze burned along my profile as we gathered them, but he didn't say anything for a long moment. We reached for a paper at the same time, our hands brushing. I jerked away, meeting his questioning brown eyes.

"Where are your boys?" Brandon said, holding out his hand for the stack of papers in mine.

"What?"

"Bailey and Wright."

"Oh." He took the papers from me and stacked them with the rest. I didn't like the casual tone he was giving me, the way he was looking at me, as if he were asking for some kind of truce between us. "What do you care?"

"I don't." He laughed under his breath and stood up. "I'm just surprised they let you out of their sight."

I stood up with him. "What's that supposed to mean?"

"Nothing," He shrugged, his brows rose as he tilted his head to sweep his eyes up and down my body. It was the same way he'd looked at me the day Alex punched him. "I have a bad reputation in this town, but you can ask any of my friends, I'm actually a pretty good guy who is finally sorting out his shit."

Surprise lit up in me, but I scowled. "Okay? Why would I care?"

He huffed a laugh, an easy smile spreading across his face. "Hit me up if you ever get tired of hanging out with them."

I couldn't decide if he was being genuine or mocking

me. It didn't matter, I still needed to calm down before I could go back to Alex and Stephen. I rolled my eyes. "Noted."

I didn't let him say anything more. I stepped around him to walk in the direction of the library again. Pushing through the door, I found students scattered around at desks and tables. As I made for the back of the library, I felt the glances and heard the whispers. Boys were nudging other boys. Girls were sitting up straighter to watch me. The librarian, who was typing on a computer at the main check-out station, paused to squint at me.

The air was different, the lights were brighter. The room was on the edge of *something*, and everyone noticed it, but no one would know how to explain it.

I found the very back corner of the library and sat down against the bookshelves on the floor. I shut my eyes and leaned my head against the shelf behind me, focusing on my breathing, trying to let all my hurt from last night and today numb over.

I didn't know how much time had passed when I heard Stephen's voice. "Bro, she's not in here."

Alex rounded the corner of the bookshelves. His face fell as he approached and dropped to a squat in front of me. "Are you okay? What are you doing here?"

"I needed to calm down." My voice sounded far away to my ears.

Alex crossed his legs as he sat in front of me, our knees inches from touching. "Calm down?"

Stephen sat against the bookshelf next to me, the heat from his mutation warmed my arm. "You need to spill, Philips. You're acting weird and we need to be in on it because it's mutant stuff."

A million thoughts spun in my mind. I couldn't catch any of them. They were like frantic blackbirds flying in a cluster in my head. I knew I needed to say something, but all I could think to blurt out was, "Why don't one of you guys ask Emma out?"

They both jerked back because that was absolutely not what they had expected me to say. I didn't blame them. I hadn't meant to say it. I'd surprised myself.

Stephen sputtered. "You… W-why… What?"

"She'd go out with either of you." I was looking at Stephen. I couldn't look at Alex or I might burst. "Why don't you guys date girls and stuff?"

Stephen was suddenly looking at Alex. I braved a glance at him too. His face was bright red, his gaze on his fingers wound together in his lap. Stephen spoke again. "Uh, why—" He cleared his throat and shifted to settle in a more comfortable position next to me. "What's up with you?"

"It's just a question." I pulled my legs up against my chest and wrapped my arms around them. "I'm just asking."

The silence stretched between us for a long moment.

Alex seemed to gather himself. His face wasn't as red anymore as he said, "For me dating Emma Henderson would be like dating a cousin. I've known her all my life and it feels weird. I'm not interested in her that way."

"Is that what upset you? That she was talking to us or something?" Stephen's voice was uncharacteristically gentle as he rested his head on my shoulder. "You didn't come find us. We were worried."

I laid my cheek on the top of Stephen's head, but Alex's serious blue eyes had my attention as I said, "My bad day is making me scared that my mutation is going to freak out."

"But we're in this together." Stephen sounded so much younger for some reason. "If you're going through something, we're going through it too. Right, Alex?"

"Totally." Alex's eyebrows knitted together and his voice was rough as he reached out and held my hand across our laps. "When you're going through stuff don't run from us. Run to us. It's important we talk about mutant stuff together. We have to lean into each other. You're not doing any of this alone, Jenny."

"Yeah, we need you too," Stephen said quietly, his head still on my shoulder. His voice was raw. "If I lose you and Alex, I've lost everything that's important to me. I think that's why I've fought to keep our secret the hardest."

I'd never been able to explain stuff the way Stephen could, but he was describing exactly what I felt. I'd grown closer to Alex and Stephen in just a few months than I'd ever been to my grandparents or my aunt. "I'm going to be there for you, Stephen Wright."

"Yeah?" Stephen's voice was heavy with emotion. "Promise?"

Alex and I exchanged a pained look. "I don't have a brother. I've just decided that I'm adopting you. Now you have a very annoying little sister." I sighed dramatically. "You have no choice in the matter. You can't get rid of me now."

Alex grinned at me. His eyes shined with happy approval.

"Oh, great." Stephen snorted, but he was happy too, I could tell. "That's what I need. Alex is so much work already."

"Dude." Alex rolled his eyes, laughing. "I'm the easiest friend ever. You're so lucky to have me. I'm the best." He paused though, his humor dissolving and voice going quieter. "I'm scared too, you know. I can't do this mutation thing without you guys. I can't share this with my dad like I want to. I used to talk to my dad about everything, but I can't. And, it's worse now because Stephen and I decided we aren't going to do sports anymore."

I blinked at him. "Wait, why not?"

"I can't gauge my strength," Alex said quietly. "I'm going to hurt someone by pitching a baseball too hard. Or swinging a bat and hitting a ball farther than humanly possible. I love sports and stuff, but I told my parents that I'm done with sports. My dad is more accepting, but my mom is upset and worried about me. She won't leave me alone about it. She knows I've always wanted to play baseball, but I can't explain why I don't want to."

Stephen nodded, everything about him quiet. "Sports are more emotional than they seem. I'm afraid of getting all worked up and lighting on fire. It's hard to control our mutations, even in regular P.E. So, Alex and I aren't going to try out for the Willow High baseball team this year."

Hollow Brook was so small that they didn't have enough resources to have their own sports teams. If kids wanted to do team sports they had to drive the forty-five minutes to the next town. It was common for a Hollow Brook student to make the drive to practice every day after school.

"This town expected Alex Bailey to step into Mark Bailey's shoes and be the next small-town baseball hero." Stephen rolled his eyes. "Everyone is going to be talking about Alex not following in Mark's athletic footsteps for the next two and half years."

"Maybe longer," Alex muttered, studying his fingers again. "Maybe for the next thirty years. Hollow Brook loves talking about the high school glory days."

The quiet stretched between us again. I was sad for them. They were boys who liked to be active. Stephen was naturally athletic and good at competitive games of any kind, but he was also resilient and flexible. Stephen rolled with the punches in life.

Alex had his life mapped out in his head. He could list his life goals on five fingers and one of them was playing college baseball.

I bit my lip as I eyed Alex. He was sad about losing the ability to play sports in a different way than Stephen was. A very real dream of his was dying. His shoulders were like stone, like he was a statue in some fancy museum, barely holding himself together.

Something painful twisted in my chest. I wiped a tear away, but I realized at the same time that last night Alex had brought me to a place where I was okay with crying in front of them. I squeezed Alex's hand until he looked up at me, his expression surprised when he registered that tears were running down my face.

"I wish things were different for you."

He looked between us. Stephen frowned, his expression making it clear that he hurt for Alex too.

Alex huffed a laugh. "I don't have anything to

complain about. You guys have been through hard stuff, but I have my parents and a nice house and everything—"

I cut him off. "I wish this town would mind their business and not try to plan your life out for you. I wish they'd let you make a mistake or two because you do a real good job of making everybody happy." Alex was a picture of confidence and control. I knew people didn't see anything weak about him. He was level, steady, and sure, but I wanted to see him. I wanted to be someone who saw beyond the solid walls he so easily put up for others. "You have time to decide who you want to be, and it doesn't have to be Hollow Brook's golden boy."

Alex cleared his throat, his thumb ran a gentle path along my knuckles as he sorted his thoughts. Finally, he said, "We can only choose who we want to be if we keep our secrets. If adults found out, they would tell doctors or the government, or whatever. They'd separate us and do tests on us. It terrifies me to think—" Alex's serious gaze sent something warm down my middle. "I won't let that happen."

"What?" I whispered.

"I won't let us be separated," Alex said, something hard and determined washing over his expression. "No matter what."

Stephen straightened, nodding in agreement. "Even if people somehow find out about us, we'll protect you.

We'll find a way to stick together."

Their declaration was hard to swallow, harder than it should have been. But I knew life wasn't predictable. We couldn't make promises to each other that everything would be okay. My parents were dead, which meant, in a way, nothing would ever be okay for me. I couldn't explain my deeply embedded fears to them. I couldn't think of how to respond honestly. I didn't want them to ask about my doubts, to dig deeper.

Alex must have read my expression. "Jenny, we won't let anything happen to you." He placed a hand on his chest. "I won't let anything happen to you."

My stomach swooped. My eyes darted down. I felt like I could always handle Stephen, but sometimes Alex said certain things and it was like he was shaking my world. I took a deep breath and forced myself to look back at blue eyes that I was sure could drown me. "Thanks for coming to find me."

"We'll always come to find you." Alex gave my hand one more squeeze. The grip I'd taught him weeks ago was perfect, sending another pulse of warmth buzzing up my arm. "Let's get you lunch, Jenny Philips."

Stephen agreed heartily. "I know we're being all mushy, but I could really go for a second lunch." Alex and I exchanged an eye roll, but we were relieved to have our carefree Stephen back.

13.

AUNT SARAH CALLED the day before I was supposed to leave to visit her to say she was sorry
because she had to go out of town on a work emergency, but my gift was in the mail.

I wasn't sad at all. I loved Aunt Sarah, but I was fine
not traveling to Coral Beach. My gift from her was a
cell phone, which sent Grandpa into a twenty-minute
lecture on the dangers of texting strangers and putting
my information on the internet. Once Grandpa was
satisfied, Alex and Stephen helped me set up the phone.

I texted Aunt Sarah and thanked her. We messaged
every day during break. It was fun to talk to her like
that, instead of having to use Grandpa's phone to call
her.

When I told her about Grandpa's no-dating rule, she sent an all-caps text back.

THAT'S THE STUPIDEST THING I'VE EVER HEARD.
YOU CAN COME LIVE WITH ME ANYTIME.
LOVE, YOUR COOL AUNT

Aunt Sarah was a corporate lawyer. She'd made sure the custody agreement gave me the choice to live either with her or my grandparents. She was my dad's sister and much more relaxed on the rules than my grandparents. Still, my grandma was my mom's mom and I felt like I needed her right now in my life.

Alex, Stephen, and I spent the first week of our break finding random stuff to do—sledding on the hills behind Grandpa's farm, snowmobiling, and igloo building—which was quite impressive and a great day's work if you'd asked me.

Christmas Eve and Christmas morning were spent with my grandparents. I survived it by smiling and saying thank you a lot. Just as Alex had said, we were invited to the Bailey house for Christmas Day dinner. Stephen, Alex, and I sat around playing with our gifts and laughing together.

Being with them was my favorite part of the holiday.

After dinner, Mr. Bailey broke out a board game.

It was the first time something sad lit up in my chest. My parents weren't here. Our tradition of snuggling under a blanket on the couch and watching a holiday movie after Christmas dinner wasn't going to happen. Stephen announced he was in to play the game and my grandparents wanted to play too. Mrs. Bailey set out coffee and sugar cookies for everyone.

This was their tradition. It wasn't mine and it was hard.

I excused myself to go use the restroom and let myself sob into a hand towel for a few minutes. The lights gently flickered on and off above the sink as if they were mourning with me. I splashed water on my face to gather myself again. I needed to go back to the kitchen looking normal. When I opened the door Alex was leaning against the wall. He looked up quickly. "Hey."

"Hi," I said softly, I couldn't handle this handsome guy with his tall, strong build that seemed to change daily. "Uh, the bathroom is open now."

When I tried to walk past, Alex's hand landed on the wall in front of me, his arm blocking my path. "Remember when I offered to be there if you needed someone on Christmas?"

I turned a little, finding him close. He smelled like the peppermint bark we'd been snacking on with Stephen in the other room. I wondered if he tasted like peppermint bark too. It wasn't something I could ask or do anything about.

"I'll be honest, I was sad, but I'm good now. Thanks, Alex."

His eyes darted to my lips before he found my eyes again as if he was wondering if I tasted like peppermint bark too. I turned to fully face him, my back against the wall. He gave me a slow smile. "We could go for a walk."

"It's okay," I shook my head.

Alex moved a little closer, his hand still on the wall next to me. "We could go into my dad's office. Chill in there for a minute."

I raised an eyebrow, surprising myself with the flirtiness in my voice. "Chill in your dad's office? What does that mean?"

Nervous laughter escaped him. He shook his head. "Uh, it means…" He laughed again, flushing red, and said with a low voice, "It means whatever you want it to mean, Jenny Philips."

Butterflies fluttered inside me. I liked this dance. It was fun. I wanted to play with Alex and explore this banter. My heart pounded in my chest.

The playfulness of the moment came crashing down when Grandpa complained loudly that Stephen had to be cheating. My stomach lurched into my throat, realizing Alex and I were almost alone together. My stomach jumped into my throat—just as electricity jolted up my spine.

The light in the hall above us flickered out.

My eyes were on Alex's chest as I said, "I can't."

The hall was dark, I could hardly make out Alex's face as his gaze drifted toward the sounds of Grandpa and Mr. Bailey talking about the power outage. Mrs. Bailey sounded flustered. "Mark, grab a few flashlights. Alex, get the candles—Where's Alex?"

"I'll find him," Stephen said. "Where's Jenny?"

I released the breath I'd been holding and the lights clicked back on. I wasn't sure how I'd done it, but I could tell by the way Alex was looking at me that he knew it was me.

He whispered. "Was that…"

I clipped his shoulder with mine as I walked away. "I don't want to talk about it."

In the kitchen, everyone was commenting on the power coming back on and guessing at why it might have gone out. Mr. Bailey raised his eyebrow at Mrs. Bailey. "I'm sure it has nothing to do with the three house remodels in the last two years."

Alex sat at the kitchen island on a barstool next to me. We laughed at the fight over the board game and the way everyone was badmouthing everyone, something easy and good falling between us again. I was grateful he wasn't pushing me to explain. He'd let me process it and talk about it when I was ready.

I missed my parents, but listening to Alex and Stephen's laughter helped.

Alex and Stephen shared birthdays in January. Alex was just a couple of weeks older. The tradition was that on Alex's birthday the Bailey family held a small dinner that included Stephen. We'd just settled in our lunch spot at school, choosing to eat outside because of the rare winter sunshine, when Alex told me I was invited to the birthday dinner. Before I could properly respond he added that he needed to use the restroom.

Once Alex's back was turned, Stephen casually cracked a joke that I was lucky to get into the exclusive dinner event. When I asked him what he meant, his eyes widened. He'd clearly put his foot in his mouth somehow. I'd grown to know the expression well in the past several months.

"I mean that it's always been Alex's parents, Mark, and me. Mrs. Bailey says it's not a friend birthday, but Alex insisted you should come."

I didn't like the thought of Mrs. Bailey disapproving of me. "Well, I'm a friend, so maybe I shouldn't go."

Stephen shrugged. "I'm a friend too and I go."

"You guys are like brothers."

"You're my sister, Jenny." He glanced around us. There was no one near us enough to overhear, but he still whispered, "We're mutants, you and Alex will be my family more than my own family forever."

Alex pushed through the door across the lawn as I said, "If Mrs. Bailey—"

"Do what you want, but I think it'd hurt Alex's feelings if you didn't go. Like I said, it was a whole conversation. He fought for you to be invited and now you are. That's all."

Still, not being enthusiastically invited didn't sit well with me. Alex plopped down to the ground next to me. "Wanna go to the arcade in Willow Sunday afternoon? Just the three of us?"

"That sounds fun." I nodded with a smile, deciding to push all thoughts of Mrs. Bailey away for now.

Stephen agreed too, plunging into an explanation of his favorite arcade games, insisting I'd think it was cool. Alex chimed in, informing me of a burger pizza they wanted me to try. Warmth washed over my chest as they talked. I loved the way Stephen's hands waved about when he was excited, his big smile always came so easily. Alex was quieter, but I'd learned to read him through his bright blue eyes, the twinkle in them gave me everything I needed to know about what he was feeling.

The thought of last summer flitted through my mind because I hadn't thought I'd ever be able to have friends again, let alone friends like them.

A strand of my hair caught on my eyelash. Before I could move to pull it off my face, Alex reached up to brush it away.

"Do you know you do that?" Stephen asked, tilting his head to the side.

"Do what?"

"A breeze picks up around you sometimes," Alex said, his gaze darting around me, as if trying to solve a mystery. "But there isn't a speck of real wind in the air."

My spine stiffened. "How often do I do that? Do other people notice?"

"You only do it when the three of us are alone." Alex shook his head.

We glanced at the groups of students in the distance eating lunch and hanging out. No one was near enough to hear us, or even really noticed us.

"It like…" Stephen scrunched his nose. "It's like you only do it when you're relaxed."

Alex nodded. "I think it's when you feel safe, like you don't have to hold onto your mutation so tightly."

"That's so embarrassing."

"It's not embarrassing," Stephen shrugged. "I feel

the same way, when it's just us, I don't have to worry about my mutation. Like Alex said, I feel safe with you two."

"Yeah, but—"

"I feel safe too." Alex bit the inside of his cheek, pausing for several seconds. "We're going to have to accept that our mutations aren't going to go away. They're part of us now, and I think the more we accept that, the more we'll have control of them."

His words were like a stone dropping into still water within me. The ripple of it spread through me. Stephen's expression turned thoughtful too. A faint ache grew in me, because Alex was right, our mutations probably weren't going to go away. There'd been consequences the day we jumped over the mutant farm's fence. The only choice we had was to decide how we would deal with those consequences. I decided to say, "So we accept our mutations, we learn to manage them and—"

"We live our lives." Stephen interrupted, his brown eyes meeting mine. "We go after what we want, and we don't apologize for it."

"Okay," It was like the ripples in the water within me stilled again. "We'll do it together."

"Together," they said in an accidental solemn unison, as if we were a band of superheroes committing to save a city from evil. Which broke the tension as we laughed, because we weren't superheroes, we were just determined to be ourselves.

Mrs. Bailey graciously greeted me the night of Alex's birthday dinner. Her body language didn't hint at her reluctance to invite me. Alex gestured for me to sit next to him at the dining table. I'd never been in the Bailey family's fancy dining room before.

There was something claustrophobic about the space with its heavy blue and white vertical striped designer curtains. The big modern lantern style chandelier cast a yellow glow over the long table, but something in the wiring was off, as if modern wires didn't quite connect with the old wires of the house, and I had to hold back my mutation from making it flicker. Mrs. Bailey had laid out baby blue napkins and flowers in low vases as a centerpiece, the colors were similar to Alex's room.

I couldn't sort why she'd chosen the color since I knew Alex's favorite color was green, and then I wondered if Mrs. Bailey even knew that fact about him.

Mark and Stephen sat across from us. Mr. and Mrs. Bailey sat on either end of the table. Each boy wore a polo with a stiff collar. I was glad Stephen had mentioned randomly it was a little formal. Aunt Sarah had sent me a box of winter clothes just days before the dinner, so I'd been lucky to have thick black tights and a forest green sweater dress.

I could feel Mark's curious gaze every so often darting between Alex and me. He was probably surprised I was there for a family dinner, but it didn't seem like he objected.

Mr. Bailey mostly talked about the way things would change now. He wanted Stephen and Alex to wake up every morning before school and do more farm chores. They'd be able to make money now.

I stifled laughter as Stephen gave me covert eye rolls and dreaded expressions over working at four in the morning before school every day. I watched with fascination as Alex listened to his dad speak, as if he held all the answers to life.

After we'd consumed the mint chocolate chip ice cream cake, Mrs. Bailey clapped her hands together announcing that all of us should go out to the shop where Mr. Bailey kept the tractors and big farming equipment.

The snow crunched under my brown ankle boots as I walked between Alex and Stephen down the gravel path that led to the outbuilding near the Bailey's barn. My breath was visible in the cold air under the industrial lights. I dug my chilled hands into my coat pockets, wondering if I was allowed to ask questions about what we were doing, but nobody else was saying anything so I stayed quiet.

When the automatic doors opened, a shiny green,

four-door truck with a big red bow on it sat in the center of the shop. My mouth dropped open as I realized this was Alex's birthday present.

Alex's eyebrows rose and a smile lit up his face, but I *felt* his reaction more than I saw it. What he truly felt was hidden under his calculated expression. The present was a painful blow to the chest, but self-control was one of Alex's greatest strengths. I didn't understand why Alex would be upset over a cool gift like that until my gaze snagged on Stephen's face.

Stephen wasn't good at covering up what he felt. I caught the initial emotion in his eyes, the mixed-up way he was happy for Alex but shaken by the fact that he would never receive a gift like this for free.

I could read them because I knew my boys, but I realized it'd been some sort of mutant thing too. My mutation had opened me up, gathered what they'd felt, and made me feel it all too.

I wanted to cry for them.

"Oh wow," Alex said, playing the part Mrs. Bailey wanted. "For me? Thank you, I—"

"Dude!" Stephen seemed to step into his role now too, saying the things he knew Mr. and Mrs. Bailey wanted him to say. "We're never taking the bus again. Our whole lives are changed forever. This is epic." Stephen ran to the truck and opened the passenger door. "Dibs eternally on shotgun. Be ready to ride in the backseat, Jenny."

Alex snorted and grinned, coming to inspect the truck. "We both know that shotgun is Jenny's seat."

Alex's face fell when he glanced at me—and I realized what I felt for them must have been written on my expression. I drew in a breath and smiled, falling into what I was supposed to be feeling too. I came to stand next to Stephen, elbowing his ribs in sisterly annoyance. "I'll decorate my seat with bubble gum air fresheners and a pink floor mat. You know, really mark my territory."

Alex laughed. Stephen wrinkled his nose. "Blasphemy, this truck is sacred, Jenny Philips."

Mrs. Bailey hugged Alex. "Well, what do you think?"

Again, I could see Alex reply with the words she wanted to hear. His smile held a familiar tightness that sometimes came when he was forcing himself to be patient as Mrs. Bailey babbled on about the story of where the truck was bought.

"The truck is used, but it's in great condition." Mr. Bailey said. Alex followed his dad around the truck, listening as he explained how things worked and the different features the truck offered. They continued to talk outside for a bit longer, but I was cold so I followed Mrs. Bailey and Stephen back into the house.

Mrs. Bailey urged Stephen to join her in the kitchen to cut the tags off the new sneakers they'd gotten him for his birthday. Not knowing what to do, I settled on the white sofa in the living room, opening up a coffee table book filled with pictures of designer rooms similar to the rooms in the Bailey's home.

When Alex came through the front door, he dropped onto the couch next to me. "Are you okay?"

"Yeah," I smiled. "I'm great."

A beat of quiet passed before he said, "I like your dress."

"Oh." I glance down at myself. "Thanks."

He grinned. "That's my favorite color."

"Yeah, I know." But that wasn't what I'd meant to say, I didn't want him to think I'd worn it specifically for him. "I mean, all of my dresses from last year don't fit anymore, Aunt Sarah sent it to me."

"It's pretty."

"Thanks," I said, the word hanging awkwardly between us. Another thought sprang to mind. "What does Stephen's dad do for his birthday?"

"I think he gives him some cash," Alex said, his eyes drifting toward the kitchen where Stephen and Alex's parents talked. "I think his dad thinks Stephen is too old for birthday parties."

I nodded, but didn't have anything to say in response.

Stephen didn't talk about his dad often. I respected it because I didn't talk about my parents much either.

"My mom is annoying," he muttered. I'd never heard Alex say something disrespectful about an adult before. "My dad told me they got me an updated game system too. I asked him to give it to me later."

I nodded again, I knew exactly why Alex asked his dad that.

He glanced at me. "I wish life was more fair, you know?"

I leaned into his shoulder, and he leaned into mine. "I wish life was more fair too."

The next day just the three of us celebrated Stephen and Alex's birthdays by driving to Willow City to go go-kart racing. I was extremely happy that Grandpa had let Alex drive us there. He'd given Alex and Stephen a long talk about safety and responsibility before we left.

I kept shifting from foot to foot as Grandpa talked, but the lecture eventually ended. We jumped into Alex's new green truck together, listening to Stephen's many ideas about what adventures we could have now that Alex had a truck.

After go-kart racing, we spent an hour playing

arcade games. When most of our money was gone, we sat at a table in the pizza parlor connected to the arcade. Stephen sat across from me in the booth. He spoke in a haughty, teasing voice, "Oh, I hope it's alright if I break the news now, but we're sixteen. We don't hang out with baby fifteen year olds anymore."

My eyes widened. "I have to find new friends?"

"Yep." Stephen looked down at a pretend watch on his wrist. "We'll hang out again in March, right?" My birthday was in March, so I still had a couple of months before I'd be sixteen too. "Until then, we can't talk to you."

Alex sat next to me in the booth with a little amused smile on his face while he waited for me to assault Stephen verbally.

"Okay." I shrugged, sitting back in my seat with my arms crossed. "I guess you won't get the gift I was going to get you."

Stephen gestured to the pizza and sodas on the table, as if something were missing. "I mean, I wasn't going to ask, but where is my gift?"

"She got us game credit gift cards." Alex rolled his eyes, but he was grinning. He was in a good mood today. Alex lived for days like this when he could hang out with his best friends and not think about responsible stuff. "If anyone is a baby at this table, it's you, Stephen Wright."

I sat up, peering around the room, trying to think of something witty to say. The thrilling sound of a jackpot win blared like a siren above all the arcade noise caught my attention, igniting inspiration within me.

I scooted over, wordlessly gesturing for Alex to move.

"What?" he asked, confused.

"I have an idea." I pushed his shoulder until he slid out of the booth.

I circled the different arcade machines, looking for the one I remembered seeing earlier. I stopped at a sleek, modern, white machine. It towered over Alex and Stephen's tall frames, its lights flickering in colorful designs behind the prizes. This game was five dollars a play because the prizes were more expensive. A couple of designer wallets, a set of popular headphones, and gaming controllers lined the shelves.

I eyed the limited-edition game system on the top shelf and gestured to Stephen. "Step up to the game."

"What?" Stephen frowned. "We don't play this one. It'll waste all our money."

I grabbed his arm, always a little warmer than a normal person, pulling and pushing him to stand in front of the arcade machine. "Put your hand on the controllers. Make it look like you're actually playing it in case they look back at the camera or something."

"Okay," Stephen said slowly, still confused.

"Wait," I stepped back to read the directions on the panel next to the red control handle. "How do you play this?"

"You have to move the lever up and then to the left," Stephen said with an edge of impatience in his tone. "You have to get the key into the hole perfectly, it cuts the string, and the shelf drops, and you get the prize. But it's impossible to win and costs five dollars a play. We don't have any money."

"I've got ten bucks left," Alex said, pulling money from his pocket. "You want it, Jenny?"

"We don't need money." I laid my hand on the panel over the instructions. "Be quiet, so I can think."

I closed my eyes, I could feel it, the wires and pulses of energy, the way power moved through the cords to make the lights flicker and the machine hum. I ran a mental finger along every electrical path, my mutation creating a map in my mind of the inner workings of the arcade game.

When I found the path I wanted, I opened my eyes, locking onto the mechanical structure of the top shelf.

Alex followed my gaze. "Wait, you think you can get it?"

"It's worth a try."

I reached for my mutation, finding the sensation

that always buzzed subtly up and down my spine and connecting with it. I directed the mutation, giving it a focus and an intention, trying to explore the different pieces of the arcade machine.

I had an awareness of electricity within objects sometimes. I noticed that kind of stuff when I was alone in a room. I liked studying how the electricity moved through the coffee maker and the refrigerator while I ate breakfast. Or, drawing the lines of the electrical cords in the outlets and lights with my mutation in class when I was bored.

I'd never taken this kind of control before.

I eyed the key, finding the panel sending signals, and played around with the idea of moving the key on the track the lever manipulated. The key moved up and down, just a few inches, stopping again where it began.

"Oh my god," Stephen's gaze whipped from the machine to me. "You're doing that?"

I shushed him. "Don't announce it to the world." I leaned against the glass. Alex crowded Stephen on the other side, as if we both wanted to hide what I was doing from everyone. We peered into the machine, watching as I moved the key. I could sense something was wrong as the key moved upward, sliding slowly left until it settled in front of the limited edition game system.

"You're really doing this," Stephen said under his breath.

"I haven't done it yet," I whispered back.

Wrong—my mutation or the machine, maybe a little both—sent me a signal that I wasn't in the right place yet. My mutation knew what I wanted, it was getting it for me, but we hadn't figured it out yet.

There was no countdown, which the game usually would have indicated while someone played it. I didn't need to feel rushed into deciding where to drop the key.

I shifted the key back and forth, left and right, up and down—

Until something felt right, and I sent the key thrusting forward into the keyhole.

The machine's alarm went off like the sound of a fire truck ripping through the room. The red siren light on top of the machine whirred in a circular motion. People turned toward us. Alex eyed the crowd beginning to gather. I was sure we were going to get in trouble for messing with the game, probably kicked out, banned from ever coming again—

Stephen bent down to open the door at the bottom of the machine, a wide smile spreading across his face. He awkwardly slid the gaming system out. "Would you look at that," He beamed as he held the game system in his hands, turning it to read the box. Excitement shined in his eyes when he looked up at me. "I won."

"You did." I laughed, leaning forward to look at the box too.

Stephen drew me in for a tight side hug. "Okay, you can hang out with us. Thanks, little sister."

I laughed again, squeezing his middle. "Happy birthday."

He flipped the box over again, reading the specs and telling Alex about the special controller it came with. A few others near our age gathered to ask questions and congratulate Stephen. A staff member came with a smile, happy for Stephen too, telling him it was well deserved. I stepped back to let Stephen have his glorious moment.

Alex's fingers brushed mine, he turned his head to whisper in my ear. "It's like you're not real, Jenny Philips.'"

"What?" I wrinkled my nose at him.

"You make me believe in magic, that's all."

I couldn't meet Alex's gaze without my cheeks turning warm for the rest of the day.

14.

A FEW WEEKS BEFORE my sixteenth birthday I stood in front of a poster with information on Hollow Brook High's annual dance. I needed to distract myself because Stephen had been called to the office in the middle of class. Alex restlessly sorted his locker across the hall behind me, he was worried about Stephen too. Emma came to stand next to me, taking a moment to read the poster before she said, "We only have one dance a year. The school budget doesn't allow more."

"Cool," I said, my voice full of disinterest.

"Its guys ask girls," Emma said with a smirk.

"I figured." I smiled back at her, clearly sarcastic. I wasn't in the mood for whatever game she wanted to play. "Since that's what I read on the poster."

She tilted her head. "Do you want Alex or Stephen to ask you?"

Alex. His name popped in my head without my consent. But I said, "You tell me which one you want. I'll make it happen."

Emma rolled her eyes at me. "Neither. Please."

"You let me know and I'll hook you up, Emma Henderson." I wasn't proud of messing with her, but I also wanted her to go away. Although, she hadn't bothered me often in the last several months, not really. I stayed clear of her path too. Somehow, we'd fallen into an indifferent existence with each other.

When I was at school I was either focused on the assignment in front of me or following Alex and Stephen around. I was content to give all my attention to them. I didn't know the school gossip, or who was dating who. It was a small enough school that I could put names to faces, give someone that I recognized outside of school a quick smile, but otherwise, no one went out of their way to talk to me either.

I was totally fine with that.

Emma didn't say anything more and turned on her heel with a little prissy sound in her throat. I read the details of the dance again. There wasn't a clear theme, just a lot of pink and purple glitter. Equal amounts of excitement and nervousness built in me as I reread the information for the third time.

Goosebumps rose on my skin, like electricity washing over the back of my neck. An awareness sparked in me. I turned and found the tall and incredibly handsome Alex Bailey standing behind me. He'd been studying the poster over my head.

He looked down, meeting my eyes. "Would you go to that?"

Flustered and caught off guard, I blurted out, "No. No way. I think it's stupid."

Alex took a second to answer. I watched his face shift in a way I didn't understand. He looked up at the poster again. "Yeah, I agree. Stupid."

I wanted to slap myself because I would have loved to go, but I couldn't bring myself to tell Alex that I'd accidentally lied to him because I'd panicked. I couldn't tell him that I was afraid he'd think I was stupid for wanting to go.

And afraid no one would want to ask me.

The bright side of my lie was that if Alex thought it was stupid, then Stephen probably thought it was stupid too. I wasn't interested in Stephen in any kind of romantic way, but I had no idea how I would feel if he picked some other girl to go with either.

My mind circled around and around, wondering what it would be like if Stephen got a girlfriend. What it would mean for our trio of three mutants. I hated how needy I felt, but I couldn't imagine my life without Alex and Stephen helping me to process my mutation.

I supposed if Alex and Stephen did end up picking other girls to go the dance with, I'd have to deal with it. I willed my mutation to calm, wrapping my resolve around it so I wouldn't hurt. I didn't want to do something obvious and embarrassing to the air and electricity around me. I kept telling myself that we didn't do sports or clubs. We didn't do school activities at all, so it made sense that we'd skip the dance.

Alex and I walked to class together. Stephen met us halfway down the hall, his shoulders slumped. "The counselor called me in again."

"Sorry Stephen," I said softly.

"Eh, it's fine." He shrugged, but it was weak. "They keep asking me about my dad. If things are good at home. People keep seeing him at the bar on the weekends late at night, and I guess they call into some agency, and it gets back to the counselor." He rolled his eyes. "He just goes and plays pool. I spend the night with Alex on those nights."

"That's so dumb," Alex muttered.

Stephen's gaze traveled past me, a rare hardness washed over his expression. "I hear someone else's dad hangs out at the same bar on the weekends. And everybody knows his mom works the nightshift at the clinic on the weekends too. But he doesn't get pulled into the counselor's office."

I turned to see who Stephen was referring to, finding Brandon Thomas shutting his locker down the hall. He caught us staring and gave us an arrogant smirk before disappearing through the door of a classroom.

My stomach turned because I knew why Brandon didn't get called into the counselor's office, but Stephen did. But I wasn't going to bring it up unless Stephen did first. He'd always respected me when I didn't want to talk about something, and I would do the same for him.

All I knew was that I'd never stood in Stephen's shoes before. I would never know what it felt like for him to live in Hollow Brook.

The dance stalked me.

Every day, the event information posters were pinned to more and more bulletin boards throughout the school. Grandpa told me randomly that he was fine if I went to the dance with a date. I just had to go with a group of people and come straight home afterward. I found that extremely annoying since I'd told the one guy I wanted to go with I thought the dance was stupid.

There was no recovery from that, I'd decided.

Alex said we should watch a movie at his house the night of the dance. There was a guarantee his brother and all his friends would be attending the dance. I'd just shrugged, but Stephen got excited. He wanted to be ironic and watch movies with high school dances in them. Maybe a horror film like *Carrie* or something from the early 2000s like *She's All That*, or maybe a real classic like *Footloose*.

I could feel his confusion when I didn't get excited about his idea. Instead of doing something like bursting into tears because I'd messed up my only chance to go to the dance, I stayed indifferent.

I pretended like I didn't care about any of it.

As the couple of weeks leading up to the dance went by, I tried to ignore all the excitement around it. Alex didn't say anything about the dance. Our only conversation about it had been when we stood in front of the poster. I hated that I would never know whether Alex would have asked me or not. I'd declared what I felt about it and we'd all moved on. But I couldn't shake my feelings around it. My mutation wouldn't stop stirring within me every time I glanced at one of those stupid glittery posters in the halls.

⟨◆⟩

After school, a few days before the dance, Brandon Thomas leaned on his shoulder against the locker next to mine. I was twisting the lock, trying to remember the code because I usually used Alex's locker.

"Go to the dance with me."

"Leave me alone," I replied dully, even though my heart skipped a beat. Brandon hadn't spoken to me since the day I'd ran into his chest, his papers scattering around us in a suspiciously perfect circle. I passed him in the halls every day, but Alex and Stephen were always with me, so there was never a time in all these months that he stopped to talk to me.

Even now, this was a rare moment that I was alone at my locker, grabbing a blank notebook for science I'd kept there for months because my other notebook was full. The lock finally clicked, my locker popped open, and I snatched the new notebook.

I started to walk away, but Brandon walked with me. "I've been working up the courage to ask you."

"Go away." I didn't look at him.

"Jenny, you're really intimidating. Did you know that?"

I stopped and turned. His voice was too genuine. It sounded way too honest. He was nervous and fidgety. I noticed the faint scar under his eye from when Alex punched him last summer. I shook my head. "What are you talking about?"

"You're pretty." His eyes landed on my books in my

hands, but then he seemed to steel himself to look up at me. "And confident. And…I think about you a lot. I've noticed these past months that Alex and Stephen are idiots. They've made no move on you."

"Don't insult my friends." I raised an eyebrow.

"Sorry. Yeah." He scratched the back of his neck. "I should be nicer. It's just that you're kind of amazing. And… I'm an idiot."

"Yes, you are."

"I agree," he laughed and a dimple in his cheek I'd never noticed appeared. "Why hasn't Alex asked you to the dance?"

I rolled my eyes. "Leave me alone—"

"You're not wondering why every single guy in this school hasn't asked you to the dance?" He stepped in front of me, making me stop, his eyes catching mine.

"What?" I asked, surprised.

"Everyone assumed Alex was going to ask you." He took a small step closer. "Everyone assumes you and Alex are dating. But I asked Mark yesterday if you and Alex were dating, and he said no. Which was a shocker because no one has seen the PDA between you two, but he's always got you crowded as if he was your boyfriend. I asked Mark if Alex was at least taking you to the dance, and he said no to that one, too."

My throat went dry. Brandon's observations were

cutting into things I'd been trying not to think about for weeks. I didn't realize the school was thinking of them too. I tried to shrug it off, but my voice was defensive. "What do you care?"

"I care because…" Brandon's eyes darted around the hall. People stood in little groups talking, or moving through the hall to leave for the day. The chatting, laughter, and obnoxious shouting filled my senses, threatening to drown me where I stood. "I can't stop thinking about you, I can't live with myself without taking a shot, you know?"

I stared at him, holding my breath, I couldn't think of what to say as I pushed down my mutation. I couldn't figure out how to calm my racing heart. The more I shoved down what I was feeling, the more afraid I became that I was going to do something crazy with my mutation.

"I'm saying that if everyone in school knew that Alex hadn't asked you, you'd definitely have a date by now. Your boys really know how to throw a mean mug at other guys to keep them away from you." He ran a hand through his dark brown wavy hair, strands falling gracefully along his forehead. "After I talked to Mark, I realized you hadn't been asked. I think that's a damn shame."

My face warmed. "Just… Stop making fun of me."

"I'm not." He smiled again, his dimple throwing

me off. The genuine light in his eyes tossed me into thoughts of possibilities that hadn't existed before. "At the swim hole last summer, I only meant to meet you and find out who you were. I saw this beautiful girl and wanted to get to know you. The whole thing turned into something else because…I'm kind of an insecure prick."

I swallowed, wrapping another layer of forced control around the uneasy feel of my mutation. "What do you want me to do with all that?"

"Give me a chance?" His eyebrows went up.

"A chance at what?"

"Friendship. That's all," Brandon said, the corner of his mouth lifting. "I thought maybe the dance would be a cool place to start."

I didn't know what to say. My mutation shifted in and around me, snaking through the crowded hallway, as if looking for an anchor. I turned to find Alex twisting at the waist as he stood at his locker with Stephen, his eyebrows pulled together. My stomach dropped as I realized my mutation had gotten Alex Bailey's attention—like a tap on the shoulder.

Despite the long hall of students leaving for the day between us, his gaze crashed into mine, whipping to see Brandon standing next to me. He didn't look at Stephen as he shut his locker and slid between a group of people talking. Stephen looked confused for about three seconds before he straightened and followed after Alex.

I didn't want them to make a scene. "I wasn't even going to go."

"So one of them asked you and you said no?"

I frowned, deciding to be honest. "No, I mean, no one has asked me, but—"

"Say you'll go to the dance with me."

I took a step away from him. "I'm not going to the dance."

"You should let me drive you home." Brandon's hand slid over my books and he surprised me by taking them from my grasp. "Want me to carry these?"

"No—" I said, but he tucked my books under his arm. "What are you doing? Give them back."

"I'll give you your books back if you promise to think about it."

I could feel Alex weaving through the crowd, an incoming storm of intensity I hadn't felt since the day he'd punched Brandon at the waterhole. I blurted out, "Okay I'll think about it. Give me my books."

Brandon handed them to me with a knowing smirk.

My hand landed on Alex's shoulder as he approached. "Slow down."

I hadn't seen it before, but suddenly I knew exactly

what Brandon meant by Alex and Stephen giving other guys a mean mug. Alex sent a message to Brandon over my head, his chin raised in a silent challenge, as if he was asking Brandon if he wanted to throw down right here in the hallway.

"It's nothing," I tugged on Alex's arm, my hand slid down to pull at his wrist. "Let's go."

I blinked, Stephen's green T-shirt blocked my view of Brandon Thomas. Alex's hand found the small of my back in a deft movement, gently pushing me in the opposite direction of my locker. An awareness washed over me, the way Alex and Stephen moved around me. I was in the midst of their shoulders and biceps, Stephen glancing over his shoulder at me to run his eyes over my face to be sure I was okay, Alex's chest brushing against my shoulder. My mutation liked this little world of safety I'd fallen into between them.

"What did he want?" Alex grumbled, the warmth of his breath whispering a sensation up the back of my neck.

"Nothing." I shook my head. "I need to get my bag."

"It wasn't nothing," Stephen said from my other side, following as I headed for Alex's locker. "Brandon had something real important to say if he conjured up the balls to talk to you."

Alex turned the lock. "Has he ever cornered you like that before?"

"He's never cornered me." I rolled my eyes, leaning into the locker next to Alex's. His locker popped open. I pushed my books in and grabbed my bag. "And, he wasn't cornering me just now."

"Jenny," Stephen said, his eyebrows raised.

"What?" I scowled at him, glancing at Alex for help, but they both wore determined expressions. They weren't going to let me keep it to myself.

"He asked me to go to the dance with him."

Stephen went completely still, his face scrunched up like his brain was malfunctioning, like the world had turned upside down.

In the same second, Alex burst into laughter.

Something about his laughter hurt. I couldn't pinpoint exactly why, just that I'd spent weeks mixed up about whether I was worthy of someone asking me to the dance or not. And now Alex was laughing about someone asking me.

I wondered if Brandon's assessment of my situation with the dance reflected the truth because it was clear that no one had asked me. There'd been time and opportunity these past weeks, and not one single guy in the entire school had asked me. My head spun because I realized there might have been time, but if I thought about it there hadn't been an opportunity.

Brandon was right, Alex and Stephen were always

with me, there wouldn't have ever been a moment for another guy to walk up and ask me to the dance. In my head, I knew Alex would never laugh at me about something like this, but in my deepest insecurities, I was confused and hurt. It wasn't their fault that no one had asked me, but in another sense, it was their fault.

"Why is that funny? Why wouldn't someone ask me?"

Stephen held up a hand. "Jenny, it's okay, Brandon is only trying to mess with you. He doesn't want to go to the dance with you."

That didn't help the way I felt either. "No, I think he was asking me."

My words sent Alex into another fit of laughter. "Oh yeah? He really asked you, huh?"

"Whatever," I said, frowning. I was angry now, my hair wisped around me like there was a breeze, but there was no breeze. "He was super nice just now. He wanted to hold my books. Like, he was genuine and explained stuff… I might go with him."

Alex stiffened. Whatever he thought was funny wasn't funny anymore.

15.

I'M READY to go home." I turned, whirling to walk away from them.

I pushed my way down the hall, passing the main office and front restrooms, then through the main doors. A breeze wisped around me in the warm air, gently swirling between trees and students leaving for the day. My mutation was waking up, responding to what Brandon had said, Stephen declaring Brandon didn't actually want to go to the dance with me, and the way Alex had laughed at me.

I didn't stop until I was standing next to the passenger door of Alex's truck. I tugged on it, but it was locked. Stephen circled the truck to face me. "You're not going to go to the dance with Brandon Thomas."

I didn't respond, pulling at the handle of the truck again.

"Like, this is some big joke, right?"

Alex stood there, studying my profile with wide eyes. I wrapped my hands around the strap of my bag, waiting for Alex to unlock the truck so he could take me home and let me calm down in my room.

"Come on, Jenny," Stephen pressed. "Talk to us. What's in your head right now? This makes no sense."

"I can do what I want," I said, remembering what Brandon had said about the school assuming Alex and I were dating. "And sometimes—sometimes you guys can back off a little too."

Stephen threw up his arms. "What does that mean? What is going on with you?"

I blinked back tears, looking away. "I want to go home."

Stephen shook his head, slipping his fingers into his dark curls. Alex dropped his gaze to the ground, as if he might find the answers there. His mutation shifted under his skin in gentle waves, as if deciding what he felt about the situation. I could feel the buzzing power radiating off him, the energy of him colliding with my energy. My hair moved in strands across my vision as my mutation continued to conjure slight breeze.

We were both tense and on edge.

I didn't want to speak because I didn't want to set anything off between our mutations. Alex was consistently patient and understanding. Sometimes Stephan and Alex got into it over little stuff, but neither of them ever really fought with me. This was new territory between the three of us and I didn't know how to navigate it.

Alex huffed, rubbing his face before he looked up at me. "You said you weren't going to the dance. You said it was stupid."

"I can change my mind." I was all emotion, all potential energy. "You guys are so much sometimes—"

"What does that mean?" Alex asked in an unsteady voice. "You said we needed to back off. I have no idea what you're talking about."

"I mean that I can have friends and do stuff outside of our group."

Hurt flashed in his eyes. "No one said you had to be part of our group."

"You know that's not what I meant."

"All right, so what did you mean?"

"I mean, I—I…" I stuttered, my thoughts racing. My mutation was confused that I was arguing with Alex, who I trusted more than anyone else in the world. "I mean, you hover. No one asked me because you hover—"

"I *hover*?" He barked out a laugh that skidded over my skin. "You're telling me right now that no one asked you to the dance because I *hover*? You're upset because no one asked you to the dance you think is stupid because I *hover*?"

Stephen held up his pointer finger. "Okay guys, let's—"

"I'm just saying that you can't march down the hallway all aggressive and ready to fight whenever another guy is talking to me."

"Another guy?" Alex gaped at me. "Brandon is not just another guy."

"Alex!" I threw up my hands. "You know what I mean."

"No, I don't." He frowned, blinking. "And—And, why do you want to talk to other guys?"

"Oh my god," I groaned, my mutation slipped like lightning in the sky, searching for its mark. "I don't want to talk to other guys—"

Alex's truck boomed to life behind us, a revving sound that made the three of us jump. I whirled around to find the diesel engine rumbling behind us.

Alex dug his hand into his pocket, pulling out his set of keys, "Did you do that?"

Stephen said, "Jenny, you turned on the truck—"

"I know!" I exploded. My voice was a burst of invisible wind and energy swirling through the parking lot. "It's because I want to go home."

The three of us looked over to see Mandy, Mark, and their friends giving us awkward glances from across the parking lot. A few of them looked around or up at the sky, as if commenting on the weird weather. Brandon stood with them. He raised his eyebrows as if to say, *See what I mean?*

My cheeks burned, embarrassed that my control on my mutation had slipped. Stephen's words, Alex's laughter, Brandon's friends whispering…

I didn't know how to calm down.

"I'm going to take the bus."

My mutation's wind slowed, the air settling into its natural breeze. With my decision made, I gripped control of my mutation again, knowing that I wouldn't have to ride in the truck with them and possibly have to keep arguing.

"No," Stephen groaned. "You're not."

Alex pressed the button to unlock the truck and reached over to open the door for me. "Come on, I'll take you home."

I was already backing away. "I'll see you guys in the morning."

Alex sighed, gesturing to the open truck door. "Jenny, it's okay, we can talk on the way home."

"No." I shook my head, wiping away tears. "Let me go, Alex."

He blinked as he realized I was serious. The hurt written across his face echoed my own. Stephen took a step forward like he was going to follow me, but Alex gripped his shoulder to stop him.

"I'll see you guys in the morning." I bit my lip.

Alex swallowed, nodding, and looked away.

I walked toward the two buses parked in front of the school, adjusting my bag over my shoulder. I needed quiet to sort out everything. I needed Alex and Stephen to know that I was part of the group, but they couldn't decide who I was friends with. I didn't know if they'd done it on purpose, but they'd been making those decisions for me for months.

"Need a ride?"

Brandon's voice made me pause. He'd fallen in step next to me. I didn't look at him, trying to settle my scattered thoughts and feelings before I did something else that would draw Brandon's attention to our mutations.

I glanced back at Alex and Stephen over my shoulder. Stephen was speaking to Alex's profile, obviously unhappy that I wasn't going with them. Alex watched Brandon and I with an unblinking expression on his face that killed me.

Except—I needed to know I could be independent of them.

"I don't want a ride home," I said, "but I'll go to the dance with you."

I turned on my heel toward the bus. I didn't look back again.

⸰◆⸰

I rushed up the steps of the bus, but quickly realized there were only a few spots left. Most of the seats were taken. I swallowed down everything I felt, trying to focus on not tripping on backpacks or knees sticking out in the aisle. With each step I took, the bus seemed to quiet. My heart pounded faster because I knew eyes followed me as I walked.

Mercifully, someone finally said, "Hey, Jenny, here's a spot." I turned to see a guy push another guy out of the seat and wave me over.

"Thanks," I slid into the seat next to him. I knew he was a freshman, but I didn't know his name.

"Where's Alex?" the guy asked abruptly.

His friend who'd been pushed out of his seat leaned into the aisle on the other side of me. Both of them were tall, skinny boys and they reminded me of when I met Alex and Stephen for the first time. The two blonde girls in front of us twisted in the seats to look at me, I realized they were Meg and Suzy.

I set my head against the backseat and shrugged at his question.

"It's just…everyone knows since Alex Bailey got a truck you get rides from him," the guy added.

I drew in a breath, trying to calm the mutation inside me, and turned to the guy trying to talk to me. I didn't want to be rude. He seemed nice enough. He was wearing a T-shirt with some sort of sports team logo across the front. "I needed to ride the bus today."

He held out a hand. "I'm Aiden."

"Hi, Aiden." I shook his hand, but I looked away to stare at the back of the seat, hoping he'd get the hint that I didn't want to talk.

"I'm Ryan," the other boy said.

I sighed. "Hi, Ryan."

Meg and Suzy were whispering to each other. Meg shifted so she was only half facing us. "Did you know that the last new girl at Hollow Brook High was Mandy Hall? She came last year as a sophomore. She and Mark Bailey started dating like a month into school."

Before I could think of a response, Suzy spoke. "Basically, the Bailey brothers always go after the new girl."

"We say that in a nice way," Meg said. "I mean, like, everyone thinks it's so romantic."

"Obviously," Suzy said. "Every girl at Hollow Brook High is jealous."

"That's why I asked." Ryan sounded like he was eager for information as he leaned closer. "You know… why you're taking the bus and not riding with Alex."

Irritated, I wanted to blurt out that it was none of their business, but I didn't have it in me to be so rude. I didn't like that they were asking nosy questions. The thought flitted through my mind that I should have ridden with Alex and Stephen instead.

Ryan tilted his head. "Trouble in paradise?"

"No," I shifted to hug my bag in my lap. "Alex and I aren't together."

Aiden sat back, his face twisted in confusion. "You're not?"

Meg whispered to Suzy. "Told you she was with Stephen."

"I'm not with Stephen either. I'm not with anyone." I straightened. "Why would it matter to you?"

The twins exchanged a look. Suzy said, "Your life is basically all everyone talks about."

My mouth dropped open. "What? Why?"

"There's just something about you…" Aiden started, but then he trailed off, his face flushing a deep red, making me feel incredibly uncomfortable.

"What about me?" My tone was a bit accusatory.

Meg's smile was slow. "Emma calls you the Disney princess."

"Yeah." Suzy smiled. "You like… it's like you walk through the halls and sparkle."

"Your skin is Photoshop-smooth."

"When you walk into a room, it's like a celebrity walking in."

"You're basically in the hot vampire group of Hollow Brook High."

"That's stupid." I scowled. The thought occurred to me that they might have been mocking me. I wondered if I was being bullied at the moment, but I didn't feel like I was. I felt their curiosity, I glanced at each of them, studying their faces. "I'm just… shy. I'm an introvert."

Except I didn't feel like a shy person, nor did I feel introverted. I felt most alive and energized when I was around Alex and Stephen. I didn't prefer being alone, I always wanted to hang out with my best friends. When I thought of my life, I always saw them in it.

"What kind of dress are you going to wear for the dance, Jenny?" Meg asked suddenly. "You're going with Alex, right?"

"I'm not going to the…" I corrected myself with another tired sigh. "I'm not going with Alex, I'm going with Brandon Thomas."

The four of them reeled back collectively and I almost laughed. Meg laid a hand over her chest. "Wait, but didn't Alex punch Brandon over you?"

"Uh, no. I mean yes, but—"

Suzy covered her cheeks with her hands. "Holy crap, Jenny Philips is going to the dance with Brandon Thomas." Her tone indicated that everyone at Hollow Brook High would know that information by tomorrow morning.

"How did Brandon manage that?" Ryan asked with a big grin.

Aiden's eyes lit up. "I'm surprised Alex let that happen."

I frowned. "Why would you say that? Alex isn't like— He's my best friend. That's it."

Aiden and Ryan exchanged hesitant glances.

"Say what you're thinking," I demanded, not caring whether I sounded rude or not at this point.

The bus slowed to a stop. Relief crossed their faces and the four of them moved to gather their things. Most of the kids got off on this stop. It was Hollow Brook's only real neighborhood. I didn't move right away to let Aiden slide past me, glaring up at him.

"Guys talk about girls in the locker room. Obviously the new girl, Jenny Philips, was an immediate topic of conversation at the beginning of the year." Aiden shrugged. "Basically, the first day of school, Alex made sure no one talked about Jenny Philips in the locker room. Stephen too, but no one is going to mess with Alex."

"What do you mean?"

The bus driver said something impatiently about Aiden getting off the bus.

Aiden grinned at me, like he was willing to play with fire. "It's easy to put together Brandon Thomas's scar on his face and Alex Bailey somehow packing on more muscle every day. He just had to tell us to shut up one time. We got the message."

I stood slowly and stepped back so Aiden could slide out of the seat.

He glanced back at me once more. "You're Alex Bailey's girl, apparently everyone knows it, except you."

I looked out the window for the rest of the ride, still angry at my friends, but also thinking I wouldn't mind living in a world where I was truly Alex Bailey's girl.

＊◆＊

I stepped off the bus at Grandpa's private drive, pausing as it pulled away, and turned to find Alex waiting across the street. He leaned against his truck with his arms crossed. Stephen sat in the passenger seat, not looking at me, obviously pouting.

Alex and I stared at each other.

My eyes flickered over him, noticing the lines of his body in light of what Aiden had said. He was tall, broad-shouldered, with biceps that fit snugly in a gray shirt. And damn, he was handsome with his blue eyes, square jaw, smooth skin, and a smile that could light up a room.

Stephen was like that too, with ebony skin that seemed to glow, full lips perfect for his pouting and beautiful dark eyes—that when used against me, could convince me to give him anything he asked.

I couldn't pin when it'd happened, but the twins were right. We were different from others somehow, as if our mutations had not only given us crazy powers but also enhanced our bodies in other ways. I'd been so focused on the little world I lived in with Alex and Stephen that I hadn't noticed all the changes that set us apart.

My face was blank because I felt blank inside. I didn't know what to make of Alex standing there like that, mirroring me without a hint at his thoughts. When neither of us spoke, I began to turn toward Grandpa's farmhouse, not interested in fighting with him anymore today.

"Can I drive you to school in the morning?" he asked with a steely carefulness. "We can still be mad at each other if you want."

"Yes, see you in the morning," I muttered, but I didn't let him see the way my face relaxed into a smile as I walked away.

16.

SURPRISINGLY, BRANDON didn't try to pull me away from Alex and Stephen again. Throughout the week, Brandon only gave me winks and quick smiles from a distance, something kind in his expression. I was informed by Mandy Hall that Brandon and I would ride with her group in a limo. She asked me about the color of my dress, assuring me that she would communicate to Brandon which color of tie to wear to match. I supposed I was lucky she and her friends took dance attire seriously, because I didn't have to worry about all that.

Although, the week leading up to the dance was miserable.

It was awkward between Alex and me, but not much changed in our days. He still picked me up to drive me to school. I used his locker. We sat in the same spot at lunch. He held doors open for me, handed me a pencil when he saw I couldn't find mine, and bought me a soda when I'd forgotten one with my lunch from home. Alex Bailey was still Alex Bailey under all of his stubbornness.

We just didn't talk to each other.

Stephen was deeply annoyed by our silence. He tried to convince us to break down and talk, but neither Alex nor I broke. Alex had laughed at me, and somehow, I'd agreed to go to the dance with Brandon Thomas—the school jerk.

Everything was twisted the wrong way.

Brandon and I walked side by side into Hollow Brook High School's gym the night of the dance. I wore a pale pink long dress that draped down my body like a waterfall. The thin shoulder straps led to a drooping, relaxed scoop neck. Grandpa had mumbled a lot of protests about my dress, but Grandma had fought for me, telling me I looked beautiful.

The ceiling was covered in a magical vision of pastel balloons in pink, green, purple, and blue. The tablecloths matched, glitter was sprinkled on every surface. Four disco balls sparkled in each corner of the room.

It was simple, they'd spent the most money on a DJ from Willow City, but Mandy and the student council had managed to give us a stunning room to dance the night away in.

Brandon gave me a charming half-smile as he watched me take in the room. "You good?"

"Yeah, I'm good." I smiled up at him, but my eyes kept darting to the decor and the way the light played off the walls.

"I'm not all bad?"

I shrugged, teasing him. "Yet to be seen."

"You're gorgeous, you know that, right?" Brandon said, pausing at the edge of the dance floor. "I'm lucky to be here with you tonight."

My cheeks warmed, I laughed a little to shrug off his compliment. "Thanks. That's nice of you to say."

"It's a fact. Not just nice." He eyed me. "You realize you look like you belong in some magazine, right? You should go be a model or actress, not slumming it in Hollow Brook. Everyone knows that you don't fit in here."

Something stung about what he'd said about not fitting in, but I rolled my eyes at him to cover up what I felt. "Don't be a jerk."

"I'm not." He reached up and ran his thumb along my jaw from my ear to my chin, leaning in and letting his eyes wash over me. "You're stunning far away but up close, you're almost unreal."

That'd been something Alex said at the arcade—

It's like you're not real, Jenny Philips.

I took the smallest step back, trying not to upset him because I didn't want him anywhere near my lips. I wondered if saying nice things about me was a ploy to give him something tonight that I wasn't ready for. But I also couldn't help the way his words sent warmth all over my body.

It was stupid how much a school dance could throw me into a tailspin of confusion. My mutation hummed along my spine, as if readying for a threat. But there was no threat. I willed myself to let his words disappear into the lights and sounds around me.

"Let's go dance." I held out my hand.

He took my hand in his. "Yeah, let's go."

Brandon pulled me into Mark and Mandy's group as they danced in the middle of the gym. We were goofy and moved freely to the fun upbeat music. Several songs in and the crowd had grown larger, the air turning warmer. After a while, I touched Brandon's shoulder and said, "I'm going to get a drink."

"I'll get it." Brandon led me off the dance floor. He

sat me down at one of the tables with a good view of the dance floor.

Mandy came and sat beside me. "That was so much fun."

"Yeah, it was." I gestured, sweeping my hand across the room. "You did such a great job. This is so beautiful."

"Thank you," She gave me a bright smile. "It was a team effort with our student council." She pulled lip gloss out of her wrist wallet, applying the make-up in an impressive two swipes. "You know, Brandon likes you a lot. He's not very good at communicating and he says all the wrong things. But I can tell he likes you. I think you'd be so cute together. You'd slide right into our group, easy."

"Oh, I don't know—"

"I know you hang out with Alex and Stephen." She shrugged, her brown curls bouncing, framing her pretty dark eyes. "It's just a thought, like you're welcome to hang out with us if you wanted."

I processed her words slowly, imagining her group. There definitely weren't any sophomores in Mark and Mandy's circle of friends. They were a mix of seniors and juniors. All of the guys were baseball players who traveled from Hollow Brook to Willow City High several times a week for practice. I sorted through the girls in my head and realized each and every one of them were the baseball player's girlfriends.

My gaze swung to Brandon's back as he ladled punch from a big bowl on the serving table into a light pink plastic cup. He was the only single guy in Mark and Mandy's group.

As far as I knew, this was a friendship peace offering between Brandon and me. It wasn't supposed to feel this overwhelming. I had no interest in being in another group, I already had a group I loved.

I began to wish Alex and Stephen were here, even though I couldn't pinpoint an exact reason why I wanted them here with me.

Everyone was being nice to me. I let the events in the last few hours play out in my mind, remembering the way I'd kept myself together by smiling and laughing at all the right times in the limo with Mark and Mandy's group. I was doing a good job of keeping a constant grip on my mutation, but I wasn't sure I could keep up the act all night without slipping up somehow.

I didn't have to keep myself in check around Alex and Stephen. They were my anchors in the sea of high school. I was used to looking to them for assurance.

I supposed I missed them too.

I was sad they weren't here for the first dance I'd ever attended. I started imagining scenarios of faking sick or pretending an injury so I could go home and start the day tomorrow by apologizing to my friends.

I blinked when Mandy moved into my line of sight, pulling me from my daydream of leaving the dance early. Somebody waved at her from across the gym.

"I think you're so sweet, Jenny. You come to me if you ever need anything. I've got your back." She squeezed my shoulder gently before I could respond and then walked over to whoever it was that waved to her.

I drew in a deep breath and let it out. A warm tingling sensation spread across my skin, loosening the tight muscles in my arms, back and legs. The air shifted and my mutation settled in my spine, as if the mutation decided to lay down and take a nap.

My mind quieted, the music seemed to muffle to a distant beat—a light pressure of air touched my temple, drawing my gaze across the room, landing on a familiar silhouette at the edge of the dance floor.

Alex Bailey was here.

Stephen stood next to him and made eye contact with me. He gave me a slow wave, obviously bored already. I waved back, giving him a little deflated smile. Alex either didn't see me or he was deliberately not looking at me.

My heart raced, knowing Alex was so close. I'd assumed he wasn't coming. I glanced around the room again until I spotted Emma. She practically floated in her princess-cut bubblegum-pink dress until she stood next to Alex. She turned to say something to Stephen, who shrugged. Meg and Suzy joined them, chatting and pointing at the activity around them.

The Small-Town Five were back together.

"They have fruit punch or water." I jumped when Brandon set a plastic cup of red juice in front of me. "Hope it's okay."

"This is great, thanks." I nodded, feeling off-centered again. I couldn't take my eyes off Alex. I wanted to walk across the gym and apologize to him, but I wasn't sure what he'd say if I tried. "This is great."

Brandon followed my line of sight. "Alex brought Emma, huh?"

"It's whatever." I jerked my eyes toward the dance floor. I tried to focus on the sensations around me, the lights moving above my head and the music blasting through the room, attempting to ignore my mutation's yearning to look at Alex again.

Brandon sat in a chair behind me and slid his hand underneath mine so our palms touched and our fingers intertwined. "You want me to make Alex jealous tonight?"

My head snapped sideways to find Brandon's face close to mine. "What? No."

"Just offering, I know you're close to Alex. I know Emma tries to torment you. Thought I could help."

"Thanks for the offer"—I gave his hand a little squeeze—"but it's all good."

He set his chin on my shoulder. "If you say so, Jenny Philips."

I swallowed, trying to concentrate on something, anything, so I could ignore everything rattling in me like an impending storm. I didn't want to burst into tears and embarrass myself, or worse—mess up Mandy's lighting by letting my mutation slip up somehow.

"Hey." I shifted to meet Brandon's eyes and smiled at him. "I want to dance."

"Me too." He pulled me up by the hand, leading me into the crowd.

We danced a lot for the next two hours.

I let the energy of the music and lights roll over me in waves until I was nothing and no one. I released everything I felt into the open air, spinning and swaying, as I laughed with Brandon and his friends.

My hands swayed above my head. The gym floor swelled with the crowd of people around me, filling my vision with faces I saw in the hall every day, but never talked to. I was color, a rainbow disco ball, light playing off light. The dark pushed at the edges of where I danced.

Mark, Mandy, Brandon, and their friends faded away.

It was just me and my mutation. I was in the room, I was everywhere, and somewhere else, too. I loosened control of my mutation, and I swore everyone around me settled into the magic of the moment too, as if I could set a hand on their minds and will it into existence. They held onto the night as if one like this might never come again.

Jenny.

I danced until I thought I heard someone say my name, as if they'd found an invisible bridge. I paused and let my gaze drift until I found the source of the voice.

Blue eyes caught mine from across the room. Alex filled my vision at the edge of the dance floor, his hands dug into his dress pants pockets, his face open and serious.

Looking at me like he knew something I didn't.

17.

JENNY," BRANDON SAID, tugging my attention back to him. "Come with me."

He took my hand, leading me from the dance floor and through a side door. My spine went rigid. He wasn't saying anything. I didn't want to be alone with Brandon. His friends and the dancing was great today, but whatever this was, it was not something I wanted.

"Where are we going?" I asked breathlessly.

He led me outside, we stood near the closed door at the side of the school. "We're all headed to the limo. There's an afterparty. I wanted to know if you wanted to go with me."

"Where's the afterparty?" I asked, watching Mark and Mandy and others spilling out of the school's front doors and piling into the limo.

"It's a couple of hotel rooms. Before you freak out, we're all going and the worst thing that will happen is someone is bringing beer." He threw a nod at the limo. "Mark Bailey wouldn't let it get crazy. He's got his baseball career to think about." He took a step toward me, his hand pushing a curl of my hair back behind my ear. "And I want you to like me on Monday. I'm not going to do anything stupid with you tonight."

"I'm tired," I said, offering an apologetic smile. There was nothing in all the universe that could convince me to get into the limo.

He huffed a little laugh, looking away. "This is it, huh?"

"What?" I blinked at him, my voice small.

"You came with me tonight, but you're going back to Alex, aren't you?" It took me a long few seconds to process what he was asking because I wasn't with Alex. He wasn't my boyfriend or anything. It occurred to me that he might have meant to ask if I was going back into the building to find Alex. When my answer didn't come quick enough, he said, "It's cool. I get it. Thanks for going with me."

I grabbed his forearm, trying to fix whatever sad thing I'd heard in his voice. "Thanks for asking me." I gave him a wide smile. His brown eyes lit up. "It was really nice."

"Yeah?" He grinned and the dimple appeared again. "It wasn't all bad?"

"None of it was bad." I dropped my hand from his arm.

"Cool." He glanced back at the limo. "Alex will give you a ride?"

I nodded. I knew Alex would drive me home, whether he'd forgiven me or not.

"I'll see you on Monday then?"

All I could do was nod again. I didn't want him to kiss me. I just wanted this moment to be over so I could breathe again. Brandon somehow knew that because he took a few steps back, winked at me, and then turned to head to the limo.

I'd had a great night, but I knew Brandon and I would never be as close as I was to Alex and Stephen. I missed them and I wanted to go find them. I wanted to see if Alex would listen to an apology from me. Before I could touch the door handle, the door pushed open. Alex stood before me as he held the door open. "It locks from the inside."

"Oh. Thanks." I glanced behind him through the opening of the door, finding it dark and empty. "What are you doing out here?"

"I don't know." He shifted to hold the heavy door open with his foot while he rubbed his face and then said gruffly, "He took off with you through the side door. His friends went through the main doors. I just… I just wanted to make sure you were good."

His presence was like warm sunshine after a cold night. I gave him a bright smile. "I don't know what I'd do without you, Alex Bailey."

Alex shoved his hands into his pockets, bunching up his suit jacket. His eyes landed on the ground. "You'd have a lot less drama, that's for sure. You were right about what you said. Sometimes I can be a little overbearing when it comes to you. Stephen and I are selfish. We want all your attention. We don't want to share you."

He went on, as if he'd been bottling up thoughts, letting me watch them bubble over.

"When people like Emma and Brandon tried to bully you at the beginning of the year, Stephen and I promised each other that we wouldn't let you get hurt. We don't exactly welcome other guys into our group, or you know, within ten feet of you." He laughed awkwardly and released a long breath. It was visible because of the cold evening. "It's a mutant thing, I think. We can't let anyone into our group. We can't be ourselves with other people. And, we don't want anyone taking you from us. But yeah, we need to chill out."

"I know what you mean," I said, tugging at the curled ends of my hair. "I don't want anyone to take you and

Stephen away from me either. I don't know what I'd do if other girls came around."

Alex snorted. "Trust me, there are no other girls like Jenny Philips."

I shook my head, wrinkling my nose at him. "I feel like I need you guys way more than you need me."

"No, no way. Ask Stephen. We'd be lost without you." He rubbed his face with his hand. "Normal teenagers don't have to have these kinds of talks."

"I know, it's a lot, isn't it?" I rubbed my arms, the chilled air making me shiver. "I don't know what happened between us. I didn't mean some of the stuff I said. I'm not actually interested in hanging out with other guys."

"You can be," he said, but he was wincing.

"Thanks, but I'm not."

His shoulders relaxed. "Was he nice to you?"

My eyebrows drew together. I wasn't sure what he was asking. "Who?"

"Brandon."

"Oh, duh." I blinked slowly. I caught the glimmer of satisfaction in Alex's eye that I'd momentarily forgotten Brandon's existence. "Yeah, it was actually really fun."

He looked back down at the ground. "At least one of us had fun today."

"You and Emma, huh?"

Alex straightened. "No, not me and Emma. Never me and Emma."

His response was far more intense than I'd expected. A smile spread across my face. "Okay, not you and Emma."

"The girls ended up hanging around us. Stephen felt bad and danced with Meg and Suzy. Emma is being all prissy and won't dance with him. I think it's because she knows I wouldn't dance with her knowing the way you feel about her."

I looked away. Tears pricked at my eyes.

"That wasn't a dig at you," Alex said, his voice soft.

"But that's what I did to you."

"No. You can go to the dance with anyone you want to go with. You wanted to go to the dance with Brandon and that's fine. I reacted badly and I'm sorry for that."

"I didn't want to go with Brandon," I said softly. "I don't know why I went with him."

His blue eyes glinted off the parking lot lights. "I don't know why you went with him either. You told me that dances were stupid. You said you didn't want to go."

"I blurted that out." I threw my hands up, but then I took a deep breath so I wouldn't cry. "I did want to go. I just… I just wasn't sure about admitting it. When you asked me if I'd go, I totally said the wrong thing. I didn't know what you and Stephen thought about dances. I think I wanted to go really bad, but I didn't want to come off as desperate."

Realization hit his face like a slap. "Oh."

"You laughed at me about Brandon." I crossed my arms, feeling exposed. "No one asked me and when someone did, you laughed at me."

"I was laughing because I thought it was hilarious that Brandon would ask you."

I flinched at the way he said that.

Alex took a step toward me. The heavy door closed behind him with a loud bang. His hands were suddenly around my upper arms. "I mean, Brandon is a pure scumbag and you are Jenny Philips. I thought you were going to laugh with me. I thought Stephen was going to start cracking up with me. It was hilarious to me that he thought he could ask a girl like you to the dance. You're so far above him."

"Oh." I had not taken it that way at all.

"I would have gone with you in a heartbeat." Alex's eyes studied my face. "If you wanted to go and needed someone to go with you. I'd do anything for you—" He cleared his throat. "As your friend. We could have had fun and made it a chill thing. I was going to ask you when we were standing at the poster, but you said—"

"That dances were stupid." My chest tightened. "I wish I hadn't said that."

"It's okay." He grinned. The weight in the air around him lifted. "It's better now, right?"

I smiled back as relief ran through my veins too. "I hope so. I missed you. This week was horrible."

"Yeah, it was." He laughed, then paused as the air changed between us again—slow and heavy and calm. He squeezed my arms softly. His eyes roamed my face and then his gaze swept over my dress. "You're so pretty tonight, Jenny."

My lips parted, but I couldn't speak. I couldn't breathe. His closeness, his calloused hands holding my arms filled every part of my awareness. My mutation wanted to reach out and pull him in because Alex was the safest place I knew.

His hands moved, sliding up and down my arms. "You're cold," he whispered, shrugging off his jacket and drawing it around my shoulders. He didn't let go of the lapels, keeping me there with the slightest pressure, asking me to take a step toward him if I wanted.

I did want to, I couldn't help it, tears stung at the edges of my eyes as I wrapped myself around his middle. He brought his arms around my shoulders, tucking me against him. I fit snug under his chin, his cheek rested on top of my head.

"I'm sorry."

Alex pulled back. "Why are you sorry?"

"I don't know." A few traitorous tears ran down my cheeks. "I didn't want to go to the dance with anyone but you, and I messed it up. And I hurt you. You are so important to me and I really screwed things up—"

He drew in a sharp breath and leaned forward, cutting me off. His mouth was so close that I could taste the minty scent of his breath, but he shut his eyes tightly. The faint groan in his throat sent a wash of warmth that traveled from my chest to my cheeks. A second passed, and then another, before he said, "I almost kissed you."

I held onto the sleeves of his dress shirt so he wouldn't step away. I'd thought about what my first kiss would be like just as many times as any other fifteen-year-old girl, but I didn't know it'd be with someone like Alex. I didn't know that it was possible to feel like I was standing on still water with a storm raging around me. In a way, a first kiss was terrifying, but I wasn't afraid because it was Alex.

What was more, based on information Stephen had overshared with me a few months ago, I knew this was Alex's first kiss too. Alex was asking me to share this moment with him.

Suddenly, everything else outside of where he and I stood didn't matter. "You should."

My hair stringed across my face as a peaceful breeze picked up around us, just like it always did when I felt safe. He lifted his hand to push the locks behind my ear, sliding his palms to rest across my jaw. "You want me to kiss you?"

"Yeah."

"Okay, good."

The press of his lips on my lips was slow, simple. But the touch of him lit a quick fuse within me that sent a sudden wildfire from the tips of my toes to the top of my head, giving me a jolt of electricity through my spine.

My mutation sprang to life, running through my veins and setting a heavy layer of warmth over every muscle. It was as if my mutation gazed up at the night sky and sent fireworks upward to explode with vibrant color—a loud, blaring sound tore through my consciousness, a repetitive blast of noise.

Alex's hands dropped to his sides as if he had been caught doing something illegal. We both looked toward the parking lot to see half a dozen vehicles flashing their lights and their alarms going off.

"Did you do that?" he asked.

I covered my burning cheeks with my palms. "I think so."

Alex took my hand. "Let's get inside before someone

thinks we're out here messing with cars."

I let him pull me down the side of the building and through the unlocked main doors. I stopped as we turned the corner toward the gym. The music and lights drifted from down the hall. Tugging him by the hand, I said, "Don't tell anyone we kissed."

"I wasn't going to." Alex smiled at me, his eyes were brighter than I'd ever seen them before. "Why would I tell anyone we kissed?"

"Emma doesn't have a date tonight, right?"

He rolled his eyes. "I heard she got asked twice and said no to both."

I'd heard the same thing, and hated myself for saying, "She would have gone with you or Stephen."

He stared at me, clearly not sympathetic concerning Emma's poor behavior.

"I mean, I know she's pouting." I slid his jacket off my shoulders and held it out for him to take. "But I came and ruined the Small-Town-Five thing you guys had, just like… make tonight a good memory for her and the twins."

Alex frowned at me, but he took his jacket back. "That's very generous of you." He looked down the hall toward the main doors and then back at me. "I get what you're saying. I'll dance with her if you promise to dance with me after." He raised a playful brow. "It's going to take a lot of dancing with me to get me to agree."

I laughed, "Okay, deal."

I started to walk past him, expecting him to walk into the gym with me. He snatched my hand, pulled me into him, and gave me a light kiss. Alex glanced up, as if noting that I hadn't set off the fire sprinkler. One hand dug into my hair and the other slid across my waist as he kissed me again, then again with a slow and intentional rhythm that toed the line of a french kiss. But he stopped and grinned at me. "I think you just have to get used to it."

"Get used to what?" I whispered, trying to catch my breath.

"Moving from base to base." He wiggled his brows and I shoved at him, but we both laughed because I knew he was teasing me. "No really, it might have to be fireworks at first, but I think you'll adjust like I adjusted my strength."

I leaned back, my eyebrows drew together. "Fireworks?"

"I mean with the car alarms," he said, clarifying. "It won't always be like that, I didn't want you to worry about it."

"Right, yeah, thank you." But I didn't know how to ask him why he'd used the word fireworks, which was the clear image of what I'd seen when he'd kissed me. I managed to ask, "What are we doing?"

"I don't know." He grinned. "But I like it."

I nodded, feeling shy. "Me too."

We found Stephen near the door leading into the gym. He glanced between Alex and me, surprised to see us together. "Where's your date?"

"Hotel party and beers." I shrugged.

Stephen's eyebrows went up. "And that's not your thing?"

"Nope. Not my thing." I drew in a deep breath, letting the air fill my chest and clear my thoughts, then turned to fully face him. "I'm sorry I went with Brandon."

He chewed on his bottom lip for a long moment as if deciding how he wanted to respond, instead he jerked his chin toward the dance floor. "You want to dance with me?"

I wondered if he had more thoughts, more things he wanted to say, but I also wondered if he knew this was a moment neither of us should push each other because I wasn't completely forgiven. He was my brother and I'd hurt him by choosing to go with Brandon. But I was his sister, and I was allowed to make decisions he didn't approve of. We both knew those facts, but I decided to say, "Yeah, I do want to dance with you."

We'd dance, and by the end of the dance we'd be good again.

Alex and Emma joined us. Suzy and Megan did too. We spun and jumped and laughed. By the end, I decided it was one of the best nights in my almost sixteen years of life.

18.

MY BIRTHDAY was on a warm Saturday at the end of March.

The sun was shining, but I wanted to go to a movie with Alex and Stephen. I wasn't fancy, I just wanted them to go to a girly movie since I'd always been out-voted. I'd seen a lot of war and spy movies since we'd become friends.

We walked into the lobby of the small Willow City theater. Alex declared he'd get the popcorn and drinks. It was still early in the day so the lines weren't long. Stephen waved me over to the little attached arcade room, murmuring that I should break into a car racing game with my mutation so we could play for free.

I shrugged. "Okay."

I was mindful of my short pale pink summer dress with little red strawberries dotted on it as I slid into the game's driver seat. I wore my new white sandals and painted my nails red for the fun of it.

I wasn't a fifteen-year-old baby anymore.

I was sixteen like them. I could see it in the way my face was thinning out, the way my curves seemed to make more sense with the long limbs of my body. I'd taken to straightening my hair down my back and wearing a little bit of makeup each day. My strawberry dress felt like a sixteen-year-old's dress.

I liked the feeling.

Stephen was merciless at the game and beat me by a whole lap. I didn't mind. Nothing was going to sour my mood. "Wanna play air hockey?"

"Yeah. Hang on a sec. Gotta use the bathroom first." Stephen walked briskly in the direction of the restroom.

I busied myself with looking at the stuffed prizes in a claw-crane game and contemplated if I wanted to steal a stuffed animal or not. I told myself that I'd stolen a video game system worth hundreds of dollars once, but I also argued that it was probably going too far to use my superpowers to steal a cute little white teddy bear. Then again, it was my birthday. I wondered if it'd really be cheating if I paid the dollar to play the game—

"It's Jenny Philips."

I jumped and slapped a hand against my chest, finding Brandon Thomas standing close beside me. "Oh, hey, you surprised me." I let out a little laugh, glad that I hadn't set off a game alarm or something else obviously mutant-like.

"I like your dress," Brandon said with a slow half-smile.

My cheeks warmed. Brandon's attention made me feel small, like prey. I took a half step away from him. "I don't wear dresses a lot."

"You should." He glanced over his shoulder behind him. Mark, Mandy, and several others from Hollow Brook High were in line a few people behind Alex. Alex leaned forward with his hands on the counter as he talked to the kid who was scooping popcorn into a large tub. "Just you and Alex, huh? That's cute."

"Stephen is in the bathroom."

Brandon's eyebrows shot up. "Huh."

"What?" I frowned.

"Nothing." Brandon looked away, biting the inside of his cheek. When he looked back at me, he asked, "Did you have fun at the dance?"

I shrugged, trying to cover the fact that my heart was pounding, but I couldn't pinpoint exactly why. "Yeah, I did."

"You and I should hang out sometime soon."

A thousand responses—all conflicting and confusing—rushed to my mind. There were parts of me that knew logically it'd be fine to hang out with Brandon, but not alone because of Grandpa's rule. I wasn't sure if he'd mock me about the rule. I couldn't think of a time outside of school that I'd want to hang out with Brandon. Alex and Stephen dominated my free time. I couldn't imagine them ever letting Brandon into our hangout time either.

There wasn't a place for Brandon in my life, and I didn't know how to process that as he stood before me. I opened my mouth, ready to possibly blurt out something stupid, when a tub of popcorn obscured my view of Brandon.

I automatically held onto the bucket as Alex said, "Where's Stephen?" He spoke to my profile, not giving Brandon a glance. He held three drinks in a cardboard drink carrier with his other hand.

"Bathroom," I said right as Stephen emerged from the restroom. Stephen narrowed his eyes as he looked between Brandon, Alex, and me.

Alex's knuckles trailed a line down my spine, sending an explosion of sensation across my back—my legs, my arms, and everywhere else. His eyes hadn't left my face. His voice was low as he smiled at me. "Ready, birthday girl?"

Brandon blinked. "You didn't say it was your birthday."

"Yeah…" A breathy awkward laugh escaped me. I needed a way to say goodbye to Brandon. Alex Bailey wasn't making it easy. "I'm forcing them to watch a rom-com."

"Well, happy birthday, Jenny Philips." Brandon's dimple flashed with his smile.

"Thank—"

"Let's go," Stephen said, not looking over at Brandon and grabbing the bucket of popcorn from me. "I like to watch the previews."

My boys were smooth, an unspoken team with the way Alex moved between Brandon and I, nudging my elbow with the palm of his hand in Stephen's direction. Stephen held back a step to wait for me, but he wasn't looking at me. He was staring at Brandon with none of the usual amusement in his eyes. At my other shoulder, Alex pretended to look casual, but I could see the annoyance written across his face.

"Jenny." Brandon's voice made me pause. I turned to find him standing where we'd left him with his arms folded across his chest. "I'll text you later and we'll figure out a time to hang out."

"Uh, okay." It was the only polite thing I could think to say.

Brandon winked before he turned back toward Mark, Mandy, and the others.

Stephen muttered something that sounded a lot like a curse word under his breath. I couldn't bring myself to look at Alex as we walked down the dark hallway to our theater room. Stephen picked a row of seats and I followed him toward the middle of the aisle until they were sitting on either side of me.

None of us spoke for very long minute.

Stephen broke the quiet first. "So, you're going to hang out with him?"

"No," I said, much more sharply than I'd meant.

Alex's leg bounced next to me, but I didn't dare look his way. The advertisements for more romantic movies played. We were the only people in the theater.

"You just agreed to a text conversation about hanging out," Stephen grumbled.

I groaned. "What was I supposed to say? Don't text me?"

"I don't know. Yeah. Maybe." He slumped lower in his seat, pouting.

Another preview played, but I couldn't concentrate on it. Stephen scowled at the back of the seat in front of him. Alex was a rigid statue of silence, except for his bouncing knee. My birthday was supposed to be fun, but this was miserable.

My mutation started to stack—brick by brick. The sensation slithered from my spine, into my arms, and began to fill an empty place in my stomach. I tried to focus on my breathing, drawing air in and out again, but I couldn't figure out how to push the building pressure within me down. I needed to do something before my mutation exploded. Scenarios of breaking down crying or standing up to storm out of the theater flitted through my mind. I needed to find a way assure my mutation that everything was okay.

I sat upright and turned to face Stephen. "It's my birthday. Stop being a jerk."

Stephen's eyes widened, his mouth falling open.

"Don't ruin my birthday or I'll ruin your face. Got that, Stephen Wright?"

"Yes, ma'am," he said, nervous laughter slipping through his words. "I won't."

"You owe her candy," Alex said, leaning forward. "It's the only way to make things better."

I nodded in solemn agreement.

Stephan's hands shot up. "All right, all right, I'll be back." He scooted in front of us to exit the theater. An awareness crept over me that Alex and I were alone. He shifted in his seat, scanning the empty room once before turning to me. "Can I kiss you?"

I swallowed. "Yes."

His hand landed on my leg, his fingers wrapped around my bare thigh, sending a million tingling spiderwebs along my skin. His kiss was sweet, soft. "I didn't get you candy on purpose."

I leaned back. "What?"

"My plan was to get a minute alone with you."

"Oh. Okay." I knew Alex always had a plan, but this was a surprise. "To kiss me?"

"Yes." He gave me another quick kiss. I craved more. I leaned in to kiss him again, but he held my shoulder with one hand as he dug into his pocket. "Yes, to kiss you, but I also got you a present. It's a secret present."

My smile was so big that my cheeks hurt. I could hear my heart racing in my ears over the sound of another preview. "You did? Why?"

"Because it's your birthday." His laugh was adorable and boyish. His hand closed over the gift as he held it out for me.

"No, I mean, why is it a secret?"

"Because it is, Jenny Philips. Hurry, before Stephen comes back."

I slid my hand under his and he dropped a square, wrapped gift the size of my palm into my hand. The wrapping paper was white with shiny gold dots. It screamed Mrs. Bailey. He must have got the wrapping paper from her.

"What is it?"

"Open it."

I ripped into it to find a pair of little rose-gold studded earrings. Alex Bailey had bought me jewelry. I marveled at the pretty pale pink gemstones in the dim light from the movie screen.

I didn't know what to say.

"They're rose quartz, I guess they're safe for allergies, I don't know if that matters to you. I told my mom I wanted to get new work boots at the Willow City mall, but really, I went to buy you a present—" He shook his head. "You didn't need to know that part. Stephen and I got you a gift card to the Espresso Hut and funny socks that we'll give you at your birthday dinner tonight." Alex paused, taking a deep breath. "These reminded me of you."

We stared at each other until light seeped into the theatre room from the hallway as the main door opened, drawing our attention to three girls entering. They walked in without giving us a glance. I didn't know them, they were probably Willow High school girls.

I wanted to say so many things, but we didn't have much time until Stephen came back. When Alex met my gaze again, I gave him a quick kiss on the lips.

"Thank you for my present."

He watched as I unclasped the backs of the earrings and put them on. I pushed my hair back so he could examine them. I liked how excited and happy he looked. It made me happy too.

He reached over to rub the hem of my dress between his fingers. "You're pretty, Jenny."

Brandon's compliment hadn't felt good, but Alex's words made me feel warm everywhere. I fluttered my lashes playfully. "You think I'm pretty, huh?"

"Everything about you is pretty." Alex slid his hand into mine as he settled into his seat. "We need to talk soon."

I squeezed his hand. "Talk about what?"

"You and me."

My stomach hollowed out and I leaned toward him to whisper, "I can't—" The door swung open behind us again. I pulled my hand from Alex's as Stephen strode down the aisle toward us.

He dropped four boxes of candy in the popcorn bowl. "I got you a variety."

"Awe, thanks." I opened the one I wanted first. "I guess you're forgiven for being a jerk on my birthday."

Stephen huffed, but I knew we were both glad the tension had eased between us. Alex didn't take my hand again, but he slid his sneaker to press against my sandal for the rest of the movie. I couldn't stop reaching up to fiddle with my pretty new earrings, both confused and happy because of the gift.

———————×❮◆❯×———————

Later that night, after my birthday dinner, I laid in bed thinking of my parents. Grandma had teared up when I casually commented that my vanilla cake with white frosting reminded me of my mom. I hadn't requested the flavors for me, but because they were her favorite and I wanted a little bit of my parents to be part of the night.

It was Alex and Stephen sitting with me at the table that made the words easy to say. They were the ones who'd brought me to a place where I could see the memories of my parents under a warmer light in my mind.

I sat up when my phone buzzed on my bedside table, jerking me from my thoughts. My stomach jumped, wondering if it was Alex. But neither one of my boys texted this late since they had to be up early for chores.

Instead, Brandon Thomas was messaging me.

I hadn't got a text from him since the days leading up to the dance a couple of weeks before. It was nearly midnight. I wasn't sure I wanted to know what he had to say. The urge to ignore it, as if I could say I was already asleep, ran through me.

Then I thought of the way he'd explained himself when it came to the day at the waterhole. I thought of how nice he'd been at the dance. In the mix of my thoughts was Alex and Stephen's overprotective-ness. Maybe it was good to have a non-mutant friend. Except, Brandon was a piece in the puzzle of my life that I didn't quite know where to fit.

Still, I found myself opening the text.

cheese, pepperoni, or hawaiian?

I stared at the text for a whole ten seconds before Brandon texted again, and then twice more.

what's your star sign?
you have 48 hours left on this earth? What do you do?
most embarrassing thing about you that you'll admit?

The thought occurred to me that he'd probably seen that I'd opened the text. If I didn't text back, he'd know I ignored him. I messaged back the only thing I could think to write.

Um... what's happening?

It took a few seconds for him to text me BACK, then they came in rapid fire, one after another.

hawaiian

libra

i shouldn't have asked the 48 hours question

i can't think of anything but camping

my mom sewed my baby blanket into a manlier quilt

because I still want to sleep with it

don't you dare tell anyone that

The last text made me laugh. My eyes trailed to my window where I could see the Bailey Farm in the distance. The house glowed with Mrs. Bailey's designer outdoor lanterns, and the surrounding industrial lights scattered around the property. It was sort of fun to have someone other than Alex and Stephen to message with. I couldn't think of a reason why it'd be wrong for me to text Brandon.

Hawaiian for me too. Are we rare for that?
Pisces obviously since it's my birthday today
48 hours left? I'd hang out with my friends

I paused to think about the embarrassing question. School before Hollow Brook was a blur of my friend Rachel, my parents, and a whole other life I'd lived. It was all far away in my mind. Nothing stuck out to me since I'd come to Hollow Brook either, at least not anything that wasn't mutant related.

I can't think of anything embarrassing

He replied a half second later.

probably because you're perfect

I rolled my eyes, but couldn't tell if it was a flirty comment or a sarcastic one, or maybe a little of both. I didn't want him to flirt, but I'd also seen something good in him during the dance. I decided to try and be as real as I could with him.

No it's definitely not that

I'm too cautious to get in embarrassing situations

And I brush stuff off quickly

He texted back again, the conversation turned easy, going back and forth as if we texted all the time.

i think not liking pineapple pizza is a red flag

Definitely a red flag I agree

i have another big question for you

Okay?

toilet paper? over the roll or under

I'm not a barbarian definitely over

right?! i agree

Sometimes in public places I switch the roll
direction
Maybe that's the embarrassing thing about me?

no that's not embarrassing that makes sense
i need to ask more questions

Why the questions?

looking for an imperfection in you
not sure it exists
i've always thought it
beautiful smart sweet
you're the whole package

A familiar uncomfortable feeling crept over me. I'd never been able to pinpoint what it was that Brandon did to make me uneasy. I wondered if it was because he was more forward than I could handle. Maybe it was because I was a sophomore, and he was a junior.

It was as if Brandon saw through me, and his gaze was intense. He saw me in a way I wasn't ready to be seen. He saw what he'd do with me if we ended up alone together. I was a challenge for him, but I wasn't interested in existing in anyone's game.

When I didn't text back right away, Brandon texted again.

let me take you out to lunch for your birthday tomorrow

It was there again, feeling overwhelmed by him.

I'd felt all right about telling Alex and Stephen I wasn't allowed to be alone with a boy, but I didn't trust Brandon Thomas with that information yet. I wondered if I could get around the rule by inviting him over to hang out while Grandma was in the house. Except I didn't know how I'd explain to Alex and Stephen that I couldn't hang out without lying to them. If I were honest about Brandon, they'd insist on coming over.

Nothing about Brandon, Alex, and Stephen hanging out at my house with my grandparents in the next room sounded fun. I could only imagine scowling, grunting, and possibly fists being thrown.

Not knowing what to say, a pressure began to grow in my chest, making me feel like I couldn't draw a full breath.

Keeping my phone in my hand, I stood to my feet and opened my bedroom window. I wore long white socks, gray sweatpants, and a Bailey Farm T-shirt Alex had given me. I slipped through the open window, carefully setting one foot on the roof, and then the other. I scooted down on my butt a few feet and let my gaze settle on the Bailey Farm.

I could see that the light in Alex's room was off. I assumed he and Stephen were asleep. I'd been jealous more than a few times that I didn't get to have a sleepover at Alex's house whenever I wanted like Stephen did. I huffed a laugh because thoughts of sleeping at Alex's house were funny and ridiculous, but also forbidden in a way that made me blush.

My phone buzzed again.

if you're against lunch maybe breakfast?
dinner?
coffee?
a snack?
or i'll just surprise you

I shut my eyes, wondering if I'd ever be able to win when it came to Brandon. A tightness spread through my limbs. My mutation was waking, an anxious breeze picked up around me, the ends of my hair tickled the tops of my arms.

But I played with the wind, it was a comfort for some reason, and I let it dance in the space just beyond where I sat. Under the moonlight, with the help of Grandpa's farm industrial lights, I created a quiet dirt-and-rock tornado. Dust and gravel swirled before me. I gave my mutation control—more control than I'd ever let it have.

I watched the slim twister move in whirls and circles into Grandpa's field and jump ditches and fences into the Bailey's field. I tested how far my power could span, cool air filled my lungs with every passing minute, a calm hum spread over me as I gave way to the mutation's leading.

Then the little tornado disappeared, but now I could see.

White and blue sparked a circle around my vision, the view beyond it shimmered like the top of Grandpa's pond at twilight. It was effortless to be like this, as if the bends of limbs and the heavy coat of skin ceased to exist.

I was on the lawn at the front of the Bailey's house somehow—it was me, and it wasn't me. I didn't need my neck to look up and down, left and right. I just moved, gliding to see what I wanted to see, as if I were floating.

I tried on the idea of moving from one place to the other and quickly realized that I had no body for gravity to fight against. I zipped and zagged, bounced and spun, and it was all in a blurry blink. I moved like a flat stone thrown over the top of water, jumping from one point to another in a smooth motion.

My curiosity led me to a specific window, and I wondered if I could find a way to enter without anyone noticing me. I aimed for the center of the windowpane, bracing myself for a potential impact, but there was no barrier.

It was dark in the room, but a sliver of light underneath the door to the hallway was enough for me to see Stephen curled up under a thin blanket on the lower mattress of Alex's trundle bed. I darted downward to hover in front of his face. I noted how adorable he was with his mouth a bit open, and his face squished against his arm.

Alex was a different story.

His blanket had twisted around his legs in his sleep, revealing his bare chest that rose and fell in deep, even breaths. I told myself that he would never know if I studied the hollows and ridges of muscle his mutation had encouraged.

The more I studied his smooth skin, the more I became convinced that I must have fallen asleep. This was impossible, even for a mutant, this could only be a dream.

Only a dream. The sound of my voice echoed around me.

And so, because it was a dream I ran an invisible hand over his chest, finding his skin cool to the touch. I traced the line of his neck, and slid along his strong jaw—

My phone buzzed, my sock slipped—I caught hold of the edge of the windowsill—realizing in a slow few seconds that I almost fell off Grandpa's roof.

"Shit," I muttered as I pulled myself up again to a safer sitting position. The phone buzzed again, my hand trembled as I picked it up. I assumed it would be Brandon, but it was Stephen instead.

> Jenny!!!!!!!!!!!!!!
> are you getting kidnapped or something

My eyebrows drew together as I texted back.

> No?
> Why would you ask that?

Stephen replied in a rapid succession of messages.

Alex was dead asleep
He just sat up for no reason
He thinks he needs to come see you
But it's midnight
Tell him you're alive so I can go back to sleep!!!!!

My gaze shot to the Bailey farmhouse again. This time Alex's bedroom light was on. The hair on my arms rose. A chill washed over my skin.

"It wasn't real," I whispered, shaking my head. "It wasn't real."

I was sure touching Alex had been some sort of intense hormonal-fueled daydream, but then I thought of the tap on his shoulder in the hallway when Brandon had cornered me about the dance just weeks ago.

I'd been dealing with Brandon in the school hallway that day. I was dealing with Brandon now through text. Twice my mutation had found Alex because of it. It was Alex who texted in the group chat next.

Stephen is annoying.
I didn't say I was coming to see you.

Stephen was quick to comment on that.

> You were putting your boots on Alex Bailey!!!
> I told him someone was going to get grounded if he went
> Texting you was smarter

I bit down on my lip, suppressing a smile that made no sense. I could imagine Alex throwing something at Stephen. They were probably arguing. It took another twenty seconds for Alex to text back, but this time it wasn't in the group, just to me.

> I think I had a bad dream.
> I think you were in it.
> I can't remember it.
> I told him I'm going for a walk.
> That's all.

I felt bad because whatever magic my mutation just performed left Alex out of sorts. There was no way I was going to be able to explain to him that I was pretty sure I'd woken him up. On top of that, it would answer Brandon's question as the most embarrassing thing I'd ever done. My mutation creeping into Alex's room to mess with him wasn't exactly something I was ready to confess. I texted him back.

> I can't sleep either
> Why?

I wasn't sure what Alex would do if I told him I was texting Brandon. I figured the best plan was to keep Brandon and Alex away from each other for as long as possible. I needed to figure out for myself what to do before my friends decided to insert themselves into the situation.

Idk exactly

Wait.
Are you sitting on your roof?

I blinked, squinting as I caught sight of Alex Bailey's silhouette. He leaned against one of the columns on his front porch.

Maybe

That's not safe you know.

Stephen taught me how to Roof Walk remember

Ohhhh I remember.
I didn't think it was safe then either.

I smiled at the memory of when we'd climbed Mrs. Bailey's trellis of flowers to sneak into Alex's room.

Alex had been shirtless, and I'd about died when the backs of my thighs touched his bed. Now I was sixteen, and a weird mutant, and kissing Alex Bailey in secret, but that would have to stop soon too.

You've been 16 three months now

Yes.

So you're basically an expert at being 16

Yes.

Any advice? It already feels overwhelming

16 doesn't have to be overwhelming.

Oh yeah just like that huh

Just like that.

How do you do that

Do what?

I mean how are you so sure about stuff

Because...

We have Stephen.
Stephen has us.
I have you.
You have me.
We're unstoppable, Jenny Philips.

I stared at Alex's answer, reading it again and again. I wanted to absorb his confidence and make it my own. But his life had never broken like mine. His parents were in bed just upstairs. My parents were buried in a cemetery in a city I no longer lived in. He texted again before I could think of a response.

I don't think I can go inside until you're off that roof.

Sorry I need another hour of contemplating life

Okay guess I'll be up for another hour.

But I yawned, remembering that any interaction with Alex Bailey settled me. His reassurance that we had each other calmed every stirring thought about Brandon Thomas.

Just kidding
Thanks for texting me

We were talking about going on a drive tomorrow. Want to?

I pressed my phone between my palms for a long moment, thinking of Brandon's invitation to hang out tomorrow. The problem was that if given the choice between spending time with Alex, or spending time with Brandon, Brandon would lose every single time. I knew it would be hard, but I had to find a way to make it clear to Brandon that I wasn't interested in him beyond the friendship we'd formed at the dance.

That sounds fun let's do it
Goodnight

Night Jenny.
Text me if you need anything.
I don't care about getting grounded.
I'll come if you need me.

Carefully, I climbed through the window. I laid on my bed and rolled onto my side with my phone in my hand. I opened the text messages from Alex to reread them. I kissed his last messages before I let the screen go black. My lips against the cool, smooth surface did nothing to ease the ache in my chest.

The next morning, I came down the stairs to find Grandma with breakfast ready as usual. A modest bouquet of clustered little yellow flowers rolled in brown paper lay on the table. Tucked beneath it was a signature homemade chocolate bar from Hollow Brook's only grocery store.

I glanced up at Grandma. "Those are pretty."

She looked past me through the front window. Grandpa and Mr. Bailey were holding coffee mugs and talking to each other in the driveway. She cleared her throat and gestured to the kitchen island at a white torn open envelope.

I reached for the envelope and read *Jenny* written in handwriting I didn't recognize. My eyebrows drew together. The envelope was addressed to me, but someone had opened it without my permission.

I slid the card out of the envelope, trying to sort out whether I was upset or not about someone opening an envelope with my name on it. I found a card that said, *I told you I'd surprise you. Happy Birthday.*

I didn't doubt it was Brandon, but he hadn't signed it.

"Grandpa called Mr. Bailey to ask if one of the boys left the gift," Grandma said, stirring what looked like dinner in a crockpot. "He said Alex and Stephen didn't do it, but Grandpa wasn't happy to see something that could be interpreted as romantic left for you on the doorstep. You're lucky he got distracted by the crop circles."

I blinked, confused all over again. I'd never seen Grandma so tense, her shoulders tight as she continued to stir the food. "Crop circles?"

"Go look from your bedroom," she said, her focus stayed on the crockpot. I turned on my heel to head toward the stairs, but Grandma said, "And Jenny? Those flowers are buttercups. They're bad luck." She pursed her lips. "The buttercups and the crops? I don't like it."

Upstairs I gasped.

Grandma hadn't exaggerated, swirls and circles and geometric shapes were pressed into the dirt of Grandpa's field. They overlapped onto the Bailey Farm. It was as if some higher force had come in the night to send a message. Except the buttercups and crop circles weren't mysterious, bad omens—they were me.

I wasn't sure what that meant.

19.

As I PACKED us lunch in the kitchen, Grandpa lectured Alex and Stephen about safe driving while on the winding mountain roads. When I sighed deeply to hint that we really didn't need the warnings, Grandpa gave me a look that said I'd better take him seriously or I wouldn't get to go.

We drove with the windows down, country music floating around me, my hand waving aimlessly in the air rushing outside the window. I kept catching Alex glancing at me with a little smile plastered on his face.

Stephen sat in the center of the backseat with the snacks. He kept saying he was Lord of the Snacks and that we had to say please and thank you if we wanted snacks. Alex and I had a lot of fun tormenting Stephen by demanding the snacks impolitely.

We ended up stopping in a spot where the mountain began to dip downward toward a valley. The sun shined through the trees and into the canyon. A river flowed hundreds of feet below the cliff edge. The air was dry. Grandpa told me that it would be unusually warm for a Hollow Brook spring day.

I turned to Stephen. "Careful with your mutation."

"Huh?" He was holding a stick, testing it, seeing if he liked it. "What do you mean?"

"She's right," Alex stood next to me to enjoy the view, his bicep brushing my shoulder as he crossed his arms, sending zings of invisible electricity across my skin. "You could start a forest fire."

"Jenny could make it rain or something. It'll be fine."

"I can push energy around." I wrinkled my nose. "I don't control the weather."

"Whatever." Stephen swiped the air with his sword-like stick.

Alex turned, raising his eyebrows at Stephen and giving him a look similar to the one Grandpa had given me earlier about safe driving.

Stephen rolled his eyes. "I'll be careful, Mom and Dad."

I nodded, pursing my lips. "That's what I want to hear, son."

Alex laughed. Stephen scowled, but then casually said, "You know Jenny, I was going to ask you about something mighty peculiar that happened last night in the fields."

I stiffened, because I knew exactly what he was referring to.

I could feel Alex's eyes land on me, gauging my mood.

Stephen side eyed me. "Did you see any UFO's when you were sitting on the roof last night? I mean, we drove all the way up here in the truck and you didn't bring up any extraterrestrial activity topics even once."

"Yes," I said, deadpan. "They were little and green and asked me to take them to my leader, so I sent them to Emma's house."

They both laughed, the sound echoed against the canyon walls, but the laughter turned into questioning silence.

"It was an experiment." I crossed my arms and turned toward the view again. "It went a little too well and I don't want to talk about it."

Neither said anything, because they knew I'd share my thoughts when I was ready. They'd learned months ago that it wasn't wise to push me to talk.

We stood in a nice, quiet spot. A hawk flew past, slicing through the sky. The evergreen pines smelled like a fresh Christmas tree. I spied a place where I could lay out a blanket in the shade. "Should we eat lunch here? Or do we keep going?"

Just as I asked, the rumble of a truck came up the road. Alex and Stephen both paused to watch the oncoming vehicle. We recognized whose truck it was at the same time.

Brandon Thomas.

Alex took a few steps closer to the road with Stephen at his side. I hung back behind them, unsure about what to do with Brandon between having ghosted him via text last night and receiving his surprise birthday gift. His head hung out the window as he pulled up close to Alex's truck. "Fancy seeing you three here."

Mark, Mandy and Emma were with him. My brows rose when I made eye contact with Emma Henderson. Her gaze darted away, not revealing anything on her face. No Suzy or Meg to be seen.

"Hey, guys," Stephen said with a sarcastic smile. "All the roads on this big mountain and you guys chose this one."

Brandon hitched his thumb back at a few four-wheelers, one in the bed of the truck and two on a trailer the truck was pulling. "Best trails up this way." He looked past Alex and Stephen, making eye contact with me. "You three should come hang out with us. We've got a lot of food and drinks. Could be a party."

Mandy rolled the window down from the backseat. "No, seriously. You guys should come. We had such a good time at the dance, Jenny."

I smiled at her. "Yeah, no, that's really nice. We kind of have a plan already. Maybe another time for sure." My eyes darted back to Emma. She seemed so much younger than the other three.

"What's your plan?" Brandon asked, a smirk playing at the edge of his mouth.

Stephen looked back at me. I gave him no indication of an opinion. I wasn't sure what to make of the situation yet. Alex kept his attention on Brandon's truck, a careful expression on his face as his mind worked on sorting the situation. Stephen said, "We're just hanging out—"

"Come for a little bit," Mandy said. "We can take turns on the four-wheelers."

Mark looked at Alex, "Yeah, come guys. It'll be fun."

I really did want our hangout time to be just the three of us, but I'd never been on a four-wheeler before and it sounded fun. I tucked my shoulder between Alex and Stephen, facing Alex. "We could go for a little bit. Mandy is nice. Mark has been cool lately, right?"

Stephen leaned close to me. "I'm down for it since Mark is here. It's up to Alex. I don't care either way. I'm chill like that."

"I'm chill too." Alex glared at Stephen over my head, but his arms and shoulders were tense. His blue eyes found mine. "I was excited for it to be the three of us today, but if you guys want to go, it's whatever."

"I don't want to go if you don't want to go," I said softly. I wanted to reach out and squeeze his hand to assure him, but I couldn't.

Alex sighed. "It sounds fun. We can go, but if any one of us wants to bail, then we bail. No questions asked, all right?"

"Deal." Stephen nodded.

I nodded too. "Deal."

We followed them in Alex's truck a few more miles up the mountain. Alex parked beside Brandon's truck. We were in a clearing with a fire pit and a picnic table. The area looked like it was popular. I could see the trails in the open field, but there were tracks leading into the trees and the nearby rolling hills.

The air had cooled as we drove higher in elevation. I wore my new brown hiking boots, black high-waisted leggings, and a cropped maroon sweatshirt. I'd thrown my hair up in a casual bun and had applied minimal makeup. I was sort of glad I'd put a little effort in because Emma was done up in pink overalls and a white tank top. Her hair and makeup was a bit extravagant for the great outdoors. Mandy was a natural beauty in jeans and a plaid jacket. She was one of those classic brunettes that didn't need much makeup.

I sat at the picnic table, watching Emma drench herself in bug spray. I bit my bottom lip to suppress laughter.

Mandy came to stand next to me. "Jenny and I have dibs on a four-wheeler first."

"I've never driven one," I said.

"I'll drive and you ride behind me." Mandy nudged my shoulder with hers. "I've been doing it since I was like seven."

"Okay. Sounds good." I looked around and caught Alex's eye. He gave me a quiet nod. I knew I didn't need his approval, but I was happy he approved anyway. My bet was that he'd been riding four-wheelers since he was young too. I trusted his judgment.

Brandon called first pick on the second four-wheeler and asked Emma to ride with him. Mark said he was going on the third one. Stephen and Alex claimed they were going to eat first. Everyone got a helmet and then started up the four-wheelers.

Mandy was opening up, shouting over the engine to make jokes and telling me to hold on over bumps and dips. She did a lot of smiling and flirting with Mark as he drove near us. They were adorable and it sent an ache through my chest I didn't quite understand, but I knew it definitely had something to do with Alex.

When we got back I opened a soda and sat on the picnic table next to Alex.

"Fun?" He handed me a wrapped sandwich.

I took it and nodded. "Yeah, it was fun. Are you going to do it?" I unwrapped my sandwich and bit into it. Stephen was up, claiming a four-wheeler and asking Mark about something that was recently fixed on the machine. Brandon didn't get off his four-wheeler.

"I think so." Alex looked over at me, his gaze running over my face. "Are you taking a break? Or do you want to ride with me?"

I pressed my lips together, trying to be chill. "I want to ride with you."

"We're taking the third one." Alex jumped off the table and grabbed two helmets. I rewrapped my sandwich and set it on the table by Mandy and Mark who'd settled next to each other on the bench seat.

After fitting the black helmet on, I climbed onto the four-wheeler behind Alex. He was obviously larger than Mandy. His broad shoulders almost obscured my view. I felt shy about pressing myself up against his back. A slow burn spread over my body at the thought.

Alex was apparently less shy. He leaned into me,

grabbing my wrists, pulling my arms around him, and then he pressed down on the accelerator.

I laughed and held on tight, very aware of his mutation's effect on his body. I desperately wanted to run my hands over the ridges and hollows of his stomach, but that thought led me to the memory of my mutation sneaking into his room last night.

I'd vowed to never tell a soul about that, even Alex and Stephen.

I focused on the smell of him instead. He'd started wearing a new cologne sometime around his birthday in January. I liked catching whiffs of it when we hung out. Somehow, I'd won the jackpot because I was allowed to bathe in the scent now.

The ride was fun because he went faster than Mandy had, but he was also more in control. He took hills and bumps gracefully, giving me a good time, but Alex Bailey wouldn't ever push it too far. He took a quick right, went off on a side trail, and then took us up a steep hill.

I scream-laughed and held on tighter. I could feel his laughter in my arms. I couldn't see or hear the other four-wheelers anymore. He drove us higher and higher up the hill and then he veered left to take us into a line of trees. I noted the area didn't seem well-traveled.

Then he slowed to a stop, killing the engine.

"What happened?"

"Nothing. Just a minute." Alex threw a leg over and jumped off the four-wheeler, taking his helmet off.

I pulled my helmet off as he slid a leg back over the seat, but he was facing me, his hands on my waist. He sucked in his bottom lip as he gripped his hands under my thighs and pulled them over his thighs, bringing us closer, sending my body into a sensational overdrive.

I realized that nothing was wrong. Alex had driven us off by ourselves on purpose. My heart raced. He was just looking at me. His face was serious, his fingers digging gently into my waist.

"This place is called Magic Valley." His gaze slowly drifted around, as if soaking in the sight. The valley was a pocket of tall grass. A little stream ran down the center a few yards away. Dark green pine trees encircled us. The sun was warm, the sky blue and clear. The usual buzz of energy I felt from constantly being in and around buildings was absent. Even the air around us was quiet. There wasn't any wind to distract my mutation. "When we decided to come up here, I wanted to show you this place."

I smiled, looking around again. "It's so pretty."

He cleared his throat. "I was trying to get you alone because I want to ask you something."

I leaned back, gripping the handle bars on either side of me, my eyebrows knitting together. "Ask me about what?"

"You and me." His eyes shot down between us as he grinned. My heart picked up speed as my stomach did a somersault. "Like I said on your birthday. But Stephen is always with us."

"What about you and me?"

"I told Stephen about the kiss at the dance."

I jerked back. "What? You did?"

"He was cool about it."

"I wish you would have, I don't know, maybe told me before you told Stephen." A breeze stirred by my mutation swirled around us, lifting my hair and ruffling his. "You should have—"

"I know, I'm sorry," Alex said. His fingers found mine, anchoring me. "He was surprised it had taken so long for me to make a move. He's known for a long time that I like you more than a friend."

"He has?"

"Well yeah," He glanced down again, a pink blush creeping up his neck behind his ear. "I told him I wanted you to be my girlfriend the first day we met you."

"You did? You do?"

"Yes, I want you to be my girlfriend and I want everyone to know it."

"Why?"

"I don't know." He chuckled. "Because I want to kiss you more. I think you should be my girlfriend if I'm kissing you."

I shook my head, opening my mouth to say words that wouldn't come. My wind picked up around us again, spreading out from where we sat, brushing back the tall grass around us.

Seeing my reaction, he added, "I mean, go out with me. You know, like on a date. Just you and me."

My mutation was confused by the blending of fear and want racing under my skin. Electricity rushed up my spine, the wind was a twist and whirl around us, a forceful swish of sound as the trees circling us moved. I pushed off the four wheeler to catch my breath, afraid of what Alex had unearthed in me with the simple offer of a date with him—which was forbidden and impossible, exciting and wonderful.

I took two steps before Alex jumped in my path, taking my jaw in his hands. "Hey, it's okay if you—"

I lifted myself up on my tiptoes, wrapped my arms around his neck, and pressed my lips to his. Alex tensed because I'd surprised him, but he didn't let me step back. He gave into the kiss, catching the rhythm of it with me and running his hands down my shoulders until they wrapped around my sides to pull me into an arch against him.

The air changed around us, charged by mutation.

Power radiated within me, shimmering invisibly around us. My mutation danced through the air, the grass, the tree branches—creating a symphony of sound, magic, and miracles. My mutation hummed in me. It was a reflection of what I felt, my heartbeat and it sounded so pretty.

Alex was breathing hard when he drew back, looking around us as the wind continued to brush against the grass and trees. "That's better than car alarms, huh?"

I drank in what his eyes looked like when he was this close, the way he smelled.

He tilted his head, searching my face. He spoke over the gentle rustling sounds around us. "It'll still be you, me, and Stephen. I want to spend time with you and me alone every once in a while. Go on dates and stuff. You know, get to know each other in another way. That's all."

My mutation quieted, leaving us staring at each other in the hot, dry air. It was painful to step back, like there was life for a second and death in the next.

"I can't date, Alex."

"Me?" His face fell, as if he was trying to absorb a blow. "You don't want to date me? Is that what you mean?"

"I can't," I repeated. "Grandpa doesn't want me to date until after I'm eighteen. He says I can be friends with guys and do group stuff. But I can't have a boyfriend."

I watched the questions and confusion cross Alex's face. "How.…What? Why? What's wrong with dating? We're sixteen. It's—It's just high school dating. That makes no sense."

"You know I have that stupid rule where I can't be alone with a boy."

"Yeah, I know." He nodded. "But you're sixteen now and that rule wouldn't apply to your boyfriend."

"Alex, that's the point, I can't have a boyfriend."

I could see the realization begin to turn in his mind, the facts settling. There was a subtle rippling effect in his arms and shoulders. He turned away and took few steps, facing the forest where it met the valley's edge. He shook his head, turning back to me. "I'll talk to Grandpa. He knows me. He knows I'll take care of you."

"I asked him about it already and he said not even you." I rubbed my face, trying not to cry. "I'm so sorry, Alex. This is humiliating—"

"You can't date anyone until you're eighteen?"

"Yes. That's what I just said."

"If you could date, then would you—"

"I'd go on a date with you." I rested my hand just below my throat, over the pulse of my racing heart.

"Not even a hesitation."

"Okay, be my best friend." Alex gestured a little aggressively toward me. "Just don't go anywhere. Be around, Jenny."

The way he was looking at me made me whisper. "Yeah, of course."

"Don't be around anyone else." Those blue eyes burned through me. "Just me." He swallowed. "And I'll be around… just you."

My face warmed. I looked down, shaking my head. "That's not fair to you."

"You don't think I'll wait?" His eyebrows raised, daring me to argue with him. "I'll just wait, Jenny. It's less than two years."

"That's not realistic for you. You can date."

"You don't think I'll wait for you." He came at me with long strides and then he hugged me to his chest. "Why don't you think I'll wait for you?"

I sucked in a breath, trying to steady myself. I wrapped my arms around him because he was the sturdiest thing I knew in my life. "It's two years. It's a long time. A lot can happen. You'll see some girl and—"

Alex moved and then he was kissing me again. I kissed him back. I was eager and needy because this was the last kiss. This was it. I wasn't going to date him. We were going to grow and change. In two years, we'd likely be different people. I knew we'd always be connected because of our mutations, but that didn't mean he couldn't date other girls.

His kisses slowed and his chin rose to settle on the top of my head. He held me as he said, "I'm not trying to freak you out, but I've always known. I'm playing the long game here. You'll see, the next two years I'll just be waiting and it'll be more than worth it." He sighed. "I'm planning on being around you every day, whether we get to kiss or not. If you can't date anyone else? That works to my advantage."

Alex never said anything unless he meant it. If he said he'd wait, then I knew he'd wait. I'd just learned that life wasn't always what we planned. My parents were gone, which meant that even now, none of this was what I'd expected life would be. I didn't say that to Alex though. I decided to say, "Okay, best friends. We'll be around."

He kissed the top of my head. "I think you underestimate how serious I am, but just give me time."

I nodded, pushing against his chest and stepping away. Alex Bailey looked miserable. I gave him a big bright smile, flirty and silly all at once. As if he couldn't help it, his face lit up and he grinned back at me. "We've been gone too long. They'll worry."

I hugged him tighter on the way back. I knew he didn't mind it. I knew he understood.

20.

WELL, THAT WAS a long time," Brandon said, leaning against the end of the picnic table with his arms crossed. "It's not safe to go off alone like that."

Stephen and Emma sat across from each other at the table with sandwiches, chips, soda and water bottles scattered across it. Mark and Mandy sat nearby in fold-out camping chairs. Mark was whispering and Mandy was giggling.

"Just took the scenic route," Alex said, helping me off the four-wheeler.

I set the helmet down on the back of it. "It's pretty up there. We should all go up that way."

"Eat something," Stephen said around a mouthful of food as he held out a sandwich for me. "Here you go."

"Thanks." I slid onto the bench next to him and unwrapped the sandwich.

Alex sat on the bench next to me, his arm pressing into mine as he reached for the chips. "Thanks for making these, Jenny."

"You're welcome," I said, straightening my back with pride.

Stephen took a bite of his sandwich. "Yeah, I'd eat your food even if it tasted like garbage." He grunted when I elbowed him. Emma laughed, but surprisingly, it didn't feel like it was at my expense. Instead her focus was on Stephen. My eyes darted between them as I realized Stephen was eyeing her back, pleased he'd made her laugh.

That was an interesting development that I would interrogate Stephen about later.

"I want to try one," Brandon said, scooting to sit next to Emma.

Alex and Stephen both stilled as they watched Brandon grab one of the sandwiches I'd made, as if they were about to tell him he couldn't have one, but they stayed quiet.

I realized the problem was that the five of us existed in a weird dynamic. Brandon and Emma had both once been my enemies, but Brandon and I were sort of friends. And, Stephen and Alex had been sort of friends with Emma all their lives. Long seconds of silence turned into minutes. Feeling a responsibility to smooth things over, I opened my mouth—

"You could have texted me last night you were hanging out with them today," Brandon said, staring at Alex before his eyes traveled to mine. "It's all good."

Heat washed over my left side, I didn't know if it was my own cheeks flushing or Stephen's mutation's reaction. I felt his eyes on me, and I knew he could read me well. He could see how uncomfortable I was. I hadn't been ready to tell Alex and Stephen that I'd been texting Brandon.

"Sorry, I fell asleep." And because I was sure he'd bring it up, I added, "Thank you for the gift. It was nice."

"No problem." He smiled. The dimple appeared. "Happy birthday."

"This is boring." Emma scowled, obviously not happy about the attention she wasn't getting. "Alex, take me up to that spot you showed Jenny."

My gaze swung over to Alex. He gave me a look and a small shake of the head. It was a promise that Emma's ride would be very different from mine. I wasn't worried about it. I gave him a shrug of approval before he said, "Sure, let's do it."

"I want to see, too," Brandon said. There was a touch

of something aggressive in his tone. "Ride with me, Jenny."

"No way in hell," Stephen said. I reeled back at his abrupt tone as he raised his eyebrows at Brandon. "She's not going to ride with you."

I looked to Alex for help, but he was staring at Brandon with a tight jaw, ready to help Stephen in whatever way he needed to deal with Brandon. Emma's mouth fell open, her helmet hovered in her hands above her head. Even Mark and Mandy had turned their attention to us. Mark straightened in his seat, gauging the situation too.

Incredulous, I whispered, "Stephen…"

"Bro, chill out." Brandon laughed, crossing his arms. "She can do what she wants." His eyes found mine. "We're here to have fun. Let's go."

I felt myself on shifting ground. If they fought, I wasn't sure I could hold my mutation steady. Inwardly, I was still recovering from what happened with Alex in the valley. And, what Brandon had said seconds ago about not texting him back the night before. Which was amplified by the fact that Stephen was out of line.

It was my choice to go with Brandon or not. I juggled the various consequences in my head based on whatever decision I'd make next. I decided riding with Brandon wasn't that big of a deal. Later, I'd let Stephen know exactly how I felt about him trying to control my interaction with other guys. He'd dug a hole for me and now I'd have to climb out of it in the least embarrassing way.

"It's cool." I raised my eyebrows at Stephen, warning him to keep his mouth shut with subtle, sisterly defiance in my tone. "You want to take the third one?"

"I want to finish my other sandwich." He gave Alex a look that said, *You're not going to let her out of your sight, right?*

Alex gave him an assuring nod.

I walked to the four-wheeler Brandon was sitting on, strapped my helmet under my chin, and climbed on behind him. I held onto the handlebars on either side of me, uninterested in wrapping my arms around him.

"Hope you're ready, sweetheart." Brandon's voice was muffled in the helmet. "Hold on."

The engine roared as he whipped around Alex and Emma. My grip on the bars wasn't enough. My arms shot around Brandon in a tight hold. It was fast, hard, and not a smooth ride. We raced up the same trail Alex had shown me. I squeezed my arms around Brandon and closed my eyes.

I already wanted it to be over. I couldn't breathe.

At the top of the hill, Brandon must have seen Alex and my fresh tracks because he headed toward the magic valley. He didn't slow down on corners, picking up speed with every passing second. I let out an involuntary scream when he hit a small bump and launched into the air, landing on the ground roughly. Pain jolted up my back, I hit his stomach, trying to make him stop so I could yell at him.

I shouted Brandon's name. "I'm done! Stop!"

But he ignored me. I couldn't see or hear anything, the engine drowning out my pleas.

The seconds felt like minutes, maybe hours. I promised myself that I'd never get on a four-wheeler with Brandon Thomas again, or a truck, or even a bicycle—

The machine stopped. A dull, but loud boom filled my ears.

The back wheels left the ground as we lurched forward.

Headfirst, Brandon and I flew off the four-wheeler. I landed on Brandon, flipping upside down, with no control, my legs flying over my head.

I tumbled—again, again, and again. Rolling and grunting, unable to do anything but curl my arms into myself. In a flash, I spotted the wide trunk of a tree, I was going to hit it, and I wasn't going to be okay.

I sucked in a breath. A swoosh of air swirled around me.

Bouncing off an invisible wall, I slammed into the

ground a yard away from the tree. Seconds passed. My mutation had saved me somehow, but I couldn't process how yet.

I groaned, trying to see if I could move.

"Jesus." Alex jerked his helmet off. It hit the ground and bounced away. He sprinted toward me, jumping over the big log we'd hit and running past Brandon. "Jenny—Jenny." He unstrapped my helmet and pulled it off. "Look at me. Yeah, look at me."

I kept blinking. I didn't want to move. "It's okay. I'm okay."

Brandon sat up. "Oh *shit!*"

Alex's hand shook. "Where does it hurt?"

I tried to sit up, but I grunted when my elbow gave way. My body felt like a mass of liquid. The more seconds passed, the more the aches crept up on me. "It kind of hurts to breathe. My ribs or something—No wait, I think I just got the wind knocked out of me."

Alex pushed my hair out of my face. "Can you walk? We need to get back to my truck."

"I think so." I trembled as I stood up. Alex slid his hand under my elbow. "I'm good, Alex. I'm okay."

"You aren't okay," he said gruffly. "We're done with this bullshit."

I hunched over a little as I walked because my ribs were aching. Alex walked with me to the four-wheeler and set me on it. I looked down to see bloodied knees and scrapes on my hands and arms.

Brandon stood up. He seemed fine aside from a few of his own scrapes. "Dude, we hit that hard." Him laughing was such a weird response to what had just happened.

Emma knelt next to Brandon, dusting him off. "Are you okay?"

"Man, that was so fun."

Alex's muscles tensed. Everything about him swelled.

I squeezed his forearm. "Leave it."

He ignored me, turning and striding over to Brandon. He grabbed him by the shirt collar. "You think this is funny? You almost killed her."

"She said she was fine." Brandon laughed again, his face flushed pink.

Alex shook him. "Your breath reeks." He pushed Brandon hard. Brandon hit the ground with a thud. "You're drunk. You asshole. You're drunk."

"I'm good, bro." Brandon did a half wave as he sat up. "Jenny's good too. Besides, we both know a girl like her wants something exciting, not some boring asshole like you."

Emma took a step back, gaping as we watched Alex

pick Brandon up by his shirt collar again. It was smooth and fluid. It was impossible.

Wide-eyed, Brandon gripped Alex's wrists. Alex had Brandon on the tips of his toes.

The mutation within Alex was a sheen over his body, muscles moving subtly under his skin. His tone was a low growl, sending chills over my body despite the hot sun. "If you ever talk to Jenny again, I swear you'll regret it."

I gasped as Alex threw a punch, it was faster than a blink, but I knew by the way Brandon's face was still intact that Alex had held back. He'd tried to throw a regular punch.

Alex turned and barked out, "Emma sit next to Jenny. Let's go." He fired up the four-wheeler as Brandon lay there, groaning. I didn't look back.

21.

ALEX TOOK IT SLOW going back.

I winced at every bump, but I was just relieved to not be riding with Brandon. When we pulled up to the picnic area, everyone stood. Stephen set a hand on the table, jumping over it to get to me. "Wh-What happened?"

"She needs to see a doctor." Alex slowly helped me off the four-wheeler.

Stephen took my arm on my other side. "What happened?"

"I don't need to see a doctor," I said with a sigh, pulling my arm from Stephen's grasp.

"Where's Brandon?" Mark asked.

Alex helped me into the passenger seat of his truck, he gently buckled me in, pulling the seat belt behind me. He was in emergency mode. He seemed to be forcing himself to stay calm as he whispered. "I'll take care of you."

Stephen scrambled to pile things into our cooler and looked around for anything else that was ours. Emma looked lost as she watched everything play out.

"Alex," Mandy said, gripping Mark's forearm, "Where's Brandon?

When Alex came around the truck, he spat out, "He's drunk. They crashed. He seems to be fine, but Jenny is hurt."

"We'll get him." Mark put his helmet on with a calm focus that matched Alex's. Mandy climbed onto the other four-wheeler and gestured for Emma to jump on with her.

Stephen slid into the backseat of the truck. Alex wordlessly started it up, rocks and dirt kicking up as he peeled onto the main road.

"Someone answer me," Stephen said, his voice gravelly. "What the hell happened?"

I didn't dare answer yet. I'd never been in a situation like this with them. Stephen telling me not to go with Brandon stirred something within me, confusing me. I didn't know what to make of the too-calm expression on Alex's face, but I could feel the rage simmering within him.

"He was out of control," Alex said as he drove, both hands wound tightly around the wheel. "Just all over and he wasn't slowing down. I watched it happen. He ran right into this enormous log and they flew." He shook his head, his knuckles turning white. "She's this little thing bouncing off the ground and rolling. It was all of my nightmares happening."

Stephen sat back against the seat, rubbing his face. "I knew it. I knew something bad was going to happen."

"He was drunk." Alex glanced at me. His tone was accusatory. "Did you smell alcohol on him?"

"No." I glared at him. I'd screwed up, but he didn't get to talk to me harshly either. "I wouldn't have gone with him if I had."

"Right." Alex nodded, his voice softer. "Duh. Sorry."

"I didn't see him drinking," Stephen said. "He must have been sneaking it in the water bottle he had. Like vodka, or something."

An awkward quiet stretched between us, but Alex kept glancing at me like he wanted to say something. Irritated, I snapped. "What?"

"You did something up there."

Stephen sat forward, looking at me. "What did she do?"

"I don't know." I winced again as I held my ribs.

"We can talk about it later," Alex said.

Stephen groaned. "What's the gist of it?"

Alex shifted in his seat, thinking about it. "There was a big tree up there. She was headed for it. I knew she was just going to hit it and die."

"Okay. Right. What happened?"

Alex and I made eye contact. "It was like she hit something invisible and bounced off of it."

"I didn't do it," I said, sinking into my seat a little. "The mutation did it."

"Huh." Stephen had always been the first one of us to process the impossible, easily accepting it as our reality. "Brandon and Emma?"

"Brandon wouldn't have seen it." Alex cleared his throat. "As far as I know, Emma didn't see either. I think, anyway. It was hard to catch and really chaotic. I saw it happen, but Emma was behind me."

"Good." Stephen nodded thoughtfully. "That's good."

No one spoke for a long few minutes, but I needed to clear my head of the things we weren't saying.

I twisted in my seat to face Stephen, the edges of my eyes stung with the threat of tears. "I should have listened to you. I shouldn't have gone with him. I made the wrong choice."

Stephen sat back into his seat with a heavy sigh. "I could of handled it better. I know it put you in an awkward spot. I'm sorry too."

"I don't know why I thought I could be friends with Brandon." I rubbed my face. "I was so stupid."

"You weren't stupid." Alex frowned. "The problem is that you're a good person."

Stephen's eyebrows pulled together. "Alex is right. You've just wanted to give Brandon a chance. We get that. But Brandon has been messing with me and Alex all our lives. We just never wanted him to mess with you the way he's messed with us."

"I get it," I said, pausing for a moment to listen to the hum of the diesel engine. I could feel Stephen watching me carefully. I finally looked up at him. "No more Brandon."

Alex released a long breath, his muscles relaxing, as if his mutation joined him in his relief. Stephen squeezed my shoulder, smiling at me. The hum of my mutation in my spine quieted. The three of us were good again.

Then I blurted out, "Alex punched Brandon."

"Oh?" Stephen said, his eyebrows raised. "Did you now?"

Alex glanced at me, snorting. "What are you, tattling?"

"I don't know." I shrugged, settling back into my

seat. "I thought Stephen should be informed that you lost your cool." I bit my lip, then said, "We have to be careful, you know? I know that punch was calculated. I know you controlled your mutation. But I also know that you could kill him, Alex."

"I know," Alex said, letting out another long sigh. "I know I need to be careful."

"I mean we all do." I looked over my shoulder at Stephen. "Brandon and Emma didn't see what I did, but they could have."

"Jenny's right, if we get caught, we go to science jail." Stephen leaned over the seat. "We're still figuring this out. We need to lay low and stick to ourselves."

"Science jail, huh? Sounds about right." Alex laughed, but then his smile faded. He reached across the seat, wrapping his hand around mine. "If people found out about us, I'd do anything to keep you safe. You know that right? I don't want you to worry."

I looked between them. "I'd do anything to keep you guys safe too. We need each other. This secret we carry is really heavy."

"We're like grownups, aren't we?" Stephen sighed dramatically. "Our childhood just went out the door when we became mutants and now we have to talk through all this stuff."

"No." Alex shook his head. "We talk through all of

this stuff so that we can protect our childhood. We've done a pretty good job of being normal teenagers, I think. It's just a lot of work."

I pulled my hair tie out, fluffed my hair, and sat back into my seat. The aches and pains were starting to dull. The sun was warm on my lap from streaming through the windshield. The cool breeze from the mountain air brushed against my skin. "I say we never grow up."

"I second that," Stephen said. I could hear the sounds of a game he had downloaded on his phone playing.

Alex laid his arm along the back of the seat, his fingers finding my hair, playing with a lock of it, but he kept glancing down at my legs again and again. We were almost to Grandpa's farm when I said, "What are you thinking about?"

"You're all scraped up, still," he said, jerking his chin toward my abused knees.

I frowned, study the scrapes on my palms. "What do you mean?"

"I mean," he said, quietly. "Remember when we told you Stephen and I were fixing a fence for my dad out in the fields? Stephen got a big cut on his arm. I knew he'd need stitches, but we watched it just… get better."

My eyes trailed over his body, the perfection of him. There wasn't a flaw to be found.

"If it were Stephen or me, the scrapes would be

gone." Worry flickered in his eyes, his jaw tightening as he turned the truck down Grandpa's private lane. "You're different from us in that way."

I stared out the window at Grandpa's fields. I understood what he was saying, but I didn't know what that meant for me.

22.

On MONDAY, the school seemed small compared to the stature of Alex Bailey. He wore his gray T-shirt and blue jeans like a champion. Everything fit him snugly.

Knowing that he wanted me to be his girlfriend seemed to amplify my awareness of him, leaving me with a dry mouth whenever he glanced at me a certain way. I wasn't sure if he noticed that every girl he walked past eyed him like a piece of meat. I just knew that whenever I looked up at him, he seemed to be already looking at me.

Stephen was almost a head taller than me, too.

He had that big bright smile for everyone as he threw nods and greeted other students. He wore a red T-shirt and blue jeans that fit a little loose, but they did all the right things for him, too. Since I'd met him last summer, he'd kept his hair styled in longer dark curls, but he'd paid for his haircut with his own money over the weekend.

Alex, Stephen, and I drove to Willow City to find a barber that knew his hair type. I listened nearby in the small waiting area as he'd asked for *a fade up the sides in the back with short curls on the top*. I'd stayed quiet as I slowly realized why Stephen didn't want to get his haircut at Hollow Brook's small salon anymore.

I wasn't going to ask him about it. I knew Stephen slipped up with saying silly stuff all the time, it was part of his charm. But I also knew there were some things he kept close, as if he were gathering clues around himself to decide what he'd do with it all as he grew into a man. There was a deeper wisdom about Stephen Wright that I admired. He saw things others ignored. I wanted to see those things too. I'd decided I would show up for him in any way he needed, but never assume I knew what was best for him.

Just before we turned the corner to stop at Alex's locker, Emma called Alex over, pulling me from my thoughts. She stood down the hall at her open locker in a yellow summer dress with little pink roses on it. I wasn't going to tell her that I actually liked the dress a lot because I was annoyed that she was shamelessly batting her lashes at Alex.

Alex turned, facing me, and said, "Come with me."

"I don't want to talk to Emma."

"I don't want to talk to her either." He shifted from foot to foot, crowding me a little against the locker behind me. "Come with me."

I glanced at Stephen, who shrugged. "Whatever."

I wondered if Alex was trying to do me a service, sending a message to Emma Henderson that she couldn't manipulate his attention. Alex Bailey's loyalty was to Jenny Philips, and I didn't know how I'd earned that spot in his life, but he was making it clear that I was the one who belonged next to him.

"Fine," I muttered, rolling my eyes.

Stephen followed us and he leaned against the locker next to Emma's. His tone was a balance between genuine interest and playful mocking. "How's your Monday morning going, Emma Henderson?"

"Great," she said dismissively to Stephen. I was not acknowledged. She faced Alex. "You have a truck."

"Ah, yes, I do," Alex said dryly.

Emma clapped and jumped. "Great! So, there's this community project that my mom wants me to find help for. She's trying to impress the new mayor since our mayor is retiring early. It's clearing out the old flower beds in the town square. I need guys with muscles and pickup trucks." She paused, looking past me. "Hey, Brandon, question for you. I need people with trucks."

I turned to find Brandon standing directly behind me. His eye was a ripe black and purple color from where Alex had punched him.

Two days ago, I'd flown off a four-wheeler with Brandon and now he stood here. I hadn't been sure if I was going to tell Grandpa about what happened with Brandon. But by the time he came home from the fields, Grandpa already knew what happened. Mark Bailey had told Mr. Bailey as soon as he'd gotten cell service. Grandpa had been too focused on making sure Brandon was held accountable to be mad at me.

Grandpa told me Brandon spent Saturday night in jail. Sheriff Bolt was going to deal with Brandon and make him do some kind of community service. Stephen had muttered, "Nice for Brandon that his dad and Sheriff Bolt are best friends. My bet is that Grandpa's police report will get dropped into a *special* file."

I'd been dumb enough to turn to Alex, confusion written across my face. Alex said, "He means thrown away. There won't be an official record about what Brandon did." And I could hear the underlying hatred in his voice for Brandon in a way I hadn't before the four-wheeler crash.

I supposed I hadn't expected Brandon to be at school, but now I realized it was silly to think he wouldn't be here.

Alex stepped in front of me, his shoulder blocking

most of my view of Brandon. His voice was gruff. "Just text me, Emma."

I watched Brandon smirk at Alex. I couldn't believe the arrogance, but Alex Bailey didn't flinch. His jaw didn't even tense as he stared back at Brandon.

They were both tall and broad shouldered in their own way. Brandon's body was on the bulkier side. He was a wall of a man, like a linebacker on a football team. Alex Bailey was lean, with generous curves of smooth muscle subtly outlined under his T-shirt. In appearance it was hard to tell who'd win in a high school hallway fight, but I knew Alex's mutation shifted under his skin and his enhanced strength could quite possibly kill Brandon.

Emma tilted her head, her red hair brushing over her shoulder. "Um, okay, I guess." I couldn't tell if she'd just orchestrated Brandon coming over or if she was simply stupid. All I knew was that nobody had accused Emma Henderson of being smart.

Alex grabbed my hand and pulled me behind him. A warm flush washed over my face, my gaze darting around the crowded hallway. People whispered and watched.

At Alex's locker, I wiggled my hand out of his. "What are you doing?"

Stephen had a familiar expression on his face. He'd

wait and watch to see how this would play out between Alex and me.

"What do you mean, what am I doing?" Alex asked, his voice edged with a growl.

"People saw that."

"When have we ever cared what people think?" He rearranged books in his locker, making room so Stephen and I could use it too. "I just want to punch him again. Give him a matching set of black eyes."

Stephen snorted, but I glared at him. He coughed and rubbed the back of his neck.

"You can't just like…" I whispered, flustered. "You can't grab my hand like that."

Alex shook his head, his expression incredulous. "That's what you're upset about? All that happened with Brandon and you're upset that I took your hand? We talked about this. Brandon doesn't get to be within twenty feet of you if I have anything to do with it."

"That's fine, but we're not like…" He was right, I wasn't upset about the handholding, not really. But I didn't know how to explain that I had a million emotions running through me all at once. One wrong word and my mutation would act up without my consent. "People are going to think we're together."

Alex seemed to force himself to soften his voice. "I just said I don't care what people think."

"It might get back to Grandpa," I whispered. "We'll get in trouble."

"She's got a point," Stephen said, raising a brow. "Don't forget we live in small-town Hollow Brook. People already talk about you two and assume stuff."

Alex narrowed his eyes at me. I knew he had a dozen more opinions on the matter, but he settled on saying, "Why is everything so damn complex?"

My lip twitched, a smile threatening to appear on my face. The building pressure of my mutation in my chest fizzled out. "I don't know."

Stephen yawned, pushing off of the lockers. "I need sugar. I'm going to grab juice from the vending machine. You guys want anything?"

Alex and I spoke at the same time, "Apple juice, please."

Stephen looked between us, then up at the ceiling. "Lord, help me with these two who are not together and are also an old married couple."

"Shut up."

I shoved Stephen's shoulder, pointing him the direction of the vending machines near the cafeteria as he grinned with satisfaction that he'd managed to annoy me.

I leaned against the locker next to Alex's. He took

the books I wouldn't need until later in the day from my arms to arrange them into his locker.

I snuck a peek down the hall, watching Brandon flirt with Emma. Usually, it was Meg and Suzy who hung around her locker, but they weren't anywhere to be seen. My gaze drifted toward Mark, Mandy, and their friends down the opposite end of the hall. Brandon was usually among their crowd and I wondered if Emma and him were getting close. Emma wasn't my friend, but an uneasy feeling spread through my stomach at the thought of her alone with him.

Alex shut his locker a little harder than necessary. I glanced up at him. He'd followed my line of sight, watching Brandon and Emma too.

And I knew he was thinking the same thing as me.

23.

THAT NIGHT I rolled over in bed, looking toward my window, and sent my mutation's air to pull the curtain back to see if it was dark outside yet. It was the limbo part of the evening when dinner and homework were over, but it wasn't late enough to fall asleep. I rolled over again and thought about reading a book, but I'd finished the book I had from the library.

The thought of calling Alex flitted through my mind.

Alex was always thinking of me. He had a spot saved for me next to him in every situation. I thought about the way he'd included me when Emma called him over today. How he'd taken my hand without a thought, making sure he kept me close when Brandon made an appearance. The more I thought about it, the more I realized I was always included in whatever Alex was doing.

My mind swirled, wondering if I was taking advantage of him somehow. I remembered Stephen telling me about Alex's fight with Mrs. Bailey about inviting me to his family birthday dinner. That night he'd simply informed me he was going to drive me to school every day with Stephen. I hadn't questioned it because Stephen and I agreed that Alex Bailey driving a truck was the coolest thing that had ever happened to the three of us. We'd won the life lottery because we'd never have to take the bus again.

If Alex bought a soda at the mall for himself, he bought one for me without a thought. At the movies, he bought the large popcorn. We knew the intention was that popcorn would be set in my lap for Stephen and me to share with him. I knew I thanked him each time. I'd even offered to pay before, but he'd waved me off so many times that I'd stopped offering.

I never really did much for Alex. That thought grew bigger than the rest of the thoughts in me. I wondered what I could do for him. It pushed me to be bold, I found his name in my contacts and called him.

He answered right away. "Jenny?"

"Hi."

"You okay?"

I laughed. "Why wouldn't I be okay?"

"I don't know," he said with a small laugh of his own.

"You've never called me before."

"Yeah. I know. I was just thinking about that."

"You called me because you were thinking about how you've never called me?"

"Yes?" I wasn't sure why my tone sounded like I was asking a question. Several seconds of silence passed. I'd called him, made this awkward, and left him confused. My heart picked up in speed and my cheeks warmed, but I needed to make this conversation less awkward. "Do you want… gas money?"

"Gas money? For what?"

"For taking me to school."

He let out a low laugh, but his tone was gentle amusement. "If I said yes, then where would you get this money, Jenny Philips?"

I bit my lip, but couldn't stop my smile. "I could get a job."

He sounded like he was sitting and shifting to get comfortable. "You're going to get a job to pay me gas money I'm already going to be using to get to school anyway?"

"Sure," I said with a quiet laugh. "I should get a job and car anyway, right?"

"What? No." I almost couldn't tell if he was teasing or serious. "Absolutely not."

My laughter was explosive, my smile big. "What? Why not?"

"It'd be a waste. I'll drive you wherever you want to go. And no, I don't want gas money, so you don't need a job."

I rolled my eyes. "Alex, I'm sixteen too now, I should be independent and stuff, right? You and Stephen are both licensed to drive, but I'm not. Aunt Sarah told me she'd pay for me to learn to drive. I mean, she said she wanted to buy me a car too, but Grandpa doesn't want stuff handed to me for free in life. So, even if I wanted her to buy me car, I'm not sure how that would go over—"

"If you got a job," Alex interrupted, "it'd be after school or something, right?"

"Yeah—"

"Or weekends?"

"I don't know. Probably."

"Nope." He clicked his tongue playfully. "Those are times we hang out. You're not available during those times. Besides, you have that trust from your parents for college. What do you need a job for?"

Something serious washed over the conversation. "I mean I get your point, but there are skills I should learn, right? I should pay my way when we hang out. Grandpa doesn't believe in money for chores. Aunt

Sarah gave me that credit card, but I told Grandpa it's for big emergencies. He doesn't want me using it for day-to-day stuff." I sighed. "There's like a principle, a lesson for me if I get a job."

"What?" Alex snorted. "To build your character? Teach you how to count money? You're perfect the way you are."

"You and Stephen have jobs." But they did farm work for money that was different from the few chores Grandpa gave me. It was the kind of work Grandpa didn't think was appropriate for me. "And don't say I'm perfect, because I'm not."

"I mean, Stephen and I work at four in the morning. It's not like we'd hang out during that time." What he said made sense, but I still felt like a fraud. "You don't have time for a job because Stephen and I need your full attention. And you work hard every day with school and with our mutations. You do enough."

"God, you make me sound like a diva." But he was right in a way. Since we'd turned into mutants, we'd spent every day after school and on weekends learning how to control our mutations. It'd always been obvious to the three of us that I'd struggled the most with controlling my superpowers. But I touched on his full-attention comment. "You realize we're always together, right? The only time we aren't is when we're forced to be home."

Alex didn't respond immediately. I wasn't sure if he'd taken what I said wrong.

"I mean, I love it that way," I assured him. "That's not what I'm saying. I think— I'm worried that I'm like dead weight in our friendship. I don't contribute in any way. I need to grow up and mature—"

"Jenny, I'm happy to work so you don't have to worry about anything."

My stomach dropped and a shiver ran over every inch of my skin. My mind and body didn't know how to process what he'd just said. "What?"

"I'm not saying you shouldn't get a license." His voice was smooth, clear. "I'll teach you to drive if you want, but I've got super strength and endless energy. Working hard is easy for me. I want—" He cleared his throat. "It's a mutant thing, all right? I work so I can be with you, take you places, experience stuff with you. I don't mind paying for stuff when we're together. It's different for us with our mutations."

My mutation perked up, as if opening one eye to see why my heart was racing. I whispered into the phone, paranoid that Grandpa could hear me somehow. "How is it a mutant thing?"

"I don't know. Maybe it's not. I just feel better when the three of us are hanging out together. If you get a job, what am I supposed to do when you're at work?"

I laughed incredulously. "Do whatever you want to do, Alex. Get a hobby or something. Do guy stuff with Stephen."

"I don't want a hobby, I don't want to do guy stuff with Stephen without you," he said, a pout in his voice. "I want to be with you. Shoot, you know I wish there were times it could be only you."

I shut my eyes as my mutation's warm breeze circled me in my room. My curtains swayed, the perfume and makeup bottles trembled on my dresser. The light from my bedside lamp flickered as I tried to suppress the ache in my chest, because sometimes Alex Bailey said things that turned me inside out. "You can't say stuff like that."

"Say stuff like what?" He muttered. "That I want to hang out with my best friend? And, there's nothing wrong with me wanting to be your boyfriend, I just *can't* be your boyfriend."

Alex was right, but I wished this conversation in itself didn't feel forbidden. He and I were standing on either side of a drawn line, both of us eyeing it and trying to define who we were to each other. "I feel better when we're together too. It is a mutant thing." I swallowed as the edges of my eyes stung. "It's like you, me and Stephen have some kind of ability to see and know each other in a way only we can. It's part of what makes us different now."

He whispered, "Why do you sound sad about that?"

"I'm not sad," I drew in a deep breath to push down the emotion in my throat. A few pages of my open textbook fluttered at the end of my bed. "It's just a lot."

"It is a lot. That's why we have each other."

It was on the tip of my tongue to apologize, but I wouldn't have known exactly what I was apologizing for. I thought of my decision to live with Grandma after my parents died, and of that first day when I agreed to fish with Alex and Stephen. Each decision I'd made had led to us standing in the garden of the mutant farm. In that garden I was the one who ate a strawberry first. My decision had tied Alex, Stephen, and I together for the rest of our lives.

"Wait, you're really thinking of getting a job?" Alex said, his tone shifting, as if offering me a path out of the darkness I was tempted to fall into. "This is a thing?"

I sighed, taking the bait with sarcasm, "I wasn't before this phone call, but now I feel like I should, just to make the point that I'm independent of you."

"Here, one minute."

The phone line went silent.

My mouth dropped open as I lowered the phone from my ear to find he'd hung up on me. I opened up my contacts, found his name, and called him again.

"Hello?" he asked with mock innocence.

"You hung up on me. Why did you hang up on me?"

"I wanted to start the conversation over," Alex said. "Somehow in our last conversation, you decided you wanted a job and I'm going to try and prevent that in the second round."

I burst into laughter. "Alex Bailey."

"What?" he said, laughter weaving into his response too. "The last phone call you asked if I needed gas money. Apparently, I said the wrong thing and you ended up wanting a job. So, no I don't need gas money, but thanks for asking. Did you call about anything else?"

I mashed my lips together. I had a dozen thoughts and responses, but I didn't want to talk in circles with Alex. He was smart. He knew if I wanted to get a job, then I'd just get one. We both knew he'd gotten his strong opinion across. He just wanted me to take note of it.

I was worried that I'd killed the conversation. I didn't want to let Alex go yet. "What are you going to do after high school? You told me you want to go to college. Do you know the degree you want?"

"Degree I want?" He said, adapting to my sudden change in subject. I could hear it, the way he didn't want to end the conversation yet either. "I want to get a degree in agricultural business. There're a few schools

I'm looking into, but my family all went to Medford University." He paused. "But you know that."

"You want to farm, right?"

"Yeah, I'm interested in farming, and I like the work. I'm now officially built for that kind of labor with my mutation."

"No, for sure."

His voice turned thoughtful. "With that kind of degree, I could run a family farm like my dad. Mark wants to get into construction, so my dad and I talk about what my future might look like with the Bailey Farm a lot lately."

"That's really cool."

"I know you're not sure what you want to do, but I have a suggestion."

Intrigued, I said, "Oh yeah? What's your suggestion?"

"Thief." Alex teased. "You know, art, jewels, and money in bank vaults. You'd unlock the vault and float out the goods. I bet you could do it all without getting caught. Not one fingerprint."

"Oh my god, that's so funny." My laughter was loud and abrupt. "That's brilliant, actually."

"Your mutation is brilliant," he said. "But really, what would you do if you could do anything? Like, if you didn't have to worry about money, but just wanted to do something to enjoy it."

My mind drew a blank, but then my mom came to mind.

I thought of the warm emerald green blanket on our couch, the orange bowl of overflowing fruit on the island, the pretty chipping black-and-white tile on the kitchen floor, and the mustard yellow chair in the corner of my old room.

I longed for the home when my parents were alive.

"I don't know about a career," I said, I'd told Alex parts about my life before I'd come to Hollow Brook in the last several months, but there were parts still left uncovered. "My mom was good at cooking. She was teaching me how to cook before she died. I don't know, I want to learn how to cook better."

"Yeah?"

"She loved to decorate the house," I said, smiling at my ceiling, letting my memories of her play like a movie in my head. "She'd rearrange all the furniture in the living room once a month. We'd do it together. Decorating for Halloween was a big thing too. She liked the scary and gory stuff like clown heads and bloody limbs peeking out of the bushes in the yard."

"Really? That's so cool."

"Christmas was over the top too. So much tinsel and garland and a real tree she made my dad cut down in the forest. We had an oversized Santa in the yard and so many Christmas lights you could see our house from space. I miss that. Grandma does a tree and your mom has the most beautiful décor. I mean it's perfect, but—"

Alex huffed. "It's a department store display, yes."

"I don't know, I just want to build a life, a family, you know? Like, I wish I could see my grandparents and Aunt Sarah like that, but I don't. I think sometimes I'm just holding my breath, waiting to have my own home, to have control over what I want it to be like."

"I feel like I haven't taken a breath since I came to Hollow Brook. You know, really felt content. It feels like I haven't had a home since they died." My thoughts rolled off my tongue in a way I could only do with Alex Bailey. "Do sixteen-year-olds talk about this? Sometimes I can't tell if we're like other teenagers because we're so different with our mutations. We've worked hard to protect the things that are important to us. I lay in bed at night…" I trailed off, uncertainty hitting my chest.

"You lay in bed at night?" Alex urged in a low whisper.

"I count off the things I want, you know—what's important to me." I sat up, grabbing my pillow to stuff in my lap so I could lean forward against it. "I try to imagine what we're fighting for. Why we work so hard to keep our secrets. I think about a house instead of a science lab. A big yard instead of the government fencing us in. I think about the way Hollow Brook is my home and that I want to fit in here, it's a world where people don't think I'm a freak. You know?"

I'd said all of it, trusting Alex again and letting him have words and thoughts I'd never given anyone else. Except I wasn't sure why I'd rambled on and on about my childhood home and the things I thought about late at night in my bed. A jolt of embarrassment pulsed through me. "Sorry, you were asking about a career—"

"I want to build a life too." I could hear the smile in his voice. "I know exactly what you're saying."

"What kind of cookies do you like?" I said, throwing Alex Bailey for a loop again, this time on purpose.

"What?"

"Your favorite cookies."

"I like mint chocolate chip cookies," he answered. "I'm a sucker for mint and chocolate."

"Oh yeah, duh, I knew that."

"Why?"

"Night, Alex."

He laughed. "You're off to bed?"

"I think so." I pretended to yawn dramatically. "You'll come to pick me up in the morning, even though I have no money?"

More laughter drifted through the phone. "That's my plan, Jenny Philips."

"Okay, thanks for talking to me." I lifted my hand, beckoning my slippers through the air off the floor next to my closet and into my free hand. I bent down to slip them on.

"I'd talk to you more if you'd stay on the phone with me, all night actually," he said with a touch of something flirty.

He earned a giggle from me. "Some of us don't have endless energy, Alex Bailey."

"Okay, well don't forget I do." His voice was soft again. "Don't forget you can call me anytime and I'll answer. All right?"

"All right." I drew air into my lungs and released it again, feeling a weight lifted off my chest just by hearing Alex Bailey's voice. "Goodnight."

"Sweet dreams, Jenny."

We hung up. Alex had my mutation buzzing under my skin. I'd lied to him. I knew I'd be up for a while longer. I headed to Grandma and Grandpa's room and knocked on the door.

Grandma said, "Come in, Jenny."

I opened the door. Grandma and Grandpa were sitting up in bed, each of them reading a book. "Can I make mint chocolate chip cookies?"

"Sure, I have everything for that. Grab my baking recipe book and follow the directions." Grandma smiled at me. "What are the cookies for?"

"Ah, the guys. Just for fun." I shrugged, then added, "They're Alex's favorite."

Grandpa raised an eyebrow, "It was Alex on the phone, right?"

I opened my mouth. I hadn't known they could hear me. "Uh… yes. Is that okay?"

"Just Alex," Grandpa said and went back to his reading.

His tone bothered me, I almost asked him how he would have felt if I'd been on the phone with Stephen, but I was afraid of his answer.

24.

THE NEXT MORNING, I slid into Alex's truck with a plastic storage bowl.

My palms were faintly sweaty. I tried to tell myself that Alex and Stephen were my best friends and making cookies was a best friend thing to do. Except I'd made them specifically because they were Alex's favorite.

I told myself to be chill, but I wasn't chill at all.

"Morning," Stephen mumbled, his voice gravelly. "I'm tired. Stayed up late playing video games."

"Do you want to stop and get coffee? I have the gift cards from my birthday you guys gave me," I said, trying to sound casual.

Alex turned the truck onto the main road. "Coffee sounds good to me."

Stephen yawned. "I already know I'm going to be nodding off in class today. Jenny, I need you to be on wake-up duty if Mr. Garrison catches me."

"Got it." I'd been on wake-up duty several times before. If his head landed on his crossed arms and his breathing deepened, I could wake him up with a supernatural tug on his sleeve, or send a magical gust of air to nudge him. I drew in a deep breath, letting my words ride on my exhale. "I made you guys cookies."

Stephen perked up at that. "You did? Let me have one. What kind are they?"

Alex had gone still, not acknowledging me yet, just keeping his eyes on the road.

"Mint chocolate chip," I said, thankful that my voice was steady. I opened the lid and held one out to Stephen. "Don't forget it's like seven in the morning."

Stephen took two cookies, biting into one quickly and speaking around it. "Who cares? These are good."

We pulled up to a stop sign, Alex looked at me, giving me a shy smile. "Thanks, Jenny." He reached out to grab a cookie. I jerked back, making sure he didn't touch me. By the way he hesitated, I knew he'd caught the movement. "You're the best." He took a big bite, wiping at a crumb on the edge of his lip with his thumb, reminding me of when I'd kissed that very spot. "These are incredible."

I grabbed a cookie for myself. I was quite proud of the big, round, soft cookies with just the right balance of mint and chocolate flavor.

I watched a spot of rain hit the truck's windshield. Seconds passed and more fell in big droplets. The sky was dark and moody, warning us of a spring storm coming. Alex turned on the windshield wipers.

"Where's your coat?" He leaned forward and adjusted the heat, shutting his side off and sliding the vents on my side open, instantly making me feel warm and cozy.

I glanced down at myself. I was wearing a long-sleeved tight black top tucked into a black high-waisted corduroy skirt that hugged my hips. I'd kept my legs bare, deciding on my new black ankle boots.

I'd casually mentioned to Aunt Sarah that I had been growing out of some of my clothes, since then she'd been sending me clothes with price tags that made me gasp. I'd told her that designer clothes had no place in Hollow Brook, but she'd insisted on certain *essential* items had to be high quality. I had to admit I looked older in them. Everything was cute and fitted well, showing off the ever-changing curves of my body.

"I wore long sleeves. I didn't know it was going to rain."

Alex grunted. "I should start texting you the weather report before I pick you up."

"Text me, too." Stephen reached around me for another couple of cookies. "I have to know how to style my hair," he said, smashing the loose bun on the top of my head.

"Hey." I swatted at him before pulling down the vizor and looking in the mirror to make sure he hadn't completely ruined my hair situation. I tugged and pulled and readjusted it. "See if I ever make you cookies again."

Stephen responded, but I didn't understand it because his mouth was full of cookies.

When we got to school, we ran into the building together, laughing because the rain was coming down in big droplets. The air was warm and muggy. We were still early, even after we'd stopped to get coffee at the Espresso Hut. Stephen handed Alex his books to put in Alex's locker before saying he was going to go to the bathroom real quick.

Alex turned to me. "I want to show you something."

"Oh. Okay."

His shoulder brushed mine as he passed me, striding down the hall. I followed him, a little breathless because this was not usual Alex Bailey behavior. We wove through students chatting in little groups around open lockers.

He didn't stop until we'd made it to the science classrooms at the back end of the school, pushing through the door of one of the two lab rooms. The lights were off and it was empty. Blinds covered most of the windows adjacent to the hall, but one was uncovered. No one could see us, but the exposed window gave the room just a touch of light from the hall so we could see each other. Dark clouds made the windows facing outside worthless for any real light.

Alex set his books down on the cabinet next to us. I glanced around the empty science room. "What—"

He took two steps, put his hands on my waist, and pressed me against the back of the closed door. "Tell me now you don't want me to kiss you."

My stomach flipped as my hands settled on his strong forearms. "There's a lot of electricity in this building. I might do something stupid."

"That's fine. There's a storm out there. It'll be a perfect excuse."

"What if someone comes in here?"

"This classroom doesn't get used as a homeroom. No one is going to come in here."

My smile was big and bright for him. "You thought of everything, huh?"

"I don't know—" He laughed low, sliding a step closer, the heat of him seeping through my thin shirt. "You made me cookies. What else am I supposed to do?"

I leaned my shoulders against the door and took the opportunity to hold Alex's gaze with mine. He gave my waist a gentle squeeze. I wondered if I listened hard enough if I could hear his thoughts because I knew they mirrored mine.

I tilted my head to the side, batting my lashes at him. "I bake you cookies and suddenly you're out of control, huh?"

He lifted his hand to tuck a loose strand of hair behind my ear. "I haven't been in control of anything since the day I met you, Jenny Philips."

I stared at his shoulder for a long moment. I thought of what Grandpa had said about my parents messing around behind his back. I decided to say, "My mom and dad would have loved you, you know. They would have let me go on a date with you. They would have been proud to have you as my boyfriend."

It took him long seconds to respond, and I could see him turning over thoughts in his mind, thinking through different possibilities. "What would you say if I said I think we should play by your parent's rules?"

I bit my lip because it was my turn to take long seconds to respond. I understood what he was saying, my parents would have let me explore the grey of life. But Grandpa had drawn thick red lines around me. I didn't want to waste time living in the shadow of his rules. I wanted to explore the blue sky in Alex's eyes, to see what we could find together, and so I said, "We're pretty good at keeping secrets, huh?"

"That's true." His voice deepened. "We are pretty good at that." He leaned in closer. "Do you want to keep another secret with me?"

My bag slid from my arm as my hands rose to land on his chest, and I whispered, "Yeah, I want to keep another secret with you."

Alex leaned in, slow and warm. He pressed the flat of his hand against my back, my arms wrapped around his neck, trying to get closer to him. His other hand dug into the hair at the nape of my neck, his fingers curling and loosening the tie holding my hair back.

Thunder boomed with lightning just behind it. Distantly, I could hear the sound of the heavy rain on the tin awning above the windows outside. I could *feel* the energy from the clouds above us, as if I was gathering power, pulling it from the air.

Alex's kisses changed.

Something charged between us the way it had in Magic Valley, building in intensity around us, but this time I was surrounded by the pulse of energy riding on electrical cords.

Air rushed into my lungs when he released my mouth, but he didn't stop kissing me. His lips touched the edge of my lips, the line of my jaw, the edge of my earlobe—until his lips found a sensational spot just behind my ear that sent a zing through my whole body. Thunder crashed just as the sky lit up outside through the windows of the room.

I was *everywhere*—the air, the walls and windows, the tables and chairs. My mutation looked for something to lock onto, something to travel on, and found the wires in the walls, which led to more wires, a highway for my power to ride on.

These weren't car alarms. This was a whole building. I'd never felt so alive, so aware of the world around me. I gasped when my mutation hit an invisible wall— free to disappear into the outside world in a sparkling explosion.

The hall light flickered off.

Alex paused, his chest heaving. He pulled away from me just an inch, and looked over at the window facing the hall. When his gaze found mine again, thunder boomed through the room. The lightning illuminated the lines of his face.

He gave me a boyish grin. "See? The storm will explain it."

I nodded, wide-eyed, trying to calm my breathing down.

"Are you okay?"

"Oh yes." I was telling the truth. Whatever had

happened with my mutation left me feeling warm and empty in a good way. "More than okay." My chest was tight, my hands framed his jaw, I tilted my head.

"What are you thinking?" He whispered.

"I'm trying to memorize this." I leaned up, taking a quick kiss. "I'm trying to memorize what it's like being this close to you."

He did the same to me, his palms flat on my cheeks, his thumbs brushing the hair back from my temples. "You know I'm going to do whatever it takes to keep you close, right?"

I opened my mouth, but laughter cut through the quiet. A locker opened and shut down the hall. I said, "We don't want to be late to class."

"No." He leaned forward, touching his forehead to mine. "We don't."

I gave him one more kiss before ducking under his arm. Seconds later, he fell into step next to me, adjusting his books at his side. I tried to look normal, pretending like I had no idea why the power was out in the entire building. I glanced up at Alex just as he ran his hand through his hair. He looked as dazed as I felt. I rounded the corner for class, knowing Alex was on my heels.

Once inside the classroom, I slid into my desk, covering my warm cheeks with my cool hands. The room was dark, save for a dim emergency light above the door.

Stephen hissed at me. "Where did you guys go?"

It was kind of funny that Stephen wasn't in on this particular mutant event, but I wasn't sure how I was going to explain everything to him. It wasn't like I'd be comfortable explaining to Stephen what it felt like for my mutation while making out with Alex Bailey, but I decided to think about it later.

Stephen glared past me at Alex.

Alex shrugged, looking deceptively chill.

I turned in my seat to grab my bag and get the study guide out for the history quiz on Friday, but it wasn't there. I stared into space for a long moment before I realized where my bag was. I leaned to whisper to Alex, he was opening up a required book for English. "I left my bag in the science lab."

Alex slid a notebook out from under his textbook. Then gave me a pen. He whispered, "Does that help?"

"Thanks." I mouthed the word, crossing my eyes, feeling flustered. I didn't have urgent homework so I could doodle in his notebook for the next fifty minutes with no problem.

Halfway into the homeroom period, the vice principal entered the classroom. He stood next to Mr. Garrison's desk. "School is going to be canceled today. The main power box is fried. The electrician we called in isn't sure how the storm could have done that, but he has to put in a rush order to replace the whole thing." He sighed, gesturing to all of us. "Call your parents. Buses will be here in twenty minutes. If anyone can't get a hold of their parents, come to the office and we'll assist you."

"Hey, that's cool." Stephen's eyebrows shot up. "Was that you?"

"I don't want to talk about it," I said, hugging Alex's notebook against my chest. "Maybe later."

Stephen followed close behind me through the classroom door into the hallway, his voice low as he spoke over my shoulder. "Are you aware that your hair is all messed up?"

My cheeks burned, I hadn't realized, but I didn't answer him. He was teasing me on purpose. I wasn't going to give him the satisfaction of watching me squirm.

The halls were full and a little chaotic. There was something urgent in the crowd because the dark halls were kind of a bizarre thing to walk through. Alex switched out his books at his locker and threw his backpack over his shoulder. No one knew it was me who'd messed up the school day, but I still couldn't help but be afraid I might be accused at any second. My mutation had made all this happen, and I wasn't sure how I felt about it.

Alex turned to me, holding out a wadded dark blue garment and letting it unwind in his hand. "Do you want my extra jacket? It's raining hard out there."

I blinked at him, surprised. "Uh, sure."

He swung the bomber jacket around my shoulders as I pulled my arms through. It was big on me, but it enveloped me in a comfortable and cozy way. He rested hands on my shoulders for a long second. "Keep it."

"Keep it?"

His smile was slow, reminding me of his kisses. "I like the way it looks on you."

"Okay."

I followed Stephen through the rowdy crowd of teenagers toward the main doors. Alex had a hold on the lower back of the jacket as if I were tugging him along with me.

I liked the feeling.

We climbed into the truck, I looked over at Alex, he bit down on his lower lip as he turned the key. He reached to check the heat again, his appreciative gaze ran up my legs, his jacket, and found my eyes. I realized I didn't mind his attention, he'd spent months learning my mind, and now I knew he was interested in the whole of who I was.

Alex laid his arm over the back of the seat as he reversed from the parking spot. We had to wait for other vehicles as we exited. I sunk into my seat and smiled brightly at him, trying to downplay what I felt so Stephen couldn't see it. I didn't mind if Alex saw it. He was mashing his lips together to suppress his own grin, the back of his neck flushing pink.

We drove through town in the rain and through the storm. Alex was careful, driving at a slower speed, with both his hands on the steering wheel. The rain was thick, it was hard to see beyond the car in front of us. I snuggled even deeper into Alex's jacket that smelled very much like him.

"Dang," Stephen said, jerking me from my hazy thoughts. "This storm is crazy." He leaned forward. "Got any more cookies, Jenny?".

"Yep." I went to reach for my bag. "Oh no."

"What?" Alex said.

"I left my bag in the science lab."

"Why is your bag in the science lab?" Stephen asked.

I felt a little bad that Stephen was not in the loop, but I didn't feel that bad. "It has something to do with the power going out. That's all I'm going to say."

"Oh. Wow." Stephen's teasing tone was there again. "Look at you two."

"Shut up." I glared at Stephen. "Mind your own business."

He wiggled his eyebrows at me. Alex pulled off the road and did a U-Turn. "We aren't far. We can go get it."

"Sorry. Thanks."

"No worries. Easy fix."

When we pulled up to the front of the school there were only three cars in the parking lot. The rain was still pounding on the asphalt.

"I'll get it for you—" Alex unbuckled his seat belt, but his phone buzzed on the seat between us. I could see from the screen it was his mom calling, she'd probably heard about the power outage somehow, and I also knew she got angry when he didn't answer her calls. "One minute."

He pressed the phone to his ear, but before a word left his mouth she asked if Stephen was there with him and demanded to be put on speakerphone so that he could listen to what she had to say too.

"Answer it," I said, for efficiency's sake. I knew sometimes it took several minutes for Alex to navigate conversations with his mom. "I'll be right back."

He went to argue, but I was already shutting the door. I glanced over my shoulder and found a disapproving expression on Alex's face through the truck's window. I waved him off and jogged a little faster, dodging puddles as I went.

I didn't know I would look back on that decision for the rest of my life and wonder why I didn't wait to let Alex go in and get my bag for me. I was a powerful mutant, but I couldn't see into the future or change the past.

25.

THE SCHOOL FELT eerily empty.

With her back to me, I spotted a secretary in the administrative office picking up her purse and getting ready to leave. I dug my hands into Alex's jacket pockets and tried to keep a quick pace. I wanted to get back to Alex and Stephen so we could talk about the fun we were going to have instead of being in school.

When I pushed through the science classroom door, I stopped to find Brandon, Aiden, Ryan, and Emma sitting around a long stainless-steel table. Three kinds of alcohol sat on the table. Bunsen burners lit around them like candles, giving the room soft light. Someone must have said something funny seconds before I'd walked in because they were all laughing, but it was Brandon who caught sight of me first.

He half stood. "It's Jenny Philips. What's up?"

"You guys look like you're having fun," I said with a tight smile, trying to hide how unsteady I felt as Brandon's eyes lit up with interest.

"Come hang out with us." Ryan lifted the beer in his hand.

I picked up my bag. "No, thanks."

Aiden groaned. "She's gonna snitch."

"I don't care what you do." I shrugged, turning to open the door.

"No, really." Quick footsteps made me pause. I looked over my shoulder as Ryan slid between me and the door. "Let me pour you a drink."

Deadpan, I said, "I'm not staying."

I wasn't going to play this game. I reached around him to grab the door handle. Ryan slid a step, blocking the handle. "I mean, it's not like we have to be at school."

The blinds over the windows looking into the hall nearby whispered with subtle movement as my mutation perked up.

"What are you doing?" I said, every muscle in my body tightened. "Get out of my way."

"I think you should hang out with us."

"Well, I'm not going to." I rolled my eyes and stepped closer, trying to show him how serious I was. The smell of alcohol on his breath hit me—It was something stronger than beer, more like the whisky my dad occasionally drank when I was growing up. "Move, Ryan."

"What if I don't want to move?" A smile grew on his lips. "Just chill, hang out with us."

"Bro, stop," Aiden said, I turned to find a scowl on his face. "She doesn't want to stay."

My gaze flickered to Brandon, expecting him to agree with Aiden.

"I don't know," A cold chill spread across my skin as I watched Brandon smirk. "I thought we were going to find a time to hangout. Why not now?"

Emma's mouth was half open, her eyes darting between me and Brandon, as if she was deciding if she was comfortable with what was happening or not.

I didn't have the patience for stupidity. I reached for the handle again as he shifted on his foot to block me.

Before my shoulder touched his, an invisible explosion of air and electricity shoved us apart. My ankles tangled together. I twisted at the waist to catch myself, but my temple slammed into the sharp edge of the counter next to us. I fell on my side, landing heavily on my hip against the yellow linoleum floor.

When I looked up, I found Ryan on his back, staring at me. He knew something crazy happened between us, but I managed to stare back without giving him a hint of confirmation about his suspicion.

"Oh my god—You can't just grab her like that," Emma said just as Aiden stood and said, "Bro, help her up."

My fear turned brittle and empty. I wasn't going to allow anybody to push me around. I reached for my bag and shot to my feet. My only focus would be to get to Alex and Stephen. From there I would decide how I would explain to them what happened, hoping I could manage to keep them from coming back to start something with Brandon.

The most important thing was to get out of this school.

"Just a minute," I blinked to find Brandon had taken Ryan's position at the door. "All we wanted was you to sit with us, Jenny. What happened with Ryan just now was an accident. Now sit for a minute."

Ryan stood, dusting himself off as his gaze narrowed on me, but then his face fell, his attention darting to Brandon with an expression I didn't understand.

"I'm all done here." I huffed, looking up at Brandon, but my mind caught up to the sharp pain along my temple, and a foreign warmth trailed down my cheek. My hand trembled as I touched where I'd hit my head, finding blood on my fingers.

"You're bleeding," Emma slid off the stool she sat on, her gaze scanning the room. "We need to get her a paper towel—"

"Sit down Emma." Brandon's deeper voice interrupted.

Emma stiffened, shock twisted her face as she used the same *mean girl* tone she'd used with me the day we'd met in the girl's bathroom. "Excuse me? Who do you think—"

"*Shut up.*" I flinched as he snapped at her, his voice ripping through the room. "You talk *so much*, Emma. Just be quiet for two minutes."

Whatever game Ryan and Brandon wanted to play wasn't a game anymore. The air grew heavy with something more sinister as thunder rolled through the sky in the distance outside. I held my breath, hoping Brandon would laugh and tell us he was joking.

But no one spoke as Brandon stared at Emma. Ryan and Aiden stood frozen too, their eyebrows pulled together as they glanced at each other. I realized too many seconds had passed for this to be a joke, and no one in the room was going to stand up to Brandon to help me.

"Alex and Stephen are outside."

"I'll bet they are." Brandon's attention turned on me as he folded his arms across his broad chest, squaring his shoulders to face me, making it clear I wasn't leaving until he was ready to let me go. "And I'll bet you'll run to Alex and tell him that blood on your face is my fault. Then he'll come looking for me, won't he?"

"No," Tears stung at the edges of my eyes. "I won't tell him I saw you, I promise."

"You know, we had a great time at the dance. I was patient. I didn't push you to go to the hotel with me afterward."

"Please, just—"

"You ignored me, Jenny. You went back to hiding behind Alex Bailey. You didn't give me a chance. You didn't even want to be my friend." He tilted his head. "Why didn't you text me back on your birthday?"

I couldn't find the ability to speak, I wanted to say the right thing to get him to let me leave, but nothing came to mind. I could only wrap myself again and again around my mutation, gripping onto it tightly.

Aiden cleared his throat. "Bro, we should really—"

"Alex Bailey and Stephen Wright are coming." Brandon said, not taking his eyes off me. "What do you think, Ryan? Should we have some fun?"

"Sure man," Ryan said, but I could hear the faintest tremble in his voice. "Let's have some fun."

Brandon pulled a gun from the back waist of his pants.

"What are you doing?" I gasped, my eyes locked on the weapon. "Put that away."

"Teaching Alex and Stephen a lesson." He pointed

the gun toward the windows facing the hallway, squinting and playing with the adjustment of it in his hands. "I'm sure they'll be here soon."

"This is not a joke," I said, glancing at Emma again. She'd covered her mouth with her hand and sat back down on the stool, tears pooled in her eyes. "Brandon, just chill, just put it away."

He *tsked* with a shake of his head. "But Jenny, you didn't answer my question."

Electricity built in my spine, I realized my life and Emma's was worth the risk of my secrets. I decided to call his bluff. I had to believe that Brandon wouldn't use the gun. I would do what I needed to do to get through the door—kick and scream and scratch. If I was wild and loud enough, I could distract them all with my mutation's help.

My decision made, I lifted my hands slowly, embracing the invisible sparks dancing on my palms—

Something in the weapon clicked, the sound smothering the rhythmic connection to my mutation, Brandon aimed the gun at my heart. "I don't want to keep repeating myself. It'd be real smart if you listened to me, Jenny."

But I couldn't bring myself to obey, the walls groaned quietly as the pressure of my mutation expanded into the room, drowning in the sound of the rain beating down on the tin awning outside. The rest of the world faded away. It was only Brandon and me. He took a step toward me, and with it I took a step back—he took another step, and another, until I was pressed against the end of a cold, stainless steel table. He wasn't more than a foot away from where I stood.

I weighed my options and decided if I couldn't figure out how to get away, then I'd help the others by bargaining with him. "Okay, let Emma and the guys leave, and we can talk—"

"Jenny?" Stephen said as he opened the door behind Brandon.

He stopped when he caught sight of us, his eyes widening.

Alex ran into the back of him. "Bro."

Annoyed, he moved around Stephen. I watched as they both took in the alcohol. The others in the room. Brandon and me.

"Oh, shit," Stephen blurted, raising his hands slowly when they spotted the gun in Brandon's hand.

Rage flickered to life in Alex's eyes when he registered the blood on my face. He took a rushed step toward us, but his boot screeched against the floor when Brandon lifted the gun again on me, emphasizing the power he held in the room.

"Alex—" Ryan said with a panicked high-pitched

crack in his voice. "Listen to Brandon."

"It's okay, he's just messing with us." I held up a trembling hand, turning to Brandon. "Right?"

"I don't have a plan." Brandon's tone was bored. "Just having fun."

I gave Stephen the smallest glance, finding focus in his expression, the readiness to help Alex. But hatred that I'd never seen before danced in Alex's eyes.

His mutation subtly rippled through his muscles under his shirt. I wasn't sure if I was the only one who could see the veins in his neck and arms slowly swell. He was a force of tension and strength, a different kind of potential than my own mutation.

I whispered to Brandon, "What do you want? Do you want them to leave? I'll stay, I'll drink, I'll do whatever you want—"

"No." Thunder boomed, and a bolt of lightning flashed through the windows outside with Alex's command. My stomach jumped into my throat. He dared to take another step. This time no one moved. "Let her leave. Let her go with Emma. If you want to settle something between us, then let's do it."

"I'm just deciding what I want." Brandon twisted his mouth as he dragged his eyes from my head to my shoes, and back up again. "I mean, I think there's an opportunity here. I think I'll take Jenny's offer. She and

I can go on a drive." He smiled, his dimple appeared, but I knew what laid behind the mask now. "I promise I won't hurt you. I just never got my date. I think I'll take it now. I can finally show you what a great guy I am."

He reached for me, but I jerked away. "Don't touch me."

"I'll kill you, Brandon." Alex grit through his teeth. "I swear it."

"Come on, Brandon." Stephen's spoke, but it was level, reason ringing through his words. "It's not too late to let us walk out of here. The consequences for taking Jenny are so much bigger than just letting us all go right now."

"Ryan, Aiden," Brandon said, his dimple disappeared. "There's rope in that drawer from the pulley system project we worked on last week. Tie Bailey and Wright up."

Aiden shook his head. "Brandon—"

"Do it," Brandon snapped, pointing his gun squarely at me again.

My hand twitched as Aiden and Ryan began to obey Brandon. I tried to say no, to beg or plead, but I only made an airy sound I didn't recognize.

Aiden's hands shook as he opened the drawer and handed a coil of rope to Ryan. Ryan approached Stephen first. Stephen eyed me as he slowly brought his hands around his back.

Aiden came to do the same to Alex, but Alex wasn't moving. Alex was like a muscled statue in a museum, as if he were made of marbled stone—as if he could stay in this standoff with Brandon for centuries before he gave in.

"You know," Brandon swung the gun to point at Alex. "I'm realizing now the key to fixing all of my problems is just getting rid of you."

I wanted to scream at Alex, but my voice wouldn't work. I willed him to listen. I pushed every ounce of my focus and energy and the magic my mutation had given me toward him. My thoughts shouted at him.

Listen. Listen. Listen. I'm begging you. He'll shoot you.

Blue eyes whipped to mine. He'd heard me.

26.

MY MUTATION had always been drawn to Alex, like the pull of magnets. I was the thunder and lightning in the sky, creating invisible ribbons of power and light, a highway for our mutations to connect. Alex was the earth, able to absorb and ground the threat of me in a way no other human could.

Drop to the ground. His thoughts were an echoing deep velvet sound, crisp and sure. His voice in my head was just like the way he kissed my lips, sweet and tense all at once. *Understand?*

Got it. My own voice echoed in my head, like speaking into a long, dark cave.

Alex finally let Aiden tie his hands behind his back, but I caught the exchange between Alex and Stephen, a quick nod backed by sixteen years of brotherhood.

Brandon jerked the gun, gesturing for me to walk toward the door. "Let's go, sweetheart."

I couldn't imagine what Brandon was thinking, just like I wouldn't have dreamed I'd find him here pointing his gun at me. I didn't know if Brandon planned to hurt me, or not hurt me and torture Alex while he took me somewhere.

I wasn't going to find out.

"No."

A gust of air encircled Brandon, tripping him backward. A second pulse of my power pushed his elbow upward, forcing the gun to point toward the ceiling. Trying to do as Alex instructed, I dropped to the ground with a grunt, my ribs taking a hard hit as they made contact with the floor.

Alex's arms sprang outward from behind.

The rope was a silly form of restraint for the strongest man in the world. He shoved a hand into Aiden's chest, sending him backward into the wooden cabinets in a force so hard the wooden doors split. Aiden's body landed in a heap of stillness.

In the same second, Stephen freed his wrists from the rope with a little hiss of heat, the ends severed in a clean line that glowed red as they fell to the ground. A whiff of burning synthetic plastic filled the room. He turned to Ryan with a flash of his fiery hands, creating a bright and blinding distraction as Alex moved.

Lightning lit up the room again through the windows as Alex charged Brandon, running into his middle. They both crashed into a stainless steel table, pushing it into other tables, creating a burst of metal clanging that mixed with Emma's scream. Bottles shattered onto the floor. Bunsen burners extinguished as they slid and fell, plunging the room into a sudden darkness.

The gun popped, the sound echoed through the room, through my entire world. I lunged forward, sure that Alex had been shot, but the gun clattered away from Brandon and Alex.

Stephen caught me at the waist and held me against his chest. He grunted, pulling me toward the door, his gentle heat washing over me. "Jenny—Run. Go. Now."

Alex gripped Brandon's shirt with one hand, his shoulders moved in an unnatural ripple as he raised his elbow to throw a punch. The audible crack of bone twisted in my stomach. Stephen tumbling behind me into the door with my mutation's supernatural push was a faraway thought in my mind.

Alex was punching Brandon. His punches were too much. The hits were too hard. He was going to kill Brandon.

Alex. I shouted, or whispered, I didn't know which, but my inner voice was like smoke filling a room, consuming both of our thoughts. *Stop.*

My mutation moved the air, willing it into action. Windows shattered—all of them at once—a million small pieces of glass rained down around us, but it wasn't enough to stop Alex.

I had to do something else. I had to do something more—

Alex's arm halted mid-punch, his muscles strained against an invisible hold. My mutation wrapped around his biceps, keeping his arm frozen in the air. It was easy, too easy, for my mutation to stop the strongest man in the world from throwing the deadly punch.

"Come on," I said, trying to take a step toward them, but Stephen's heated hand wrapped around my upper arm. His body shook with restraint against his own mutation. "Let's go. Please let's go."

Alex grunted when my wind knocked him off Brandon. He rolled to his side, looking up at me with something crazed in his eyes before he pushed off the ground. I vaguely registered the blood soaking into his shirt at his side. Alex glanced back at Brandon's limp body for only a second.

But I didn't want to look too closely, I didn't want to know if he were dead or alive. "Come with me."

Stephen's grip loosened on my arm as Alex reached out to take my hand, pulling me with him through the door. Stephen followed behind, a gentle wash of heat along my back.

We made it several yards down the hall when I said, "Emma."

Alex blinked at me as if his mind were beginning to uncloud after attacking Brandon, and he looked at Stephen. Stephen was already turning on his heel to go back for Emma.

But Ryan stood in the middle of the hallway, pointing Brandon's gun in our direction with a shaking hand.

Stephen's voice was even as he said, "Just let us get Emma, that's all."

Alex stepped in front of me.

"What was that? With your hands…" He said, swinging the aim of the weapon between Alex and Stephen. "The fire came from nowhere."

"Calm down, Ryan." Stephen held up two hands. "We can talk about all of this."

"And I *know* you did something in there, Jenny." He said as I took in the paleness of his cheeks, his lips a ghostly white. I realized he was terrified, but it wasn't of Brandon, it was of us. "You're a freak," He spat out. "You're all freaks."

Time slowed as I squeezed my eyes shut because now Ryan knew about our mutations. I always knew we were bound to be sideshow freaks. It had always been our destiny. Our lives were about to change forever.

My mutation built inside me again—anticipating, coiling, and threatening to do something that would overwhelm my control.

Brandon strode through the science doorway into the hall, his face gushing blood that dripped down his T-shirt. He dragged Emma by the hand with him. In a blink, he grabbed the gun from Ryan, shoving him aside.

"We weren't done." Brandon stalked toward us. Alex pushed me a few steps back, but Brandon was there several feet in front of us now, holding Emma against himself.

"Brandon," Stephen said. "For real man, don't be stupid. Just let Emma come with us."

Brandon jerked the gun and pointed it at Alex.

"Here we have Hollow Brook's darling, sweet little Alex Bailey. Self-righteous prick thinking he can do no wrong. I know you've got everyone fooled." Brandon moved a step, catching my eye while keeping his gun pointed at Alex. "Especially her." He shook his head, giving us an empty smile. "I don't know why Jenny hasn't seen right through you. Everyone knows how controlling and manipulative you are with her. Everyone knows that you're desperate and won't let anyone near her. There's something weird about you three and no one says anything. No one questions it. Nobody wonders why Jenny worships the ground you walk on."

Brandon tilted the gun, raising it to aim at the center of Alex's forehead.

"But I could, I think," Brandon shoved Emma away. She crumpled to her knees. Her crying was quiet and pitiful, making me feel sick. "I think I could go to prison for the rest of my life knowing that you're dead."

Time warped and wrapped around me again, and I took control as Brandon pulled the trigger, releasing my mutation to do its work. My mutation shoved Ryan and Emma in opposite directions. They slid against the smooth yellow linoleum floor, away from Brandon.

"You're done, Brandon," I said in a strange, strangled voice.

Wind whipped around us, the air was mine to manipulate, creating a hollow sound in my ears. White sparks of light snapped from my fingers. I funneled everything in me through my mutation to stop and distract—to take the authority I wanted.

My mutation tore violently through the hallway.

Bam. Bam. Bam. Bam. Bam—

Locker after locker flung open around us like a tsunami crashing over the shore in a storm. Papers and books flew around us. Jackets and bags thrown upward with my mutation's wind. Shards of glass whirled around us as they glinted with the green emergency lights above the classroom doors. Metal slammed into metal—a horrifying rhythmic boom.

Brandon and I stood in the center of my storm. His arms raised above his head to protect himself, but when we met eyes I knew he understood he was no longer in control, we both knew he no longer held the gun.

The world turned quiet again.

It was a long silence before Stephen whispered, "Drop the bullet, Jenny."

I looked down at my hands in confusion, finding them empty of any bullets.

"It's okay," Alex said from my other side, but I didn't understand his careful tone. "It's over now. You did good."

I blinked, then blinked again as I realized the bullet meant for Alex hovered in the air above the ground halfway between Brandon and me. It turned in place with a slow rotation, as if waiting for my instruction. At my feet laid the handgun, my mutation had brought it to me, setting it at my feet like a gift.

With half a thought, the bullet dropped to the ground.

My attention jerked toward Brandon falling onto his knees, palms laying flat on the ground as he drew ragged breaths in and out again. A second later my legs buckled under me too.

Alex caught me by the arm, it was an awkward hold, but he shifted to help me settle on my knees. He faced me, squatting down to meet my eyes. My mutation sent an apologetic breeze around us, my hair whispered across my face as I held Alex's gaze with my own.

They know about me. I didn't have to tell him this was my nightmare because it was his, too. *They know about me, Alex.*

Alex leaned forward and kissed my forehead. He let go of my arms to turn and run into a locker with his shoulder, creating an outrageous dent. He ripped a locker door off its hinges. The only sound in the room was his bootsteps as he came to stand in the center of the hallway. He dropped to one knee, throwing a single punch to the linoleum floor, a plume of white dust bursting around him. The ground was an empty crater of damaged concrete when he lifted his fist.

Brandon, Ryan, and Emma knew about Alex now too. They're expressions matched with opened mouths and wide eyes. I realized I'd never seen terror so pure before.

Stephen lifted his hands, turning his palms upward. His brows went up and his grin was a bit mad as his arms lit on fire. Balls of flame hovered in the air before him, glinting against his dark eyes. I caught something that was almost like pride in his expression, because we'd earned the control we each held over our mutations. He was unafraid and brilliantly blazing for us all.

Now they knew all three of us were mutants.

Sideshow freaks.

I flinched when Alex moved, surprising me as he walked toward Brandon, stopping where the bullet laid. He was like a Greek god standing in the midst of a ruined battlefield, the damage of what he and I had inflicted surrounding him.

"We're going to walk out of here. Emma is going with us. You will never speak of what you saw today, or I will come for you." He looked over at Ryan too, making it clear he was talking to them both. Aiden hadn't emerged from the classroom. The last I'd seen him he'd been on the ground in the science room. "I'll slam my fist into your face once, and this time you'll be dead."

"I'll be there, too." Stephen took a step forward. I raised my arm to cover my eyes as his dancing flames pulsed in a white explosion around him, disappearing just as fast as he closed his hands. "We'll drag your bodies to a field, and I'll light you up until you're nothing but ashes. It'll be easy. You never should have messed with Jenny Philips."

Alex turned, coming back to me, but he paused to pick up the gun. He stared at the weapon for a long second.

"I hate guns, I always have." He looked up at Brandon with icy blue eyes. "Everybody loves them in this town. I never knew why I didn't like them." He glanced back at me, taking in the way I knelt on the ground.

I'd walked into school, thinking I was safe, but I hadn't been safe at all. "I know why I hate them now."

Alex unloaded the gun, pocketing the bullets. Using two hands, he ripped the gun in half as if it were a piece of paper before handing the two pieces to Stephen. Stephen stared at Brandon as the gun melted through his fingers, dripping to the ground with a silvery, sizzling effect. Stephen shook his hands clean of the molten metal.

"Emma, come on, let's go."

Emma whimpered, half stumbling into Stephen as she rushed to him. He wrapped an arm around her and pulled out his phone. He held up the back of the phone to face Brandon and Ryan.

He snapped a picture, the image would reveal Brandon and Ryan, framed by the rubble around them. Evidence, I realized, if they betrayed us.

Without a word Alex bent to lift me into his arms, marching down the hall like a storm clearing from the sky. We didn't stop until we came to his truck. Alex's movements were gentle as he pulled the lap belt across my chest. Stephen opened the door, helping Emma slide into the backseat with him.

Alex peeled out of the parking lot, turning in the opposite direction of our farms. He was heading toward the forested hills. I turned to survey Stephen to make sure he and Emma were okay. Seeing they were unharmed, I turned to Alex.

"You're bleeding—" I gasped, reaching for him.

Alex lifted his arm as I pushed up his shirt. "No, I'm not bleeding—"

I pulled his shirt up to find where the bullet had entered through the fabric. His skin was smooth, smeared with blood, but there wasn't a wound of any kind. I looked up at him. I couldn't form the words to ask the questions I wanted to ask. Alex took my hand from his side, turning his eyes back to the road, and kissed my fingers. "I'm all right."

Emma's voice was small. "Where are we going?"

I sat back, but nausea rolled in my stomach. I leaned forward, grabbing Alex's backpack on the floor. I dumped the contents and vomited into the bag. Alex reached over as he drove, scooping up my hair and gathering it at the back of my head, letting me lose what was in my stomach into his bag again.

"What's wrong with her?" Emma asked.

Stephen shushed her. "We'll get to that. Just wait."

27.

THIRTY MINUTES LATER, Alex pulled into a muddy parking lot. Wooden picnic tables scattered around the area with basic coal grills for barbecuing. Pine trees thickly knit together circled the area. The space was meant for picnicking in the day, but no one would come here during a storm.

Alex got out of the truck, the vehicle shook back and forth when he slammed the door shut. He strode toward a larger picnic area with a dozen tables. It was meant for group events, and was the only place shielded from the rain by a tin roof.

"I guess this is where he wants to talk," Stephen said with a long sigh. "Jenny, are you okay?"

I watched Alex pace, muttering to himself and shaking his head.

"We need to help Alex." I pulled my seatbelt off and opened the door.

I took Alex's backpack in my hand and chucked it into a trashcan nearby, deciding I'd find a way to buy him a new one. I hugged his jacket around myself and joined him. He didn't stop pacing. Stephen came to stand next to me, shoving his hands in his pants pockets. Emma followed a few feet behind him, her brown freckles prominent against her pale face.

Stephen sat on one of the picnic tables. "What do you need, Alex?"

"Why." He stopped abruptly, looking at his best friend. "I need to know why."

Stephen's shoulders slumped. "I don't know."

Alex threw his hands up. "What did I do wrong?"

"Nothing," Stephen said quietly. "You didn't do anything wrong."

I sat on a picnic table bench near where Alex stood, dropping my gaze to my lap. I didn't know what to say. Alex squatted in front of me and reached up to hold my face. "I'm so sorry, Jenny."

I wrapped my hand around his wrist. "It's not your fault."

"I know, but I…" He shook his head, the words he wanted to say didn't come. Alex sat next to me, looking over at Stephen. "What do you know about those guys with Brandon?"

"Ryan is the one who saw our mutations," I said. "The other was Aiden." My gaze whipped to Alex. "Aiden never came out of the classroom."

Alex leaned forward to drop his face in his hands.

"He's fine," Stephen said, his eyes swinging to where Alex parked the truck, eyeing the little dirt road that led to the highway. "He probably just got knocked out, or maybe he was hiding or something." Alex looked up at Stephen with a sharp question in his eyes, as if asking him what we would do if Aiden wasn't okay. Stephen shook his head. "Don't go there, Alex. We need to assume he's okay."

Alex pressed, "What are we going to do if he's—"

"No," Stephen said, his tone hard and sure. "Don't say it, don't talk about it. I'll text people. I'll find out when we get back. We'll deal with the problem if there is one."

I could see that Alex wanted to push it, the guilt was already threatening to drown him, but he gave Stephen a nod instead.

"Mark and Mandy blocked Brandon's phone number." Emma wiped tears as they fell. "They blocked him on everything. You know, since the four-wheeler incident. I think he might have got kicked off the baseball team. He's been hanging out with Ryan and Aiden for the last few days. Brandon and I—We've been hanging out for a while now."

Stephen studied her with furrowed brows for a long moment before he turned back to Alex. "They'll stay quiet. We have dirt on them. They have the dirt on us. That was a good move you made, Alex."

"You did a good job too," Emma said, clearing her throat. "I mean, with taking the picture."

Stephen shrugged. "Anyway, if they talk, who is going to believe them?"

Alex's jaw ticked. "It was make a deal or kill him. Literally."

"You weren't going to kill him," I argued, drawing back to face Alex squarely.

"If you hadn't stopped me, I would have—"

"We never found out because she stopped you." I could see Stephen was trying to help Alex, keep him from falling apart. "And I wouldn't have blamed you if you had."

"Don't say that." I scowled at Stephen.

Stephen glared back at me, but fear flitted across his face too. "He held a gun on you. Hell, he was trying to kidnap you. What else do you think we were going to do?"

"Not kill anyone." I rubbed my face, exhaustion was beginning to settle into my muscles. "We aren't out here fighting crime. We don't use our mutations. We manage them."

Stephen rolled his eyes but didn't say more.

Alex huffed a humorless laugh, shaking his head.

I knew Alex was taking on the brunt of the blame. I replayed it all in my head again. It was Alex who Brandon was trying to hurt. Holding the gun on me, threatening to take me, it'd all been to punish Alex for the past. The day Alex punched Brandon at the waterhole over me was the day he made his bully feel small. But it wasn't all Alex's fault, we'd all played a part when it came to Brandon.

"I exploded." I said, turning to Alex. "You had to make a deal with them because I exploded."

"I moved first." Alex reached for me, pulling me against his side, wrapping his arm around my waist. "I exposed us first when I took Aiden down the way I did."

"That could have been explained." Stephen blew out a long breath. "He could have fallen just right, or whatever. I used heat to get Ryan out of the way. I was trying to throw Brandon off for you."

"We always said we were in this together." Alex looked from me to Stephen. "We always promised to reveal everything together."

Our attention drifted to Emma.

She shivered as she rubbed her arms to warm herself. Her pale pink cardigan wasn't any thicker than my shirt. The rain still poured in the mud puddles around us, and the cold was creeping over my skin.

I couldn't sort out how I felt about Emma Henderson knowing our secret. The thought of Emma having any kind of upper hand over me was sharp and brittle in my chest. Despite the resentment I felt, I said, "Are you okay, Emma?"

"Brandon is going to be able to go to school again," Emma said through a shiver, I wondered if her trembling was more from the cold, or the shock. "What does that mean? And…what are you guys?"

"We don't know, we just know what we can do." Stephen lifted his hand until his palm faced upward. A globe of flame ignited, growing to the size of a basketball between the four of us, but he was offering more than what we could see. The warmth of his mutation washed over my face, quickly spreading to the rest of my body. Emma's shivering calmed and her shoulders relaxed, the color in her cheeks returned to normal. Stephen closed his hand, but I could feel the warmth he'd left generating off his body to maintain a comfortable temperature for us. "We just know that we ate strawberries on the farm behind Jenny's farm. We all got sick like we had food poisoning and within a couple of weeks, the three of us were different from everybody else."

"We call them mutations," Alex said. "We nick-named ourselves mutants."

"That's the story." Stephen shrugged again. "It happened just before school started last year. It's grown inside of us. We've practiced controlling it. It's part of us now. Just the three of us know about it. Until today."

Emma blinked. "It's hard to take in."

"Oh, we know." Alex let out a shaky laugh. "It's hard to live with it."

"What are you going to do now that I know?"

"We aren't going to do anything." Stephen sat next to her. "But we do need you to keep this a secret. It's our lives. Can you do that?"

Emma's eyes widened. I could see the fear still lingering in her expression. "Do I have a choice?"

"Yes," Stephen gave me a sharp look, I added, "You do have a choice. We would be forever grateful if you decided to take this to the grave with you, but Alex isn't going to punch your face in. Stephen isn't going to light you on fire. And you'll never see my mutation explode like that again either. I know you won't forget what you saw, but we'll never hurt you. We promise that."

"We absolutely promise that," Alex said.

Stephen nodded, his voice softening. "We would never hurt you."

"Okay, so what are your… What can you do?"

"You know what I can do with the fire," Stephen said, snapping his fingers to show off again with a little flame. "Alex has crazy strength. And Jenny—" Stephen smiled. "Jenny is magical."

Emma bit the inside of her cheek. I couldn't do anything else for Emma, she'd have to decide how she was going to handle our mutations just as we had last fall. I leaned into Alex, resting my temple on his shoulder, but I winced and reached up to touch a tender spot along my hairline.

"Damn," Alex pushed my hair back. "You might need stitches."

"I don't need stitches," I said, leaning away. "It stopped bleeding. I just need somewhere to clean up."

"We should watch her," Alex said to Stephen, ignoring me. "What do you do if you think someone has a concussion?"

"I don't know." Stephen rubbed his face. "But we can't bring her to Grandpa without an explanation."

Emma stood up and leaned forward to look at my forehead. "We can go to my house. My parents are both at work. We can look up how to treat a concussion and ice it. I can give her a haircut to cover it up." She gestured to Alex. "There's a donation box in my garage my mom hasn't taken yet. She's getting rid of some of my dad's old T-shirts. They'll be small on you, but you could clean up and at least go home in a shirt that isn't covered in blood."

My eyes ran over Alex, a new shirt for him was probably a good idea.

Alex narrowed his eyes. "What do you want to do, Jenny Philips?"

"You need a shirt." I shrugged. "I could use a haircut."

Stephen shrugged too. "And, most important, I want lunch." Stephen's inappropriately timed humor drew a small smile from me. He winked at me, knowing he'd won a small victory with my quiet snort. Alex didn't think Stephen was funny, nor did he like the plan.

But, he nodded, it was the best solution for now.

28.

MMA HELPED clean me up.

I sat on a kitchen chair while she stood behind me brushing out my hair in her parent's master bathroom. "You just needed some foundation. Also, I'll give you a little bit of a bang and some layers to cover the cut."

I cringed. "Not too short."

Emma was one of us now. We'd talked in the truck on the way here. She knew our secret. She promised to keep it. I'd decided to trust her with my life, but I wasn't sure if I was ready to trust her with my hair.

"Not shorter." Emma tilted her head. "Your hair is so pretty, Jenny. It's thick and healthy. But it could use a little life and lift."

"Okay." I drew in a deep breath, bracing myself. "It'll grow back."

Emma laughed, "Yes, it will. But trust me, I can do this. I've been doing my mom's hair for years. Meg and Suzy's too."

"Okay." I said, taking another deep breath. "I believe you."

Emma laughed softly and started to slowly cut my hair little by little. It was quiet. The images of what we'd just been through kept flipping through my head. My school bag, Brandon, Ryan, Aiden, the gun. Alex punching Brandon. Stephen's fiery hands. My mutation. The glass shattering and the way it'd turned the hallway into a tornado—

The way I'd held Alex back from killing Brandon.

I had to stop my thoughts. Something Emma had just said made me ask, "Where are Meg and Suzy?"

Emma eyed the ends of my hair as she pulled them up and clipped them. "They moved away."

"Moved away?"

"Yep, moved far, far away." She kept cutting, not looking at me. "I'm trying to slide into Mandy's group, but Brandon ruined that with his drunken four-wheeler stunt."

"Why are you still hanging out with him?"

"I don't know." She stopped, meeting my eyes through the mirror. "I mean, I guess I do. Meg and Suzy moved away. I hadn't been hanging out with Brandon long enough to be accepted into Mandy's group. I've been a nightmare to every girl in our class for years. It's a small school. No one is going to give me a helping hand in the small social world of Hollow Brook High. Brandon was basically what was left for me."

"Oh." I didn't know what to say. I knew Emma probably didn't want my pity, but I couldn't think of something kind to say to her either. Our relationship had been complex since the first day she tried to bully me in the girl's bathroom, but now she knew about our mutations, and she needed a friend. I didn't want to admit that there was someone real under Emma Henderson's red hair and cold personality.

Absently, she said, "You're definitely the prettiest girl I've ever met."

"I bet." I rolled my eyes.

"There's something about you," Emma brushed out my hair, parting it a different way. "You're like a Disney princess or something."

I snorted. "I heard you call me that behind my back."

"I said it sarcastically before, but people just like you, it's hard to spread rumors about you." She laughed. "I mean, I'm not stupid, I've created the monster that I am knowingly. I'm the evil queen of Hollow Brook High."

I frowned, Emma wasn't my favorite person, but I didn't want her to beat herself up. "Emma, you're not—"

"I'm being honest when I say I prefer it." She pointed at me with her scissors. "But you? You sort of sparkle when you walk through the halls. You're all long legs, cute little butt, and perfectly proportioned boobs. Alluring brown eyes, straight pretty nose, and sports illustrated model lips—You know, Disney princess."

"Stop it." My mouth fell open, but laughter escaped. "Just stop talking."

There was no apology in her expression. "As I said, I know who I am. But I don't think you have any idea how people perceive you. I don't think you know who you are, what power you could have over people."

I opened my mouth again, but wasn't sure what I was going to say when Stephen pushed open the door and sat on the bathroom counter to watch. "How do you know how to do that?"

"I'm naturally good at hair and makeup. I want to own a beauty salon someday."

"Oh. That's cool." Stephen kept watching.

Alex had been cleaning up the lunch mess we'd made earlier in the kitchen, he came to lean in the doorway. "What's going on in here?"

I glanced up at him, smiling. "Well, as you can see, I'm getting a haircut." Emma was at the back of my head now and so I pushed my new subtle bangs forward. "See? No cuts."

Alex frowned, nodded, and left the room.

I looked at Stephen. "It's not the most fun haircut I've ever had, I guess."

"I'll go check on him," Stephen said, jumping off the counter. "He's going to carry this thing on those big shoulders of his forever if I don't talk him through it."

I was grateful we had Stephen. "Thank you."

He gave me a grin in reply before he left.

"I don't agree. This is totally fun." Emma waved a hand in the air. "It's to cover your dramatic wound, but also you are going to love this when I'm done." She pushed hair over my shoulders. "See how it changes your face? It gives those cheekbones of yours definition. Everything is a little sharper about your features."

I ran my fingers through my hair, playing with it. "I actually like it."

"Good." Emma laughed, but then we met eyes through the reflection, something shifting between us. I'd learned more about Emma in the last fifteen minutes than I'd learned in the last year of knowing her.

I turned to Emma and hugged her. "Thank you so much."

She was stiff at first, but then she hugged me back. "Thank you for being nice to me right now."

Emma began to clean and pack her things that were

laid out all over the counter. I found Stephen rifling through the fridge in the kitchen. "Where's Alex?"

"We talked," Stephen said as he spread peanut butter across a slice of bread. "It was good. He's frustrated, but mostly just worried about you. He's on the back porch."

"Oh. Okay."

Stephen smiled at me. "I like your hair like that."

"Thanks. I should leave Alex alone, huh?"

Stephen jerked his chin toward the sliding glass doors leading to the backyard. "No, go talk to him. He needs you."

I grabbed Alex's bomber jacket from the back of the couch and slid it on. I found Alex sitting on a cushioned porch swing under an awning. It was the only piece of furniture that wasn't wet from the rain.

I sat next to him and looked over the yard as he pushed the swing with his foot gently. Emma's mom had a big garden and a water feature in the middle. Beyond that was a spacious lawn until it met a wooded area.

We were quiet for a long time. I didn't know if Alex wanted to talk or just sit here with me. Finally, he said, "I wish I had made so many different decisions this morning."

"None of this was your fault, Alex."

"Maybe if I hadn't snuck you off into an empty classroom so I could make out with you, you wouldn't have forgotten your bag and the lights wouldn't have gone out. Then they wouldn't have been messing around in the science lab. And I knew, I had a gut feeling that I should have gone in there to get your bag for you, and I don't know why the hell I didn't."

I sighed. "Alex—"

"It's all just playing in my head over and over again. All I can see is Brandon holding that gun on you." He looked at me, his eyes shining, tears on the verge of spilling over the rim of his eyelids. "I can't get over it. I never will."

I thought I might drown in his bright blue eyes, but he'd always found a way to hold me up when I'd felt lost. What Brandon had put us through was heavier than what I could carry, my thoughts about all of it tangled together, and so I blurted, "It's a good thing I'm so scary."

He stared at me for a beat before he barked a laugh, the sound of it washed through me, all the heaviness lifting from my shoulders. "That's true, you are very scary, Jenny Philips." He shook his head, but he was still grinning. "You've always scared me, at least."

I nudged his arm with my shoulder, giving him a teasing smile. "Have I really always scared you?"

"Yeah really, you're terrifying." He leaned in closer, but his face fell again. "Those things he said about you and me—"

"Are nothing," I said with a rare sureness in my voice. "They mean nothing." Another thought crossed my mind. "And I don't feel bad about any of it. If Brandon hadn't of done what he did then the hallway wouldn't have been destroyed. We did what we had to do to stay alive. That's what matters." I could see he wanted to argue, to beat himself up more, but I added, "No hear me out, Hollow Brook High needs a remodel, the whole school is old and ugly, we did them favor."

I knew I'd got him again when he smiled, but I didn't want to lose the smile again. I pushed my lips against his, insistent, trying to assure him that all was right between us. The wind chime above us sang as my breeze danced in the air.

I drew back, holding his eyes with mine, trying to keep us both afloat, trying to sound as confident as Alex Bailey usually was. "We need each other. We'll figure this out. We're in this together."

I didn't blink as I held his gaze.

"Okay, together." His grin didn't go away this time, making me feel weak and strong all at once. He leaned in to press his lips softly to mine, but I wanted him to kiss me. I wanted to be sure Alex Bailey was alive. I wrapped my arms around his neck and deepened the kiss. His hands found the soft skin at my waist, answering my silent pleas, pulling me into his arms, and holding on too.

29.

THAT EVENING during dinner, Grandpa and Grandma talked about the bizarre things that happened at Hollow Brook High that day. Lockers were blown open, student's possessions strewn about, and glass everywhere.

My phone buzzed in my pocket. It was Grandpa's rule that I couldn't have my cell phone at the dinner table. My knee bounced while they talked. My gaze kept darting to the front yard and drive. The sky was blue and the sun shined again. The storm had faded away, leaving the air hot, drying the wet ground.

"At first, they thought it was the storm that caused the electrical problem. But, when the electrician got into it, it looked like things were melted and fried. They think someone did all of it intentionally," Grandpa said, wiping his face with his napkin. "There's going to be an investigation. School will start as soon as they get the electrical work done. It sounds like it'll take more time for the science hallway itself to be ready."

"The ladies in my prayer chain think it was a prank from those Willow High kids. Hollow Brook High has good farming kids. Willow kids all have those two working parent households and no supervision," Grandma said with a worried frown. She looked over at me. "How was Emma's house? I wasn't sure that you got along with her."

"We sort of misunderstood each other before. It's better now," I said casually. I was getting good at throwing out lies to appease my grandparents. "Anyway, can I go up to my room? I'm finished."

"Sure, Jenny." Grandma nodded.

Grandpa said, "You still have chores."

"I'll get them done." I took two steps at a time as I ascended the stairs, shutting my bedroom door behind me. I landed on my bed with a bounce and slid my phone out of my back pocket. Stephen had texted Alex and I just before dinner time, but I'd missed it.

Aiden is good!!! i texted his sister
I'm restless let's hang until curfew

Alex had texted right back.

Thanks for letting us know about Aiden.
Dinner and chores I can come in an hour.

Stephen sent another text while I was eating dinner.

jenny??? hang?
clubhouse????

Fifteen minutes later Alex texted.

Jenny see you at the clubhouse if you can?
If you can't no problem.
We'll see you in the morning.
Text when you can so we know all is good.

It was 5:20 now. I held out my hand for my sneakers. One-by-one they each floated across the room from where I'd kicked them off by the door, landing neatly in front of me on the floor as I swung my feet off the bed to sit up.

Sorry no phone at dinner table

Half an hour

Need to do chores

Alex sent a message back immediately.

Perfect see u soon.

Stephen's message came a second after.

do chores fast!!!

I shoved my phone into my back pocket, threw on Alex's jacket, and sprinted to the barn. I hoped Grandpa wouldn't notice the sloppy job on my chores, but I didn't want to waste time I could have been spending with Alex and Stephen.

Once I was finished, I popped my head into the living room to say to Grandma and Grandpa, "Just going to the clubhouse to hang out with Alex and Stephen."

Grandpa frowned. "Maybe you should be home tonight."

Something deflated inside me. "I'm…I'm good, Grandpa."

Grandma waved Grandpa off. "She's a teenager, all she wants to do is see her friends. There's no school tomorrow either."

"Be back before nine." Grandpa raised an eyebrow at me.

"Okay." I smiled. "For sure."

As soon as I was through the door I took off running. I was a little out of breath when I got to the clubhouse. Alex, tall and handsome, hands in his pockets, stood with his back to me. Stephen stepped past Alex and waved at me.

"Hi," I said, trying to catch my breath. My mutation's breeze swirled around the three of us, making my hair dance around my face.

"Hey," Alex wrapped an arm around my shoulders, easy and natural, giving me a hug. "How are you?"

"I'm good," I said, hugging him back, letting him settle the air around me. "Grandpa almost didn't let me come. I feel like he's catching on that stuff is happening or something."

"Nah." Stephen waved me off. "No one knows we had anything to do with it."

Alex squeezed me again, keeping me against him. "Yeah, don't worry about it."

"The damage at the school is all over the local news." Stephen crossed his arms, eyeing the mutant farm across the flat fields. "I wanted to check in with you guys. Did anyone see you come in, Jenny? No one was in the office when we came in. We got in because Alex has a key from when his dad built tables for the library."

"Ah, I was supposed to give it back a few weeks ago," Alex said sheepishly with a glance at me. "I keep forgetting."

"There was a secretary in the office." I turned into Alex, looking up at him, curling my fingers into his T-shirt. "I know she didn't see me though. She was facing away from me."

Alex's free hand moved my new bangs aside to see my cut. I was glad to sense the steady confidence he usually carried was back. "As long as no one saw you. We're good. Right, Stephen?"

"I think so." Stephen picked up a stick to play with it, catching the end of it on fire with a snap of his fingers.

"Emma?"

Stephen gave me a quick nod. "I texted her while I was waiting for you guys. She's good with the story. We're all good."

"Yeah," I paused to think, and then nodded. "I trust her."

"Me too, if anything, she's scared of Brandon." Stephen took a few steps to swish his firestick as if it were a sword, he paused and looked up at Alex. "What do we do if the police show up at one of our doors?" He threw a nod at me. "What should she do if cops come to her door?"

Alex sighed and shifted me so I was in a full embrace. He stared at nothing over my head as he thought about Stephen's question. I hugged him back and looked up at him, my eyes tracing the line of his jaw. We were all silent for a long moment. I supposed there wasn't a good or easy answer to Stephen's question.

"It won't happen." Stephen shrugged. "No one thinks we had anything to do with it."

Alex let out a breath he'd been holding, frowning down at me. "You say as little as possible, if they want you to get in a police car or something, do it. Stephen and I will come for you."

"Okay," I whispered, smiling at him. I was afraid, but I wanted to stay optimistic for them. "We'll figure it out."

✕ ◆ ✕

We hung out for the next couple of hours.

We pushed away all the serious stuff, leaning against the clubhouse together. Alex and I sat on either side of Stephen as he showed us videos on his phone. His favorites were animals doing funny stuff and car crashes in foreign countries.

It was an easy and safe feeling, sitting there with them like that.

Those couple of hours were somehow magical,

healing me from the nightmare of Brandon in the hallway. I'd never felt so helpless in one moment and then powerful in the next. I'd been afraid of Brandon for months, but I decided I wasn't afraid of him anymore.

Soon, it was almost nine.

"How about I head back home and let you guys work out the mind-reading stuff?" Stephen said when we stood. He took a few steps backward. His dark eyes moved between us. He knew it would be a long time before Alex and I got the chance to be alone again.

"Thanks, Stephen." Alex gave him a wave.

"It'll be okay, Jenny." Stephen narrowed his eyes on me. "You're not allowed to worry."

"Okay," I smiled. "See you in the morning."

We watched in silence as Stephen made his way down the path, disappearing into the trees toward the open fields.

Alex and I turned to face each other. He held my eyes, not blinking. We stood at the edge of the way things used to be and what it might be like if we took our secrets further. If we inched closer.

I knew I should have looked away, taken a few steps from him, told him that we couldn't do this. We needed to talk. Draw lines. Make decisions. Alex and I needed space and breath, distance and time.

His hand twitched, I caught the movement with my eyes.

My mutation reached out to read him. I could feel the constriction in his chest, the way his blood pulsed in his veins, and it was everything I felt too. I wrapped around him, my mind touched his— I was all of his thoughts, warm and heavy and wanting. One thought of his cut through the rest, crisp and smooth, like velvet across my skin.

I don't know how to go back to the way things were.

I don't either. I sent the thought echoing through his head.

He fisted his hand at his side. *I don't know what's next.*

Alex and I had always been magnetic. There was an invisible rubber band stretching between us. I'd always known eventually something would snap when it came to him and I.

Grandpa's rules, right? He said, eyeing my lips. *Not your parents?*

I don't know. I bit my lip, allowing seconds that felt like minutes pass, and with a one-shouldered shrug I said, *What's one more secret?*

We crashed into each other.

Leaves and branches rippled with my mutation's wind, giving us a shimmering sound that filled the air. My hair whipped about us, Alex's shirt lifting. Power pulsed through me, trying to upend me. He held onto me. Steady hands wrapped around my ribs while I used his shoulders to pull myself onto my toes.

We'd kissed before, but not like this—mouth and teeth and tongue were promises. His hands told me he wasn't going to let me go. I was here for it. I wasn't going anywhere either, I'd always run to Alex Bailey. I'd always give—

"Jenny Phillips."

I shoved Alex away.

Grandpa was here. He'd seen us kissing.

Alex stood next to me, his chest heaved with deep breaths. Grandpa crossed his arms, standing a few dozen feet away from us. The wind was gone, the air dry and empty of the magic I'd conjured up seconds ago. I was terrified that Grandpa might have noticed, but he pinned his gaze on Alex.

I spoke first. "Grandpa—"

"Get to the house." Grandpa's voice was ice. "Go on home, Jenny."

My voice shook. "We can talk about this."

"I said *go home*." I felt the full force of his fury beyond what I saw, as if my mutation absorbed the energy of it.

I lowered my eyes but kept standing there. I didn't want to abandon Alex. I wanted to take the verbal thrashing standing next to him, letting him know that I was with him in the consequences. I wrapped myself around my mutation. I fell into a numb and unfeeling place. I needed to protect myself and Alex, not let my mutation do anything stupid because everything I'd felt just a moment before was gone.

Alex spoke quietly. "Grandpa wants to talk to me."

"I know." I looked up at him.

Alex's eyes were clear as he looked back at me. "I can handle it."

I won't go. I sent the thought to him.

He gave me a wave of something tender as he sent his thoughts. *I care about you, Jenny. You know that. Go home. We'll get through this. I'll listen. I'll apologize. Everything will be good again eventually. I promise you. And if not, we'll still play by your parent's rules. I'll come get you the day you turn eighteen and we'll run away together.*

I didn't look at Grandpa as I took off in a run.

Grandma stood up from the porch swing, asking me what was wrong as I passed her. I didn't answer her. My vision tunneled, I slowed only to swing open the screen door and push through the front door. One step, another, and again. Up the stairs until I was on the landing.

Opened my bedroom door. Shut it. Landed on my bed.

I turned to lay on my back and stared at the ceiling. I sunk into myself. I touched my swollen lips, but I couldn't feel Alex's kisses anymore.

I drifted into a place where I didn't hurt.

I couldn't see Brandon and his gun or Alex and his blue eyes. I could only see the ceiling—I only knew my next breath, and that's how I would survive Grandpa's punishment.

30.

MY PUNISHMENT was brutal.

I wasn't allowed to see Alex or Stephen for two months outside of school. In Grandpa's fury, he had wanted it for two years, basically until I was eighteen. There was a lot of negotiation, Grandma got it down to two months. I'd get my second chance on the last day of school.

We'd *discuss* what summer would look like then.

Grandpa wanted me to know he was serious. He was serious about my school, my future, and the fact that I had to heed his rules if I was going to live in his house. He couldn't trust me to hang out with Alex and Stephen. I'd abused his rules, and he was protecting me from myself.

He said I was lucky I wasn't getting sent to live with my Aunt Sarah.

The punishment reminded me of last summer when I was alone and my parent's death was new. I couldn't tell Grandpa that he'd thrown me back into the darkest part of my life again.

When I closed my eyes at night, I saw Brandon and his gun. Ryan and Aiden were there in my nightmares too, waking me up in a cold sweat. Emma moving into my friendship with Stephen and Alex made me feel uneasy.

I clung to the grip around my mutation. It was the only thing I could control. I was always somewhere else, drifting through nothing in my head. I couldn't hear music, I couldn't taste food, or feel the electricity in the wires in the walls. Missing homework stacked in my teacher's gradebooks, because I couldn't concentrate on the words in textbooks, and I wasn't asking Alex to check my answers anymore.

"Jenny?" Alex's voice drew me from the whirl of empty thoughts in my head.

I leaned against the locker next to his, giving him a weak glance. Every time I looked into his eyes, they threatened to make me cry. "What?"

Alex sighed, I'd heard that sound from him many times in the last month since my punishment began. "Stephen is asking you a question."

My gaze swung to Stephen and I sounded way more defensive than I'd intended, as if he were accusing me of something. "What?"

Stephen's brows shot up in surprise. "We're going to work through the study guide together for history. I mean, Alex is going to do it and we're going to copy him. Do you want to grab yours? Emma is getting hers." He gestured down the hall where she stood at her locker. Mandy was standing with her and talking excitedly about something.

I wished I could explain that I didn't want to do the study guide at lunch because lunch used to be reserved for listening to Stephen's funny rants and talking about random stuff. Homework used to be done after school at Alex's house around his kitchen table. Every little thing led back to the day Brandon had held a gun on me, and I didn't know how to deal with that pain.

"You guys do whatever, I'll do mine at home."

Stephen slumped, rolling his eyes. "I guess I'll go tell Emma we aren't doing the study guide at lunch because, for some unknown reason, Jenny Philips wants to do it at home." He turned slowly on his heel, somehow morphing his body into a sarcastic movement.

"Stephen..." Alex frowned with disapproval, but Stephen didn't turn around.

My chest tightened, I wished I knew how to call him back and tell him what was wrong with me, instead the air in my lungs locked.

Alex moved closer, his fingers brushing mine. A spiderweb of sensation exploded up my arm. "Jenny—"

"Please don't." I sucked in a gulp of air, shifting to face him. "Don't, okay?"

I just want you to talk to me.

He'd tried so many times to speak to me mind to mind, but I always pretended like I hadn't heard his thoughts.

"I left my lunch in my locker. I'll meet you at the spot."

Minutes later, I waited alone against the tree we sat under in warm weather. Emma emerged from the double doors at the back of the school with a wide smile on her face. Stephen was on her heels, looking pouty. I assumed it was because of the attitude I'd given him. A second later, Alex followed him, his head ducked low as he walked with his books tucked under his arm.

Emma sat next to me and handed me a flyer. "Mandy is having an end-of-year party at her house. She wants everyone to wear a costume. She has prizes for the best one. She wanted me to tell you that you're invited."

"What about Alex and me?" Stephen said with mock offense as he sat crossed legged in front of me.

"I guess Jenny and I could bring a plus one each." Emma said, but I couldn't conjure up a response. "Come on, don't look like that, Jenny, you won't be grounded anymore. We can go and have fun."

I knew Alex was watching me, but I didn't look over at him as I said, "I doubt Grandpa is going to let me go."

"I don't get it." Emma sat up, setting her hands on her hips. "You'll be free. Right?"

"It's a party for juniors and seniors."

"Why does that matter?" Emma's hands flared out on either side of her. "There's no rules against sophomores going. You're quite capable and old enough to attend a cool party. Mandy is the girl in this school. She'll be a senior next year. She likes you a lot and that's a big deal."

I pulled my knees up and wrapped my arms around them. Alex's quiet probing attention was starting to irritate me. He was looking for some glimmer of hope that I might be excited about this party.

"I get what you're saying," I said, attempting to sound patient, but everything was bubbling up inside of me. "I'm probably not going to go."

Emma insisted though. "Socializing is important, Jenny. It's part of the high school experience. This isn't something to be unreasonable about. You and I are friends now. You have obligations to me, like going to this party and having a lot of fun…" She kept rambling. I tried to block her voice out. I tried to push down the tightness building in my chest again, but I couldn't breathe. I wanted her to stop talking, but words wouldn't come out of my mouth.

The hold on my mutation cracked within me, electricity whispered up my spine. Stephen and Emma's gazes shot upward over my head as they scrambled away.

Then I was on my back, held by a pair of endlessly blue eyes.

Seconds felt like forever as I studied the way Alex hovered above me, an elbow next to my temple, his other arm bent and twisted above me. He was holding up half a tree trunk, blocking the sunlight from my eyes. A bolt of lightning shot through me, finding the solid ground Alex always provided. His eyes flashed in response. His lips parted—

"Jenny." Stephen whisper-shouted. Alex pushed the heavy piece of trunk aside. "Oh my god, are you okay?" He paused when I kept staring at Alex. I lifted myself to rest on my elbows. Stephen huffed a breathy laugh. "I'm glad Alex was here because apparently my instinct was to run away and let a tree fall on you."

Emma let out a nervous snort, but the joke didn't land with Alex and me. Alex offered his hand to help me stand. I glanced around at students in the distance whispering and watching.

That was me, Alex. I did that.

I know. He took a step closer, offering his hand again. *You've got the best superpower, I'm jealous.*

I ignored him and jumped to my feet on my own. *I can't do this.*

I can't do this either. Alex dropped his hand. *I know you can hear me when I talk to you like this. You're grounded, but it doesn't have to be like this at school. I know you're not okay. Talk to me. I'll help you.*

"Guys," Stephen kicked the fallen trunk as if assessing the viability of a teenage boy lifting the trunk of a very big, old tree. He frowned when it didn't budge. "Please share your thoughts with the rest of the group."

I'm not your responsibility. I turned to walk away.

"What?" Alex fell into step next to me, whispering, "Is that what this is about? You feel bad because you think you're some kind of an obligation to me? That you're a burden?"

"Hey! Are you guys okay?" Mr. Garrison was jogging toward us, other students drew near with him to study the fallen tree. "Holy crap."

Stephen stepped up. "We're good. That was crazy."

"I'm glad you guys are okay. I'm going to call maintenance. Whose books are under there?" Mr. Garrison asked.

"Mine," I said, rubbing my face.

"We'll get them out," Mr. Garrison said, walking away. "I'll be right back. Don't touch anything."

"Jenny." Alex moved into my line of sight. "I'm confused. Talk."

I gave him a harsh laugh. "I'm not allowed to talk to you. Remember? Leave me alone. I just want to get to the end of the school year so I can get away from this place." Alex's eyes widened in surprise. I didn't mean those words. They'd come out of my mouth to push Alex away. I was pushing him away so I wouldn't feel anything. I didn't want to feel anything because it was the only way I knew how to control my mutation. I moved past him and glanced at Emma, who had been watching Alex and me. "Please hold my books till I come back? I need a minute alone."

"Sure." Emma nodded.

I made my way into the building and headed to the bathrooms at the back of the school. I ignored the leftover damage from the month before when my mutation had exploded. The hallway had been cleaned up, but the mangled lockers hadn't been replaced. Yellow construction tape hung in an X across the science room's shattered windows.

Once in the restroom, I washed my face in the sink, staring at myself in the mirror for a long moment. I focused on wrapping the numb around my mutation again until I only knew the sensation of air through my nose and out my mouth. Breathing was the only sign I gave myself that I was alive.

I left the bathroom, pausing to lean forward to drink from the drinking fountain.

"What's up, Jenny?"

I whirled around to find Brandon Thomas a few feet behind me. I backed into the water fountain, my heart pounding. This was the first time he'd approached me since the day in the science room with the gun. "Don't talk to me."

Raising both hands up, a cruel smile lit up his face. "Just getting water. Don't freak out and do something magical now."

I tried to step past him, but he stepped with me, blocking my way. "I want to hear more about what you can do."

"Alex told you—"

"Alex really does have a leash on you, doesn't he?"

"Go away."

He moved closer, filling my vision. "I saw what you did to the tree. What Alex did. Don't worry though, I've made sure Ryan and Aiden kept their mouths closed."

"What do you want?" I hissed. "What more do you want from me?"

"Emma gets to be in your club." His smirk was arrogant. "Why can't I?"

"Move." I tried to step around him again, but he reached for my forearm. Before his fingers brushed against my skin, his hand jerked away from me, my mutation stopping him. "Don't you dare touch me."

Brandon studied his hand, as if marveling at what I could do.

"You were told not to talk to me. I can do a lot more than open lockers and split trees." He yielded a step at the gentle press of air against one shoulder, and then the other. "Leave me alone."

"Do something." Brandon's eyebrows went up, but his eyes were hollow, sending a chill over my skin. I could see now that some of the scaring Alex inflicted a month ago would be permanent. He wasn't afraid of me in the way he should have been. He was my mirror, something cold and numb and empty in him. Except he'd done this to me. The day he'd held a gun on me was the day he'd stolen everything. "Do something to me. I dare *you*."

Within my mind, I stood on a ledge. It was a cliff. I was tempted to jump, to show Brandon Thomas how much he'd hurt me—but I'd promised Alex and Stephen that we wouldn't use our mutations to *fight crime*. We weren't going to enact justice, we were going to manage our mutations, and chase a normal life.

"No." I shook my head. "I think what goes around comes around. I think something way worse than what I could do to you will come, Brandon."

His jaw worked as he pressed his lips together, but the door leading to the outside swung open. Our attention darted to Alex coming through the door. "Step away asshole."

I shoved past a startled Brandon, coming at Alex as his mutation rippled under his skin. My hands landed on his chest. I pushed against him. He paused so he wouldn't run me over. I said, "Let's go outside."

"I made him a promise." Alex's voice was a boom, thundering through the hallway. A group of students down the hall turned to watch and whisper. We had to be careful to not say anything that would cause more suspicion than we already gave off every day.

"I need your help." I held his jaw in my hands. "I need you to take me outside."

"There aren't any more chances," Alex said through his teeth. "This isn't a game. You talk to her again and I won't hesitate."

He took my hand, slamming through the heavy door leading to outside harder than humanly possible. We rounded the corner and Alex turned on me. "What did he say to you?"

"He knew I cracked the tree. He saw what you did." The numb feeling I was surviving on was a dam about to burst, I was holding back a flood within me. "He saw it and followed me just to mess with me."

"I'm not playing, Jenny. I will literally—"

I hugged him. "Everything is a disaster."

The stiffness in Alex melted against me. His arms moved around my shoulders. I settled into his closeness as he spoke into my hair. "I know."

"I miss you so much. I can't breathe," I said into his chest. I squeezed his middle tighter, holding on so I wouldn't explode. "I can't let myself breathe."

Alex kissed the top of my head, squeezing me back. We hadn't touched like this in weeks. I hadn't realized how much I needed his skin against my skin, how much my mutation settled while I was near him like this. "I can't breathe either."

"Just give me the rest of the month." I looked up at him. "Let me be sad. Don't be mad at me. Just give me the month."

"Okay." He studied me, pushing my hair to the side. His thumb ran along where the cut had almost completely faded away. "One month. Then we'll figure out where we're at." He hugged me against himself once more. "Please don't go anywhere."

"Where would I go?"

"You just said you wanted to get out of this place."

"I didn't mean it. I don't want to go anywhere. Everything just hurts."

"I know it does." He tucked his face into my neck, drawing in a deep breath. "You have Stephen and me.

Tell us how to help you."

"I just need a month."

"Okay, a month."

The maintenance man said he couldn't see why the tree had split down the center like that. He said the tree might have been sick, but he didn't see any rotting or usual signs. It was a mystery. Just like all the other crazy things happening around Hollow Brook High lately.

I felt his words in my bones.

Alex kept his promise.

He was still always there, but he stopped chasing me with his eyes. Anxious energy that he'd had before was now peaceful. Alex was a stone in the river. The world could rush by him, but he would never be moved. I knew he'd be there at the end of my mess. I'd always known he'd take me back when I was ready.

After that day, I could breathe a little easier.

31.

AT THE LAST minute, I asked Grandma if I could go to Mandy's end-of-year party since my sentence had ended the day before. She handed me my phone and told me she'd tell Grandpa where I went. I was glad I didn't have to ask him myself. Before I left, I paused at my open closet and made the quick decision to grab Alex's jacket.

I was ready to wear it again.

Grandma dropped me off at Mandy's house. The music was loud as I walked through the front door. It was odd to see costumes in June, but there was something Victorian and haunted looking about her house.

It worked somehow.

The place was already full of high school kids and a wide variety of costumes. Mailmen, doctors, and police officers. Teletubbies, superheroes, and retro 80s. Monsters, werewolves, and vampires. I only recognized a few people. Many of them weren't from our school, probably Willow High kids. I'd overheard people talking about the party at school for the past few weeks. Everyone said Mandy's parties were legendary.

Mandy's pool shimmered in the center of her backyard. I scanned the crowd surrounding it until I spotted Emma Henderson dressed in a sparkling light blue ball gown. Standing next to her on the back deck was a princely Stephen Wright. Before they saw me, I watched Stephen kiss Emma on the cheek, they leaned against the deck railing together.

I guessed they were a thing now.

It made sense. I was cool with it. While Alex and I had been wallowing these past two months they must have grown close. I was glad they'd had each other to process everything. I owed it to Stephen to be supportive of his relationship with Emma.

Emma saw me first and she tapped Stephen on the shoulder. He grinned. He waved me over to join them. "You're here."

"I'm here," I said, looking around. "Where's Alex?"

"Uh, he's at home." He frowned at me. "He wasn't going to come if you weren't here. Emma picked me up."

"No worries. I'll text him."

"Where's your costume?" Stephen looked me over in black biker shorts, a graphic T-shirt with a vintage flower on it, and Alex's jacket.

"What do you mean?" I winked at him. "I look great."

He grinned again. He could see I was trying to come back.

⋅ ◆ ⋅

I decided to let Emma and Stephen keep flirting without me.

I slid through the back door and into the kitchen. The music was loud, the air warm from costumed teenagers. Mandy's house was a maze of connected rooms. From the kitchen, I found a dining room. Through another door, I stood in a room with a black grand piano, and then crossed the hall into a formal living room. I was trying to find a quiet spot to call Alex, but the music seemed to reach every room. I wasn't brave enough to venture upstairs, especially at a high school party with a bunch of juniors and seniors in attendance.

I decided my best bet was the front porch.

I walked around a group of people sitting on fancy furniture. A tall, lean guy with dark hair and bright green eyes straightened against the back couch and blocked my path. "Hey, you."

"Excuse me," I said absently, trying to step around him.

He stayed in my path. "Do you go to Willow High?"

"No." I sighed, speaking to the gold star on his chest. He was wearing a police officer costume. "I don't."

"How do you know Mandy?" He ducked his head, trying to make me look at him. "Do you go to Hollow Brook High with her?"

"Sorry," I tried to step around him again, but he stepped with me. "I'm trying to find someone."

"I like your costume," he said, his voice turning deep and smooth. "Casual hot girl looks good on you."

Suddenly I regretted coming, Alex wasn't here to ward off jerks for me. I needed to turn around and find Stephen, maybe ask Emma to drive me home. I looked up at him to give him my best unwelcoming glare.

"I'm Bryce," His white teeth glowed against tan skin. "You should let me get you a drink."

"Bryce."

A chilly sensation washed up my back. Every hair on my neck stood straight. The music stopped and the lights in the room flickered off.

The world was dark and silent as I twisted to find Brandon Thomas behind me. Groans and shouts of protest rose through the house. But his expression softened. I blinked, my mutation allowed the electricity to charge through the house again. Cheers and shouts echoed as the lights turned on and music played again.

Bryce raised his hand above me to exchange a high five with Brandon. "What's up, bro?"

Brandon high-fived him back, but gestured to me. "This is Alex Bailey's girlfriend."

"Ah, you're Mark Bailey's little brother's girlfriend?" Bryce stepped back with a laugh. "That's too bad."

"I'm not—" I began to clarify that I wasn't Alex's girlfriend, but Bryce wasn't in my way anymore. He turned back to the group of people he'd been talking to in the first place.

Brandon's mouth twisted, revealing a hint of the dimple that'd tricked me into going to the dance with him. He stepped aside, letting me pass by. I would never forgive him for hating Alex, but I was determined to forget he existed.

I needed Alex's thoughts.

I needed him to come to the party and be with me. I started walking again, not stopping until I was sitting on the top step of the front porch. The street was quiet despite the muffled pump of music in the house behind me. I pulled my phone from my pocket and texted Alex.

Where are u

It took a few minutes, but Alex texted back.

You have your phone?
What's up?

I smiled to myself. I missed seeing his correct capitalization and punctuation in text messaging. He'd always been so effortlessly himself without apology.

Mandy's weird costume party
Come

It was taking Alex a long minute to text back again. I glanced at the door to the house, wondering again if I should call Grandma to pick me up. I wasn't sure I could handle being here without Alex.

I rubbed my face with my hands. I was waiting like an idiot for Alex to text me back when I should have been independently going into the party alone. I hadn't learned my lesson at all about Alex in these past months. I was sitting here in his jacket, waiting for him to be with me like a lovesick puppy.

I opened my phone, scrolling to find Grandma's number to call her when Alex finally texted me back.

On my way to come see you.

Something dropped like a stone in a well within me. The music faded into a softer sound in my ears, the porch light above me dimmed, and my lungs drew in the clear summer air. My mind and body and the universe were right, knowing Alex Bailey was on his way.

I didn't care if there was something wrong with that.

32.

MANDY LIVED toward town.

It was a twenty-minute drive from the Bailey Farm. I watched Alex park his truck down the street. He wore a forest green baseball cap, and his hands were in his pockets as he walked, his head ducked low. I couldn't see his expression. Taking the porch steps two at a time, he came to stand in front of me. "Hey."

"Hi." I smiled as I stood up, but his expression made me frown. "You okay?"

He rubbed the back of his neck. "Uh, yes. I just wasn't sure if I should come or not."

"I thought you'd be here with Stephen and Emma," I said, trying to push a normal tone between us. "Otherwise, I would have texted you I was going to be here."

Alex looked away toward the street. "They're a thing now, I guess. If you weren't coming tonight I didn't want to hang around. Even when you texted I wasn't sure I should come."

"Why?"

He didn't answer right away, his attention drifted to a white lifted diesel truck with way too many teenagers riding in the truck bed as they hunted for a parking spot.

Gruffly, he finally said, "It all changed the night of the dance when I kissed you. I didn't know how to go back to the way things were. And I didn't know how to act after everything that happened with Brandon. How do we just be friends again? What if I mess up again?"

I sent him a thought. *Last time we talked about this I asked for the month. It's over now. We're back to normal.*

"We need to talk about what normal is for us."

I gestured to the swing. "Sit with me?"

Alex eyed the swing like it was a bad idea in itself but decided to sit.

Music blared each time the door opened and shut. People in costume came in and out of the house. I scooted away from Alex, facing him and bringing a leg up under me so I could sit comfortably. I hugged his jacket around me because the evening was starting to cool.

"You're wearing my jacket," he said as he eyed two guys shouting across the yard, as if naturally assessing if they were going to be a problem for us.

"Do you…" I moved to take it off. "You can have it back."

"No." His blue eyes went wide as he held up a hand. "No, keep it. Please. I want you to have it. I'm glad you're wearing it."

I swallowed and drew the jacket around me again. I was ridiculously relieved he didn't want it back.

"Let's make this simple," I smiled at him, trying to get him to smile too. "No being alone. Leaving when it's an accident. No kissing. No hand holding. No hugging."

He nodded. *What about being in each other's heads?*

What's wrong with that? I tilted my head.

"I don't know," His hand moved toward mine, but then he seemed to cover it by pulling his hat off to run the hand through his hair. "It's our thing. But is it wrong?"

We're allowed to communicate and be friends, right? There's nothing wrong with it. I shrugged.

His smile was slow, a little dangerous for my heart. *That's true. This is allowed for us, then?*

"I think so," I held out a hand for him to shake.

"We're friends until further notice."

He shook my hand, warm and familiar, helping me to come alive again. "Deal, Jenny Philips."

"Do you want to go inside and hang out?"

"Yeah, I do." He stood, sticking his hands into his pockets.

I didn't have to worry about guys moving into my path as I walked because Alex Bailey was on my heels. We weaved through teenagers being loud and laughing with red solo cups in their hands. I found Stephen and Emma in the kitchen with a group of people who were all listening to Mark tell a story with Mandy laughing next to him. Mark and Mandy wore togas, some sort of Greek costume. They were an impossibly cute couple.

There was something so perfect about them.

I watched Stephen and Emma, how aware they were of each other, the way Emma leaned into Stephen's shoulder without fear that she might be grounded for the rest of her life.

Another perfect couple.

Mandy raised her voice over the music. "Who wants to play beer pong?"

Stephen declared he wanted to play. One of the senior guys dressed like someone in the military also wanted to. We shuffled outside to gather around the ping pong table.

I leaned against the deck railing to watch the game. Emma stood on one side of me and Alex on the other side. Alex kept his hands in his pockets.

"I have to go to the bathroom," Emma said. "Want to find it with me?"

"Sure."

I followed Emma through the house until we found a guest bath under the stairs. I stood against the wall with my arms crossed and watched teenagers dancing obnoxiously to music in the living room.

When Emma came out of the bathroom, she asked, "Do you need to go?"

I shook my head. "Nope. Want to go back and watch?"

She nodded and I followed her outside again. Alex had moved to stand next to Mark. They were watching Stephen and a senior guy dressed as Elvis Presley play. It looked like Stephen had won the first round.

I glanced around and caught Alex looking at me, but his eyes darted to the red solo cup in his hand instead, giving the impression he didn't mean for me to know he was watching me.

Stephen lost this round and stood by Emma and me. "I almost had him. I was so close."

"You're really good," Emma said brightly, smiling.

My mouth dropped open behind Emma as I watched Stephen's flirty grin back at her. "Well, I was trying to impress you, Emma."

It was at that moment that I realized Stephen had never once flirted with me. Every smile he'd ever given me was brotherly, intentionally platonic. He'd never offered me the hot look he was giving Emma right now. My gaze trailed back to Alex, wondering if Stephen had stayed away because his best friend had liked me from the beginning.

Emma wiggled her brows. "Well, it worked. I'm impressed."

I pretended to shove my finger down my throat, making Stephen roll his eyes as he grabbed our cups. "More?"

"Just water for me," Emma said. It was a good choice, she was a little flushed.

"I'll have more soda," I said.

When he left, Emma turned to me. "Stephen and I like each other."

"Oh, I couldn't tell. You guys hide it so well." My sarcasm was good-natured, though.

"What do you think? Are you good with it?"

"I'm good with it. I'm happy for you guys."

"Thanks so much." Emma hugged me a little more

enthusiastically than necessary. "Your approval is everything."

I glanced at Alex again, something painful and very irrational struck me. He was nodding and listening to a blonde girl I didn't know. Mark was laughing. Alex was smiling and shaking his head.

It threw me into a weird train of thoughts.

Alex could date that girl if he wanted. He didn't have rules about dating like I did. He was the best at hiding his mutation. Stephen and I struggled with keeping the evidence of our mutations quiet. Alex was the only one who could even think about exploring a relationship without worrying about exposing us.

I knew that because I was the girl who taught him how to hold someone's hand.

She was definitely into him, I could tell by her eyes and body language. She flipped her blonde hair and knew how to move in her little cheerleader outfit just right. My stomach soured watching her bat her lashes up at Alex.

I wondered if I wasn't here, if he didn't feel responsible for me, he could date that girl. I kept pulling Alex around in circles that didn't go anywhere. There was nothing stopping him from going off with that girl. He had every right too.

The day I'd eaten that strawberry, was the day I'd tied him to me.

I looked away, but Emma and Stephen were in some sort of eye-flirting-situation. I didn't belong here, there was no place for me—no person who was all mine to stand next to. "I'm going to circle the house and come back in a little while."

Stephen opened his mouth as if he was going to say something, but Emma squeezed his arm. His face fell and he nodded.

The house seemed even louder than before, teenagers still poured in through the front door. I was sure this was some kind of fire-code violation. Or that someone was going to call for a noise complaint.

I didn't look over when a Willow High guy called out for me to come hang with him and his friends. I passed another who stepped into my path to talk to me. I found myself walking out the front door to get away from the stuffy house and into the cool air again.

I sat on the porch steps and pulled out my phone, annoyed with myself for being so pathetic. I wanted to be happy. I wanted to be content and hang out like a normal person, but Brandon had held a gun at me two months ago. I wondered if my world would always circle back to the power he held over me that day.

Where did you go? Alex's soft thought drifted into my mind.

My heart leapt. It felt good to know he was looking for me. *Just getting air.*

You left the backyard to get air? His humor drifted with the thought.

I'll come back in a minute—

Alex sat on the stairs next to me. I glanced behind me toward the door to the party. "Why'd you leave beer pong?" I didn't mean to, but I blurted out, "Who was that girl?"

Alex's eyes widened in surprise. "What girl?"

"No one. Nothing." I shook my head, rubbing my face with my hands. "Sorry."

"I don't know her name," Alex said, trying to shift and catch my eye. "She was talking to Mark. I wasn't even listening to what she was saying."

I looked down the other side of the street. "You didn't need to leave to come looking for me."

"I know I didn't need to leave. I wanted to leave." He took a moment before he spoke again. "I left ping pong because you left ping pong." He touched my arm, a spiderweb of warmth whispered over me. "I came here because of you." His hand dropped. "You know me, Jenny. I'd rather be watching a movie with you, Stephen and Emma on my couch right now. You're the only person in the world who could convince me to come to my older brother's girlfriend's stupid costume party."

My heart pounded in my ears. I wanted so badly

to rest my head on his shoulder. I didn't respond right away, so he looked toward the street too.

"I'm sorry." I blinked, feeling the sting of tears at the edges of my eyes. I drew in a sharp breath. "I'm not sure I was ready to come back into general society again. I'm going to do something stupid with my mutation. I think I'm going to call Grandma to pick me up."

"Yeah?" He looked over at me again. His brows scrunched. "Really?"

"Emma and Stephen get to just jump into their relationship. Mark and Mandy are like this solid high school sweetheart pair." I wiped a tear running down my cheek but forced a laugh to cover it. "I sound so shallow. I'm not boy crazy. But a lot has happened, and I think I'm kind of sad."

He gave me a pout with his lower lip. *I'm sad too. And, just so you're aware, I'm absolutely Jenny Philips crazy.*

I didn't deserve Alex. I curled into my bent legs and set my cheek on the top of my knees. "I'm sorry it's hard."

"I'm sorry too," He frowned, but then nudged my shoulder with his elbow. "I'm not going anywhere. There's only one girl in this town I'm interested in. I'm here for you even if we aren't together."

I hated the distance between us, of the conflicting

arguments circling my mind, the doubts about the future. Instead of voicing any of it, I said, "Thanks, Alex."

"You're really going to leave?"

"I don't know what to do with myself. I think maybe this isn't my thing."

Alex glanced back at the door. "It's not my thing either. But it's been so long. Just…just come hang out with me?"

I studied the dark gravel road, watching the pink blossoms fall from the trees in the breeze, realizing I hadn't noticed flowers in a long time.

"I want to hang out."

We stood together. I followed Alex through the crowded house, resisting the urge to reach out and hold his hand. We spent the rest of the night standing next to each other. No hand holding, just unintentional touches as we moved about the party. No kisses, just eyes meeting eyes. His smiles flipping my stomach again and again.

Just hanging out together, and it was really nice.

33.

LATER THAT NIGHT, after Mandy's party, Stephen sent me a text.

Can i call you???

I frowned, Stephen hadn't ever wanted to talk on the phone with me. He was strictly a texter, and all of his texting had to do with gathering Emma, Alex, and I together to hang out face to face. I texted back.

Yeah one minute
You okay

He was quick to text back.

Gotta talk to you about mushy stuff...

Intrigued, I slid Alex's jacket over my T-shirt and athletic shorts, sticking my phone into the pocket. I hoped it was advice about Emma. As his little sister I knew I'd enjoy the female-superiority of that kind of conversation.

My grandparents were already asleep. I knew Grandpa could hear me when I talked on the phone in my room so I crept down the stairs and found my sandals. Silently, I tip-toed in the kitchen and pushed carefully through the squeaky back door.

"Jenny?" The kitchen light clicked on, I turned to find Grandpa behind me. "What are you doing? It's two in the morning."

Without thinking, I blurted out, "Stephen wants me to call him."

Grandpa's mouth turned into a hard line. "Why do you think it's okay to sneak out the back door in the middle of the night and call Stephen? You've only been ungrounded for a day."

Suddenly, I was someone else.

Someone far more confident than myself as I raised my phone to hug it to my chest, facing Grandpa more squarely. "Because he's my best friend. Because he needs his friend to call him."

I raised my eyebrows, daring him to argue with me. I was ready for a fight. I was ready to scream at him. I was ready to tell him that it'd never been okay for him to tell me to be careful of Stephen. Grandpa had always been wrong about Stephen.

He wasn't a bad kid. He was my big brother.

"I'm going to call him real quick and then go back to bed."

Grandpa let the silence stretch between us for a long moment, as if he could see my silent challenge. As if he knew that if he didn't let me talk to Stephen tonight, he'd lose some part of me forever. If he fought me on this, I'd never forgive him.

"All right. It's summer." He cleared his throat. "No more than half an hour then get up to bed."

I didn't move an inch as Grandpa turned and climbed the stairs. I didn't let myself breathe until the door to his bedroom shut with a soft thud above me.

✶ ◀◆▶ ✶

The industrial light above the barn doors caught my eye. I decided that was a good place to make a private phone call. Inside, I sat on the stool next to the horse stalls and pulled out my phone, finding Stephen's contact to call him.

He answered with a hushed hello, making me note his deepening voice. I liked watching him grow from boy to man. It fascinated me.

"You have to talk to me about mushy stuff?"

His laugh was breathy as he said, "Alex was going on and on about you in the truck on the way home. He said something that I can't stop thinking about."

Surprised, I asked, "Where are you?"

He paused, as if looking around himself. "Bailey's front porch, sleeping over. Why? Where are you?"

"I'm in Grandpa's barn. Do you guys talk about me a lot?"

"Of course. You're the center of our world, obviously." Sarcasm caked his words, but then he added, "Actually, not really, Alex is tight-lipped about you most of the time. I guess, especially since you've been grounded. But he wouldn't shut up about you after the party tonight."

"Oh," I said, feeling awkward. "So, why did you want to talk again?"

"He said…" Stephen hesitated, as if sorting out what he wanted to say. "He said you keep… I can't remember how he put it, but basically that maybe you think Alex only likes you because our mutations have clumped us together. That you think he feels bad for you because of your mutation and all the work it takes to control it."

All my thoughts eddied out of my head, quieting my mind.

"I thought you should know something."

Speaking around emotion in my throat, I said, "Know what?"

"Remember the day we met you?" I could hear the smile in his voice. "We went fishing."

I glanced around myself, realizing I was sitting in the same spot where I stood that day when Alex and Stephen had come through the barn doors looking for their fishing poles. I remembered it clearly. The way Stephen had called me Weird Girl and Alex had forced Stephen to invite me fishing.

I remembered the pain of last summer, how dark and lonely it'd been. And yet, Alex and Stephen had come into my life and taught me how to see sunshine again.

"Okay, so here's the mushy part, I remember it because he'd shocked me." His words were flowing freely now. "After we went back to your house, Alex insisted he and I walk home instead of driving back with his parents. He said you were the prettiest girl he'd ever met. I mean, I thought you were pretty too, but he said he liked the sound of your voice, and you were funny and he'd touched your hand, and you had the softest skin he'd ever touched." He laughed. "I wanted him to shut up so bad, but he never talked like that. I knew this was a big deal for him."

My body tensed and I sucked in my bottom lip.

"Anyway, he said he was going to ask you to be his

girlfriend the next day." Stephen laughed again, louder this time. "He said he'd beat me up and never forgive me if I made a move on you. I told him you weren't my type, which is true, you're one hundred percent sister material." I huffed at that, but he didn't give me any room to comment. "He made me swear that I'd never do anything to mess this up for him."

My spine ached, listening to him as I held my mutation in place. "Why are you telling me this—"

"Let me tell you the whole story first," he said, talking over my question. "I was there when he told his dad that he liked you and wanted you to be his girlfriend. He was looking for advice, I guess. Mr. Bailey said that it was great that he liked you, but your parents died a few months before and the thing you needed was a good friend. He told Alex to start off by being a good friend, and then when the time was right, he should ask you out on a date." He paused. I imagined him shrugging. "Alex was cool with that plan, he told me you were in our group now. I agreed because I didn't have much of a choice—"

"Oh, wow, thanks—"

"Not finished, Jenny Philips," he said sternly. "We decided that being our friend meant you got to see the clubhouse." His voice caught, turning quieter. "I thought of sneaking us onto the mystery farm last minute. I thought I was helping Alex by doing something cool to impress you."

I could hear the way it hurt him to tell this part of the story. My shoulders slumped as the memories of that day blossomed in my mind.

"You know the rest..." Stephen said, trailing off.

I whispered because everything he'd just said was a blur of information my mind didn't know what to do with. "I still don't know why you're telling me this story."

"You don't?" He groaned, annoyed. "God, you're such a girl. I'm saying that you know Alex as much as I do. You know that Alex never says or does anything he doesn't mean. He wants you for you. You're not an inconvenience, or whatever."

"He's told me that before—"

"Then why don't you believe him?" He scoffed, sounding annoyed again. "When we were driving home tonight, he said the best thing about our mutations is he gets to share the secret with you and the worst thing about our mutations is that you keep doubting his feelings for you. I called you to talk about this mushy stuff because you need to start believing him. Alex liked you before our mutations, that's it. Stop being dumb, Jenny."

My mutation perked up, a little defensive. "None of this matters, we can't be girlfriend and boyfriend."

"Do you like him back?" His question shot through

me, clearing away the smoke and fog within me. "I know he's intense and stubborn and way more serious about stuff than he should be. You can be honest with me if you don't like him back, I won't say anything. If I knew you didn't like him back, then I could be prepared to—"

"I like him back." I didn't need to think about my answer. "But, it's more complex than—"

"You sound like Alex. You two are both dumb. It's not complex."

"It's two years, Stephen." A breeze picked up around me, making the tools and chains hanging around me clank against each other. "I'm going to be in love with him and he's going to realize I'm not worth the wait. He's going to date other girls and I can't go through that. My mutation would never be able to handle that. I feel like I'd have to curl up and die. It's complex because I feel everything. My mutation feels all of it, and it's impossible to explain to anyone. I mean, if Alex was with another girl, who'd want me? I mean, god, Stephen, I already know it—I know that my mutation wouldn't want anyone else. I only want Alex and it's terrifying."

Stephen didn't say anything at first, letting my words settle between us. Finally, he said, "What if he waits?"

"What?"

"What if things work out for you and Alex?"

The wind around me slowed into a cool breeze that played with the hair around my face. "I don't understand the question."

"I used to complain a lot, you know, be down on myself." Stephen said, and I could hear the sureness in his voice, the wisdom that went beyond his sixteen years of life. "I know better than anyone how small this town is. For some people, Hollow Brook is their whole world, but it's not to me. I know Jenny, I know more than anyone that life isn't fair. And, I know there's no easy answer for me, but I'm going to stick with you and Alex, and I'm going to do my homework and see where life takes me. I have to believe it's going to all work out, just like you can."

I sniffled, wiping away tears. "I mean, I like that, but what if it doesn't work out?"

"Easy, no one messes with my little sister. I'd beat up Alex."

I laughed at the thought. "Oh yeah? You'd be able to beat up the Strongest Man in the World?"

"Bro, I'm the Man Made of Fire. It doesn't seem like we're a match, but you'd be surprised. Remember when our mutations were new and we still tried to wrestle out in the Bailey's backyard? I'd heat up and he'd let go every time." He said, laughing and I laughed too. I did remember those days. "But really, I'll always be there for you. You're stuck with me. You need me, you call me. If I had to choose between you and Alex, I'd choose you."

"No you wouldn't." I rolled my eyes. I'd always been grateful that they'd brought me into the group, but I'd also always felt like an afterthought. "You and Alex have been friends forever and—"

"I would, I'd choose you. Alex and I are friends, but you and I are family."

More tears spilled down my cheeks.

"You're never going to be alone, I'll always be there." He paused. "Alex would absolutely choose you over me a thousand times over. We actually talked about it once, we both vowed we'd be on your side if we had some kind of big fight. It was after the thing with the dance and Brandon when you and Alex were fighting."

"Okay well, I didn't know that."

"You know most stuff. Alex and I have to keep a secret or two from you." I started to object to that one, but he spoke over me again. "And, it's not about being mutants, it's about the way you care about us. It's because you've become vital to our lives, and we'd do anything for you. You need to get that through your head, alright?"

I didn't know how to respond because I felt the stubbornness within me, the way my mind had dug into my fears. One conversation with Stephen wasn't going to change that.

"What if Alex waited for you, Jenny?" he asked again. "What if you lived your life believing in what Alex says about the two of you?"

"I don't know." I used the sleeve of Alex's jacket to wipe at my runny nose. "I guess I could be happy."

"Be happy then, Jenny."

"Okay, okay," I said, giving into his insistence. A quiet stretched between us. My supernatural breeze picked up, bits of hay floating around me as I thought of how thankful I was of Stephen. I didn't think he'd ever understand how much I loved him. I would never be able to explain in words what he meant to me. I whispered as I spoke, "You know I'd leave this town with you, right? If you ever wanted to go somewhere else, I wouldn't hesitate."

"You mean when we're eighteen?"

"Yeah, or tomorrow." I said, tucking a flyaway strand behind my ear. "Right now, I'd pack my stuff and we'd go anywhere you wanted."

It was a long time before he responded. I wondered if he knew why I hadn't mentioned Alex. I wanted him to know that I would set aside everything I cared about for him because of the way he'd treated me from the first day we'd met.

Finally, he whispered, "Thanks, Jenny."

The rest of the conversation was Stephen's stream of

consciousness about his ideas for the next few months. It'd be me, Alex, Emma, and him. We'd have the summer of our lives. We'd adventure in the mountains and swim and go to the movies and go bowling. He was going to convince Alex to convince Grandpa to let us go to Medford, which was three hours away, and we'd walk around the big downtown area doing random stuff. He had a list of buy-one-get-one activities so the four of us could get into places cheap. I let him name all the activities on his list because I loved hearing the hopefulness in his voice, I tried to make that hope my own.

When we finally hung up, I kept sitting on the stool, staring at the spot where Alex and Stephen stood when I'd first met them, wondering if I was brave enough to be happy.

34.

THE NEXT MORNING, I laid in bed staring at the ceiling.

The sunlight reflected off the perfume bottle on my dresser, projecting little rainbow dots, creating something that reminded me of magic and miracles.

I let the things Stephen said to me last night wash over me again and again. I let myself feel his words. I let myself feel everything—the heat of the water on my skin in the shower, the taste of my coffee and toast, the sunshine on my face as I stepped out onto the front porch.

Everything that'd happened this last year was still a heavy thing within me, but this summer was going to be different than last. I wanted to see the future the way Stephen saw it. I wanted to believe that Alex was okay with being my friend for the next two years. That he'd still want me when we were both eighteen.

I was still thinking of these things after breakfast as I sat on the front porch swing. I pushed the swing in a gentle back and forth movement with my dirty sneaker along the gray wood plank floor.

Grandpa pushed open the front door, pausing to look at me. He made a little gesture, asking if he could sit next to me, I nodded. I fought against the resentment that sat like a stone in my stomach.

"Thank you," he said gruffly. "Thank you for trying these past couple of months. I know it was a hard lesson."

I cringed, bracing myself because I didn't want to talk about this. I never wanted to talk to Grandpa about Alex Bailey ever again. After last night, I'd tucked Alex snugly into my mind as my best friend again, and I was going to protect his place in my life no matter what.

"I think it was a hard lesson for me too," he said. My gaze whipped to his face. He was staring at the red barn across the gravel drive. "I've been thinking a lot about your parents. Your dad was a good man. He loved your mom and was always good to her, but I couldn't see past what'd happened with your grandma and me. You know?"

I nodded the slowest nod in the world.

He frowned, but there was a smile in his eyes. "The way I showed your grandma I loved her was quitting school and working for no money on a farm. We had some really hard, painful times." He coughed a little into his fist. "I pushed your mother, I pushed your father, and when they were allowed to be free of me, they left." He met my eyes with his. "How can you and I both win? How do I make sure you're safe and focused on school, but won't drive you away from Grandma and I?"

"I get it, I understand why I shouldn't be sneaking around." I'd gone through two months of punishment. Grandpa's message had been sent. "I just want to be allowed to be friends with Alex and Stephen, that's all."

The wrinkles around his mouth deepened. "I don't want you getting pregnant."

"I know," I said, exhaling. "I understand—"

"There will be rules when it comes to Alex Bailey." Grandpa raised an eyebrow. "You can continue to get to know each other while you're at the Bailey house or here, but I don't want you two spending an excessive amount of time alone." He scratched the top of his wrinkled hand, crossing his arms. "I talked to Mr. Bailey this morning."

"You did?"

"He thinks Alex is ready and responsible enough to court you."

A stone dropped in a well within me creating a rippling effect through my body. "*Court* me?"

"Ah," He waved his hand. "Date, or whatever they call it these days."

I caught hold of my mutation to keep it from picking up wind but couldn't stop the way my heart raced in my chest. "You'd let Alex be my boyfriend?"

"One thing at a time." Grandpa's frown deepened even more. "You two… The two of you can go on a date alone once a week. All right?

I tried to clarify, I didn't want to misunderstand a word of this conversation. "We can't be boyfriend and girlfriend, but we're allowed to go on a date once a week?"

"One date a week," Grandpa said. "We'll start there."

"Okay, but what about—"

He stood to his feet. "One date a week."

Stunned, I watched Grandpa head toward his truck, climb in, and drive off toward the back fields without looking at me again. I didn't know what to make of Grandpa's vague permission to date, except that I'd take anything he'd give me when it came to Alex.

I pulled my phone out, thinking of calling him, but I quickly realized he'd been trying to call me. I swiped past seven missed calls. I'd made sure it was on silent after my late-night conversation with Stephen so I could sleep in.

I opened my phone to call Alex, but it rang until the

voicemail came on. Wherever Alex was, Stephen was bound to be with him. I found his number and called him.

"Hey," Stephen said, I could hear commotion in the background. "You okay?"

"Yeah, I'm great," I said a little breathlessly. I paced the length of the porch. "Where's Alex? Can I talk to him?"

Stephen let a few seconds pass before using his careful tone to not hurt my feelings. "Ah, I picked Emma up for breakfast this morning. Alex let me take his truck. I know the four of us are hanging out later today—"

"Where's Alex?"

"Home, I assume."

"Oh…" I said, processing that information slowly. "Okay."

"He's not answering his phone?"

I waved Stephen off even though he couldn't see me, trying to piece myself together. If I had to wait to talk to Alex, then I'd just have to wait. "No, he'll call me back. He probably—"

"He'd never not answer your call, Jenny." Stephen said, the phone muffled. It sounded like he was asking a waitress for a check. "Do you need us to come to you?"

"No, no, I'm okay, I just—"

Movement in the distance caught my eye.

A tall, handsome figure with light brown hair in a gray T-shirt was running up the drive. He was a boy and a man all at once. He was silly running toward me like that, and gallant too, making me want to laugh and cry. I was aware that I was only sixteen and stupid in so many ways, but he was the answer to every question I'd ever had about life.

"Alex is here."

"I'm confused," Stephen said. "What's going on?"

"Everything is good. Enjoy your breakfast." I clicked off the phone.

Alex grinned at me, coming to a stop at the bottom of the porch steps, his breath a little quicker than usual. "Hey."

"Hi." I smiled back, feeling the twinge of tears in the corner of my eyes because Alex Bailey was like fresh air to my lungs. "I tried to call you—"

"Is it creepy that I ran here?" The skin behind his ears bloomed pink. "I tried to call you, but I knew you said you were going to sleep in. I'm not sure what my plan was if you were going to be asleep when I got here, but Stephen has my truck and so I—"

"I called him looking for you."

"Oh," He nodded. "He's at breakfast with Emma."

"Yes." I nodded back.

We stared at each other. He was taller than me, but standing two steps up on the porch, I was looking down at him slightly. He was still panting. My mutation studied the way his heart raced. It matched mine, even though I wasn't the one who'd just been running.

I knew one of us should say something, but I bit my lip, deciding to force him to say his piece first.

"My dad talked to me. He said Grandpa was going to talk to you—" He ran a hand through his hair. "I mean, did he talk to you?"

"Yes. It was vague though."

"I couldn't get a solid answer from my dad either, just that this is a big step for Grandpa and I needed to not screw it up." He dug his hands in his pockets, glancing away. When he spoke again, his voice was deeper. "I mean, do you want to go to dinner with me tonight?"

"Yes," I said, a burst of laughter riding on the word. "I want to go to dinner with you tonight."

Everything about him lit up—his eyes and face and body.

He tugged me to him, wrapping his arms around my ribs, and spun me off the porch. I squealed when he spun me again, and then a third time for good measure. He glanced at the barn where Grandpa's truck was usually parked. "Grandpa's not here?"

I shook my head. "He's out in the fields. Technically, I don't think we're alone? I mean, I guess I don't know if we're allowed to be alone. Grandma is upstairs napping because she wasn't feeling good—"

The windchimes sang as my wind swirled around us because Alex had caught me up in his arms again, pressing his lips to mine. My hands snaked around his neck, deepening the kiss. I knew Grandpa's permission was confusing, but nothing had been as clear as this kiss.

I gave myself to it.

I let myself dream of Alex holding my hand in the hall, of date nights, school hallway kisses—and private kisses that sent fireworks through me. When we came up for air his forehead touched mine, his minty breath tickled against my nose. "I'm not sure what the fine print is on kissing you."

"I don't really care right now." I lifted up on my toes again and took another long kiss.

The sound of a big engine drew our attention toward the road in the distance, the rumble disrupting the quiet farmland around us. We both looked in the direction of the main road over the short stalks of corn.

Alex slid his arm around my waist just as the logo of the first semi-truck came into view, knocking the breath from my lungs in a gasp.

I whispered, "*Abilities*. It's *Abilities*."

Abilities was back and on their way to the mystery farm. They were a caravan of trucks, SUVs, and cars. There were more of them, a lot more of them since last fall.

Alex slid in my view, holding my jaw. "It doesn't matter."

"They're back—"

"Our mutations don't matter," He shook his head. "None of it matters. We keep our secrets. We live our life."

"What if—"

"Jenny," He kissed away my protest. "You and me, we'll protect that, all right? We get to decide what kind of life we want to live, not them."

"Brandon, Aiden, and Ryan know about us."

"We've got that covered. They mess with us and I mess with them." He hugged me to himself. "Besides, they have no idea we're connected to *Abilities*."

"What if *Abilities* finds out about us?"

Alex shook his head again. "How could they? This is a secret we could really keep. We stick to working on our mutations. Like you said before, we don't use them, we manage them. That's how we play this."

My eyes followed the *Abilities* caravan, the diesel engines of the semi-trucks were quieting. I let the soft sounds of Grandpa's front yard settle me because Alex's arm was wrapped around me.

He and I were going on a date tonight. And, I knew my parents would be proud of me for choosing Alex if they were alive today, everything was right again. "What if they never know about us?"

"What?"

I wrapped myself around him. "It's something Stephen said to me. That I could live my life believing everything will work out."

"I like that," he said, but he touched my chin with his thumb. "Don't let them take you away from me."

I pressed my cheek to his chest. "What do you mean?"

"Don't pull away from me, don't be afraid of them." I looked up to study him, his strong jaw, his bright blue eyes, the firm set of his lips. "Trust me, trust Stephen. We'll keep doing this together."

I looked toward the road again, watching the vehicles as they made their way past the Bailey farm, turning on the road that led in the direction toward the Wright Farm and then the mystery farm.

"We'll run," Alex whispered, drawing in slow breaths, as if trying to stay in control of his own fears—his own mutation's stirrings. "If they find out about us, I'll take you away."

"I trust you," I wanted to wipe away the uncertainty in his eyes. "I won't be afraid."

He looked down at me again, a soft smile played at the corner of his mouth, his shoulders relaxed. "Good, Jenny Phillips."

I let our secrets bury me in peace, accepting the truth Alex had been trying to tell me since Magic Valley. He'd be next to me no matter what we faced. Stephen would be, too. I didn't know what the future held, but I knew the lengths I would go to keep them in my life. My mutation wouldn't give me a choice anyway. We'd create the lives we wanted without apology.

At least for today, I'd let myself be happy.

The End

SHADOW MAIL

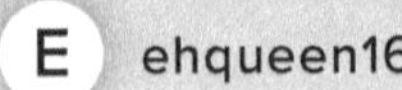

ehqueen16

Write New Email

✉ **Inbox**

Drafts

Sent

Important

More

charlotte.tucker@hollowbrook.gov

Secure Forwarder ⌄   **Select Secure Forwarder**
To hide your real reply-to address.

Subject: Concerned Student from Hollow Brook High

Dear Mrs. Charlotte Tucker,

I am a student at Hollow Brook High, but I found a website that teaches you how to write an anonymous email. That might be weird to you, but please read this whole email before you put it in your trash file.

I heard from my mom that you are going to be Hollow Brook's new mayor. I am hoping you care about Hollow Brook High's safety. I did a lot of research on how to keep schools safe from gun violence. One big thing I learned is that students telling teachers and adults they trust about someone who they don't feel safe around is important.

I am scared, but I'm writing to come forward about someone who doesn't make me feel safe. Attached to this email are screen shots of forums and posts on radical political sites Brandon Thomas is very active on. Also, private messages from Brandon Thomas to me. I blurred out my name. In these pictures you will see him make jokes about taking out certain students and teachers because they made him mad.

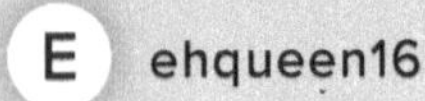

ehqueen16

Write New Email

✉ **Inbox**

⊙ Drafts

✉ Sent

✦ Important

∨ More

I also know Brandon has got a new gun every year on his birthday since he was twelve years old so it's easy for him to get a weapon. As you can tell from the picture, he was the one who vandalized the lockers and caused the fire in the science room. I cropped out another student because they didn't have anything to do with it. I'm sure they have not come forward because they are as scared of Brandon as I am. I can't tell you how I got the picture, but I promise you it's real.

I know you are moving to Hollow Brook with your husband and your daughter who will be a junior at Hollow Brook High this coming year. I trust you will think of your daughter's safety and investigate Brandon Thomas's behavior. I think you should know that if you report these things to Sheriff Bolt it will be ignored. He is one of the biggest secret keepers in Hollow Brook and that fact is scary for every citizen in this town. In conclusion, I want to say my mom birthed me in the bathtub in the house I have lived in my whole life. I say that because no one knows Hollow Brook like I do and I want it to be a better place. I have done my part to keep our school safe, now it's your turn to do your part.

Thank you,

A Concerned Student at Hollow Brook High School

I'M LIKE A quiet, steady stream that takes its time to carve a path down a mountain. Eventually, after years of contemplation and dreaming and hesitation, I get to where I want to be. I wanted to publish this book, and I *finally* got here.

You, Justin, are the crashing, wild, stormy waves. Do you remember that fishing show we watched when Hensley was a newborn? They'd have those storms and the water would wash over the fishermen in those yellow rain suits. And we waited for them to be pulled into the dark waters? Basically, I'll say this: You've never been afraid to rock the boat. And, I'm so thankful for that, because you've kicked down every closed door I've ever faced.

To Meg Delagrange-Belfon of Blended Mix Publishing, I can't believe I found you, you're so magical and cool. You're business savvy, insanely creative, and in possession of a kindness that makes me hopeful in this uncertain world. I met you, and I instantly knew I could safely place *Hollow Brook Mutants* in your hands to bridge the book from a Google Doc and into the hands of readers.

To Sarah Pagano, thank you for the immense amount of time you've invested in *Hollow Brook Mutants*. You gave me space and invaluable feedback to write this book. And what's more, I'm pretty sure *Hollow Brook Mutants* has its title because you bullied me into it. Reluctantly, I'll admit you were right, it really is a great title.

To Evan Cardoza, you filled me with confidence every morning as we started our day in a classroom full of one year olds discussing *Hollow Brook Mutants*. So much of Alex, Jenny and Stephen's personalities were shaped through those conversations. Thank you, you mean so much to me.

To Alejandra Fine, thank you for your love of Alex, Jenny and Stephen. I remember whenever we talked about *Hollow Brook Mutant's* plot it felt like we were talking about real events with real people. I could feel your genuine warmth as we discussed, and it gave me hope that maybe others would enjoy getting to know them too.

To Sarah Fuller, I'm so thankful for your time and thoughts. I could see the excitement in your eyes as we talked about this book, and I absorbed every word of your feedback.

To Amy Larger, I admire how brave and tenacious you are, I love the way you set me straight when I drop into the group chat with my unnecessarily-dramatic-panic.

To Christie Livermore, you were the only one to passionately express the flaws of the ending in the first draft. I felt pretty stubborn about keeping it the way it was, but your feedback haunted me (pretty sure it was like literally years of haunting) and so I found a way to keep it the same, and change it too.

To Katie Halface, every time I feel like *Hollow Brook Mutants* might fade from reader's minds you randomly pop up in my comments section, unintentionally reminding me you haven't forgotten about the book, and so maybe others won't too.

To Taurenelle and Martin Cullen, you guys were my first writers group and it was such a special experience. I remember the moment you two confirmed that this book was where I could hit my stride as a writer.

To That One Summer School Teacher I Met Because I Failed Freshman English, I told you I wanted to be a writer. The only essay I'd turned in during that previous semester had been covered in horrifying red marks. (red pens are still my nightmare). But you pushed me to keep rewriting the haiku poem you assigned. It was called 'Red', and you kept telling me it wasn't good enough and to go make it better. You taught me what feedback felt like, what revision was, and that I had the capability to write something worthy enough for someone to connect with.

To Ken Bastian, at thirteen years old you let me ramble on about my ghost story. It wasn't a 'short' ghost story, but you leaned forward with real interest, and you said, "You know what, with that kind of storytelling in your head, you should write that down. You should write books." And so I did. The book was horrible, but I discovered the magic of writing from sunset to sunrise. It's 20 years later, and that story lingers in the dusty, spooky, witchy corners of my mind, and I'm pretty sure I'm going to write it one day.

I'd also like to thank Taylor Swift for the song *Miss Americanna* and *The Heartbreak Prince*, its sound and lyrics are woven into this story.

Finally, to my family, these acknowledgments are already pretty long. So I'm just going to say thank you to the Days, the 'Snethen', the Davis's, and the Merciers. I'll give you guys more sentences in the next book because I know you'll all be there in the future. But really, thank you so much for your investment, I can't convey how much I appreciate my family.

To Hensley, I love you, holding you in my arms is the most precious gift I've ever been given.

JESSICA MERCIER is a writer from Boise, Idaho, where she resides with her husband, Justin, and their daughter, Hensley. She enjoys long walks, exploring bookstores, and spending time in coffeeshops, where she often gathers inspiration. Growing up, Jessica spent her days sneaking through cornfields, exploring hidden worlds with scraped knees and dirty sneakers. This childhood sense of adventure and curiosity informs her writing, adding a touch of magic and wonder to her stories. Her latest book, *Hollow Brook Mutants*, captures these experiences, inviting readers into a world of mystery and imagination.

CONNECT WITH *Jessica Mercier*

@JESSICAMERCIERBOOKS

JESSICAMERCIERBOOKS.COM

JESSICAMERCIERBOOKS@GMAIL.COM